A BLADE AND A RING

THE CHAIN BREAKER BOOK 7

D.K HOLMBERG

ASH
PUBLISHING

CHAPTER ONE

The massive bloom of light caught Gavin off guard.

He ducked, rolled to the side, and started to reach for his sword before thinking better of it. He wasn't supposed to be using his weapon. Gavin wasn't supposed to be diving out of the way of the magic blasting toward him either, but he couldn't help his instincts.

He scrambled to his feet, starting to focus on the part deep inside of him that he called his core reserves. The space buried within him allowed him to access what he now understood to be magic, and he could channel that through himself. The challenge was knowing what he could do with it after he summoned it.

As he tapped into the core reserves, Gavin pulled on power. There were specific patterns he could use to augment the magic he managed to summon, but for the most part, he didn't even try. He lacked the skill—and the knowledge—to do something as simple as that.

He instead braced his arms, crossing them over each other, and pushed the energy of his core reserves up through his body. The way his arms were crossed seemed to augment the power and permitted him to pour it out of himself and into the world.

The magic blasted free.

And completely missed the bloom of light.

"Terrible," a creaky voice said from nearby.

Gavin spun quickly in surprise. What was the old master doing here? As far as Gavin knew, the man had been back in the settlement, leaving him to work through all of this on his own.

"What did I do wrong this time, Master Jaremal?"

The man dusted his silver hair back from his forehead, managing to make his pale eyes seem icy as he glowered at Gavin. "What did you do *right* would be a better question. You have completely failed at the simplest aspect of drawing on the power within yourself. Can you not see that?"

Gavin found that he couldn't move. He didn't need to, really, but the feeling was unnerving. Master Jaremal held him with an invisible band of power that looped around his body, sealing him inside.

Gavin suspected that he could break out of this trap. He *was* the Chain Breaker, after all, and had learned to use his power against magic—but he didn't dare try. He was here for a specific reason, and he wasn't going to learn what he needed to know if he overwhelmed his instructor. At least physically. There was no way he could do so magically.

"All I know is that I'm able to pull the power through myself the way you've described."

Master Jaremal walked over and wiggled two of his bony fingers at Gavin, and they landed like a punch to his chest. Gavin didn't see anything but the energy that struck him and pounded through him, forcing him to gasp with a sharp intake of air as he struggled to withstand the assault.

"You pull power. That was never the issue. When you first came here, you were able to access that part of yourself. Even a child can do that, though." Master Jaremal clucked softly and turned away, though Gavin knew his attention was not fully off him. He had learned all too often that the man was aware even when he didn't look in his direction. "But you have no focus. I don't know what she sees in you."

"She thinks I'm the Champion," Gavin said.

Master Jaremal turned back slowly, swiveling and looking at him—and the ring on his finger. The simple, smooth band was constructed of a white material and impossible for him to take off. Master Jaremal claimed that over time, Gavin would learn how to do so. The problem was that he had not yet learned what that was going to entail, and he had not been given any specific guidance as to what he needed to do.

"Yes. Well, the Shard thinks a great many things, but unfortunately for you, they are not always accurate. If they were, then our people would've been united long ago."

Gavin stood motionless at the admonishment. He'd heard it before. "What should I do differently?"

"What did you see, Gavin Lorren?"

Gavin smiled tightly, reminded of his earliest lessons all those years ago from his first and most brutal instructor. "I saw a bloom of pale-blue light, and I ducked out of the way, not wanting to be struck by it, so I—"

"What did you *see?*" Master Jaremal asked.

The question was the same, but Gavin sensed there was something distinct about what the man asked, though he had no idea what it was or why it would matter.

"I saw some shape of magic," Gavin replied.

Master Jaremal nodded once, and he made another small sound in the back of his throat. "You saw magic. Well, what you call magic. It is not magic when you are born to it, though, is it?"

He turned quickly and dragged Gavin with him, practically floating him above the leaf-covered floor of the forest. Trees on either side stood nearby, guardians protecting Master Jaremal—not that he needed it.

"Do you believe it to be magic that your heart beats in your chest?" Master Jaremal glanced at him, before turning and heading deeper into the forest. They were venturing away from the settlement, though Gavin didn't worry about that. He knew his way around well enough now that he didn't have to fear getting lost anymore. "Do you believe it to be magic when you take a breath while you're sleeping?"

"My body does that for me," Gavin muttered, the same way he had responded whenever Master Jaremal had asked that in the past. Not that the man recognized Gavin's irritation. And if he did, he didn't show it.

Master Jaremal waved his hand, shaking his head. "Your body. What does your body do when you call on what you refer to as magic?"

"I have to focus on it," Gavin said. "It is a part of me, but I have to draw it up intentionally."

"Why must you use it intentionally? Why is it not part of you at all times? Why must you focus on something that you should be calling on consistently?"

Gavin didn't have a good answer for that, and he knew that Master Jaremal didn't expect him to either. These were rhetorical questions, the kind that he had been asked ever since they had started to work together, designed to encourage him to focus. He had no idea why these questions were important, only that Master Jaremal was specific on what he wanted Gavin to think about.

That was in sharp contrast with the kind of training he'd had when he was younger. Whereas before it had been about perfecting his body, his instincts, and his reaction so that he could be the most skilled fighter he could be, this training worked his mind in ways he had not considered before—a fact that Master Jaremal constantly reminded him about. He treated Gavin as if he were some dullard. In that, the man and Gavin's old friend Gaspar would've agreed.

"I was trained not to draw on it constantly because I ran the risk of weakening myself," Gavin said. "You know the story behind it as well as I do."

Master Jaremal turned and focused on him with intensity. "I know the story. And I know that you are what they believe to be the Champion." He waved a hand as if that meant nothing. "But it's what you were that matters. It's what you are that is important. It is how you think that will set you apart."

"Where are you taking me?" Gavin asked.

They were heading into a deeper part of the forest, the trees now arching overhead, blocking out the daylight. The musty air smelled of damp earth mixed with the stench of decay and even something musky that Gavin couldn't identify.

"I am taking you to where you can continue your studies. That is why you are here, after all."

He flicked his fingers again, and Gavin felt another punch to the chest. Though he had trained his entire life to withstand pain, there was something quite demeaning about having this frail-looking man handle him as quickly and easily as he did. Would he even be able to take Master Jaremal down in a real fight? Maybe if Gavin drew upon magic—all the magic he had available to him—he might have a chance, but even that wasn't a guarantee.

"You've been with us for the better part of several months," Master Jaremal said. "I've tried to teach you the techniques necessary to hone your mind and to emphasize the skills that everyone with your abilities should possess. But in that time, you've only just progressed beyond where you were when you first came to me, and you can barely handle the basics. And now, I fear we are running out of time."

Gavin clenched his fists. "What have you seen?"

Master Jaremal turned to him, and for a moment, the brightness of his pale eyes seemed to change. It was as if some part of the ocean washed through them and part of the sky reflected within them, but then the effect faded. "I have seen nothing, but I fear for what has transpired so far," he said softly, then turned away. "The divide between the families deepens. There has been much anger for far too long. It should have been over by now, but it persists despite my best efforts to stop it, along with the attempts of others like me."

He clasped his hands in front of him and looked at Gavin with vibrant eyes. "And you. The Champion." He managed to make it sound like an insult as he said it, though as far as Gavin knew, the title was supposed to be one of honor within the El'aras people. "You have done nothing other than prove yourself unworthy."

"I don't know, I think thwarting several attempts to destroy the Shard has proved me worthy."

"Focus on that power within yourself again."

Gavin opened his mouth to argue, then clamped it back shut again. This was the reason he was here. He was supposed to be learning how to draw on magic, but being able to do so was not as easy as he had believed it to be. Not the way Master Jaremal wanted him to do it.

Gavin focused. Finding the core reserves within himself was simple now. He had known about them for many years, though he hadn't realized that the power was magic until recently. It was a simple matter of tapping into the energy and pulling it out, or perhaps pushing it out—he wasn't sure which way it worked. As he did, the power bubbled up and outward, rolling over his entire being, filling him and strengthening him. That was the way he had been taught to draw that magic out by other El'aras he had traveled with.

A burst of energy struck Gavin in the chest again, and though he hadn't been prepared for it, the force of the blow was not nearly as hard as it would have been if he had not been calling on his core reserves.

Master Jaremal's brow furrowed for a moment, and in that brief flash, something seemed to shift within him. Almost as if he became more youthful. He took a step back and held his hands before him, making a triangle out of his index finger and thumbs, though they didn't touch. The space between them crackled with a blue energy that built in intensity, like he was holding some point of power between his hands.

"Can you recreate this?" Master Jaremal asked. This was not one of the techniques he had demonstrated before.

"I can try," Gavin said carefully. He had learned not to argue too much with the man, especially when it came to his lessons on how to call on power. He attempted to move his hands but could not. "You need to release my arms, though."

Master Jaremal merely watched him.

"It's like that, is it?" Gavin muttered.

He focused on the core reserves within him again, letting that energy bubble up and strengthen him. Adding that strength to his arms, to his bones, to his entire being, had been a simple matter from the very first time he had realized what he was doing. It had gained him the nickname of Chain Breaker, a reputation he had earned long ago but seemed unnecessary once he'd come to the El'aras. There was no chain that magic couldn't break.

But perhaps Master Jaremal was trying to show him that the kinds of chains and the types of power he would be using on Gavin would be different.

Gavin tried to push his arms outward, to help himself stretch out as he pushed on the barrier that surrounded him, but he quickly realized that Master Jaremal wasn't testing him with physical strength. This was magic.

Gavin focused his core reserves, letting them continue to bulge outward and flex against the resistance. He couldn't see what Master Jaremal was doing to hold him. Until Gavin could break free, he wasn't going to be able to place his hands in front of him the way Master Jaremal wanted him to, so he wouldn't be able to generate the power Master Jaremal wanted from him either. He had to find some other way, but doing so would involve drawing on magic he had specifically been instructed not to use.

Would Master Jaremal even know? Gavin wasn't sure if he would recognize it.

Gavin ran his thumb around the surface of the ring he wore on his left hand. The band felt tight on his middle finger, almost as if it were trying to cut off the blood supply to his hand, but he had been wearing the ring long enough that he no longer thought about it that way. Now it was just a part of him.

The ring also granted him connection to some other power, something that was beyond what he could call on naturally. He had access to what seemed like a new source of core reserves, one he was meant to access but was difficult for him to do easily.

In the time he had been working with Master Jaremal, Gavin had been specifically instructed not to draw on that power. Master Jaremal wanted him to master his own power first, to have the ability to use all magic within himself before he started to summon anything additional. Gavin had tried to do as he had been told, but he still struggled. As much as he wanted to follow the man's instruction, the ring gave him access to something more.

He attempted to draw just a bit. Though it was little more than a trickle, the power Master Jaremal was using around him constricted more tightly. Gavin glowered at him.

"Did you think I wouldn't know?"

"I won't be able to break free of what you're doing on my own," Gavin said, keeping his voice tight and controlled.

"And why not?"

"Because I'm not El'aras like you."

The bands continued to constrict, and Gavin struggled to breathe. He had felt something like this before. His first instructor had made a point of trying to demonstrate a technique like this.

"You need to be El'aras like me to be able to escape?" Master Jaremal taunted.

"Isn't that why I'm here?" Gavin couldn't see anything of the forest around him, though he felt as if the trees were closing in on him, as though they were part of these bands squeezing him. He wouldn't put it past Master Jaremal to have some way of connecting to the power of the trees to use them against him. Though he had never seen an El'aras use power like that, it wouldn't surprise him to learn that something like that could even be possible.

Master Jaremal took another step toward Gavin, and the power continued to constrict. "What do you think I am doing that you cannot do yourself?"

Gavin attempted to flex. When he had been bound by physical chains, he'd been able to easily use his connection to that power so he could burst free. When he had been bound by magic, there had only been a few times when he had struggled to withstand it.

This time, the energy squeezed him and continued to make it difficult for him to breathe. He had been warned that this would be difficult training, but he hadn't taken it as seriously as he probably should have. This was far more challenging than he had anticipated.

"You have greater control over your own power," Gavin said. His breaths came slowly as he controlled himself. He didn't want to exhale too much because each time he did, the power around him pressed against him even more.

Master Jaremal simply watched him with a casual expression on his face. In that way, he reminded Gavin far too much of his first mentor. "And you think you cannot do this because you did not learn to during your childhood?"

"I've told you I cannot."

"But you have demonstrated a facility with all the various techniques."

Gavin hesitated. What was he getting at?

Master Jaremal's statement was true. Gavin knew many techniques, mostly because part of his training had been in identifying patterns, replicating them, and using them after seeing them only a single time. Sometimes, he had extrapolated from those patterns and tried to come up with new ones. That was part of the training that Tristan, his mentor, had instilled in him, something that had made Gavin an incredibly gifted fighter. Learning how to fight and adopt different combat styles had been out of necessity, though—so that he would not suffer.

Was that what Master Jaremal was implying?

"I can use the patterns," Gavin said, making a point of speaking softly. He wanted Master Jaremal to come closer to him.

"And what about this pattern?" Master Jaremal still had not moved his hands, the blue arcing from fingertip to fingertip, from thumb to thumb, and creating a powerful burst within his hands as if preparing to release that ball of energy.

"I can't do that," Gavin said.

"What would happen if I were to unleash this upon you?"

If he did that, Gavin would have to draw on the power within the ring immediately. He suspected it had enough strength to allow him to withstand any magic that this El'aras master might be able to throw at him. That wasn't what Gavin was supposed to do, though. He had his connection to the ring, but he had to find and master the El'aras ability within himself now, despite how much he had been struggling with it.

Anna had taught him techniques, basic aspects of his magic using the core reserves he could feel, but drawing on his power in other ways had proved challenging for him.

And he had to be careful that he didn't harm the master, so he couldn't attack him.

Unless that was what Master Jaremal wanted from him...

Perhaps Master Jaremal had been holding back.

He hadn't demonstrated anything to him. Gavin had tried to use the power within himself, and he'd shown he was a skilled fighter, but they didn't want him to fight. All of the El'aras were skilled at fighting, at least with a sword. What Gavin had, and what he *was*, was something different.

He was the Champion—whatever that meant. He had seen evidence of a prophecy, but it had been manufactured.

Still, it seemed as if Master Jaremal believed there was something more to it.

Gavin focused on the core reserves and let himself fill with that power, feeling every bit of it as it began to build within him. The power flowed out through him while he concentrated on the energy. He stayed connected to his core reserves, and as he did, he started to flex that power outward, trying to first draw it deep within him and then push it out with as much strength as he could summon.

He felt resistance and started to push again... and again.

Gavin closed his eyes. Master Jaremal had mentioned something about patterns. That had to be significant, though why would it be? Something about what he had done to Gavin had to matter in all of this.

Energy sizzled around him, and he could detect a pattern to it. He hadn't paid attention to that before, but recognizing the pattern, he immediately understood how to defend himself.

And he understood what Master Jaremal was getting at.

The defense was simple, a technique he had demonstrated to Gavin repeatedly. Gavin traced it with just his fingers, much like the attack Master Jaremal was using on him. As he did, he pushed a tiny amount of his energy out through his fingertips and into the pattern to activate it.

His magic struck the barrier around him, shattering the energy, and Master Jaremal fell back. He locked eyes with Gavin and tipped his head in acknowledgment.

"That's it?" Gavin asked.

"Did you expect something more?"

"I did what you wanted."

Master Jaremal snorted. "You came here to learn, Champion," he said with a sneer on his face. "And you have just accomplished what a child can do. Congratulations."

CHAPTER TWO

The El'aras stronghold of Arashil sat in the heart of the forest, surrounded by towering oak and pine, though there was a smattering of unfamiliar trees as well. When Gavin had first come to this part of the forest, he had found himself drawn to the trees. Their massive trunks were coated in a rough, irregular bark, and the smallest of them were twenty feet around. Branches stretched out from them, covered with velvety leaves. The ground was littered with small wooden thorns that none of the El'aras wanted to get close to. Gavin had attempted to touch one when he had first come upon them, but he had been advised to avoid them. He wasn't sure if they were poisonous or sacred. With the El'aras, either one was a possibility.

The rest of the settlement was built out of a dark gray stone that seemed to have been quarried from someplace far away. He hadn't seen signs of stone like that anywhere else, though the structures themselves looked to be impossibly old. Moss and vines covered a few of the tall, stone structures, but for the most part, the forest left the settlement alone.

This place had an ancient quality to it, which gave it a sense of age, though there was also evidence of life and the people who resided here. When Gavin had left the city of Yoran, he had thought he'd be going to one of the El'aras cities, not a settlement like this. But Anna thought he needed more time training before they went to a city.

Master Jaremal had reached the settlement ahead of Gavin, leaving him to wander through the forest on his own, almost as a punishment. Luckily, Gavin had paid attention as they had gone deeper into the forest, so navigating back to the settlement had been simple, but perhaps the reprimand was justified. Master Jaremal was not wrong, and Gavin should have understood what was going on sooner. As soon as he recognized the pattern used against him, he had been able to counter it easily using a basic skill. Maybe there was a more complicated technique that Master Jaremal wanted to use on him, but so far, the technique had been easy for Gavin to manage.

He looked around and spotted several other El'aras, but it was the ones he couldn't see that he focused on. He knew there were others surrounding the entire settlement, hiding within the trees and providing protection, which made him feel strange. Gavin was accustomed to being the one offering the protection, not receiving it.

Along the road stood an older building near the far edge of the settlement, where the Order of Notharin had taken over. He had not seen them nearly as much as he thought he would have since coming to Arashil. He needed to understand more about what the Order knew of Tristan and what he might have done, but Gavin had not taken the opportunity to do so yet. Perhaps that was a mistake. More than that, he had a sense that Anna and Master Jaremal didn't necessarily trust the Order. Given everything that had taken place, he wouldn't be terribly surprised to learn that there were unreliable El'aras, even those who claimed to be interested in helping. And they *had* actually helped.

"You seem upset," a voice said from beside him.

Gavin turned to see Anna making her way over from one of the nearby buildings. She was dressed in a cloak that matched the colors of the forest, and her fluid movement suggested that she was calling on her own power constantly—which Gavin suspected she was. He still hadn't mastered that aspect of his power, not knowing how to hold it consistently, or continuously, to essentially enhance and enchant himself as he did something as basic as walking.

"I think Master Jaremal wanted to give me a lesson in humility," Gavin said.

She smiled slightly. "That has long been his favorite strategy. I remember learning from him when I was a child. He made a point of showing me how little I knew."

Gavin thought he caught sight of Master Jaremal in the distance, but the man disappeared quickly. "First, he wanted me to demonstrate what I can do, then he made a point of telling me how much I lacked, and then he wanted me to show him how to get free of the hold he had on me."

"Did you do it?"

"It took a while."

"You should have known the technique to escape from anything he would use to hold you."

Gavin nodded slowly. "I tried to use the ring—"

"That is not why you are here, Gavin Lorren," Anna said.

He glanced over to her. He had always thought Anna lovely, impossibly beautiful, and even among the El'aras she was breathtaking. There was a hardness to her as well, which he found equally attractive.

"I understand that he doesn't want me to use that power so he can teach me the right way," he said.

He thought about the kind of power Master Jaremal had been working with him on, and the way he had described that power. It was a technique Gavin was supposed to control, one that would help him master his magic. And there was something about the way that Master Jaremal had said the word "Champion" that alluded to something more.

He sighed. "The problem is that we know there's more danger coming."

Anna frowned. "We've been looking. There is no evidence of anything."

"I should be part of the search."

"Just because your old mentor is the one who suggested that there's something more to fear doesn't mean that you need to be searching." She rested a hand on his arm, and it felt as if she called on her own magic and pressed it into him, leaving his skin tingling. That might only be his reaction to her, though. "You need to understand who and what you are. You have been away from the people for too long, Gavin. This cannot be rushed."

He didn't pull away, but he felt as though he needed to. He didn't have the answers he wanted, and he wasn't sure if Anna would be able to provide him with anything more.

"I'm not trying to rush anything," he said. "What I am trying to do, though, is to fully understand the power I have. All of it." He placed a hand on the hilt of his sword. So far, since coming here, he hadn't even had the opportunity to use it. Being able to fight was another part of his role as Champion, and he was still surprised that the El'aras would want him to abandon it. "I have this ring, the blade, and my own ability—"

"Ability that you have not yet begun to fully understand," Anna said softly. "Certain things take time."

Gavin smiled at her. "If I take the time you want, or that Master Jaremal wants, I'll be studying with the El'aras for decades." Or longer, he didn't add.

"You have made that same objection before."

"It doesn't change the truth of it. We don't necessarily have decades."

"You don't know that."

He resisted the urge to explain the obvious.

When he had last seen Tristan, he'd warned Gavin that there was something worse coming. Gavin didn't know what it was, and Tristan had been unnecessarily opaque about it, likely because he feared the El'aras for some reason that Gavin didn't fully understand. But he increasingly felt as if Tristan had been training him to do something far more than what he knew. Maybe it was simply about becoming the Chain Breaker and doing what he had managed to do so far. Gavin had prevented powerful sorcerers from succeeding in their goals, but that didn't seem to be the entire purpose behind what Tristan wanted from him. It couldn't be.

He chose not to argue with Anna. "I don't think I have as long as you do. And I'm trying to learn at the pace that you and Master Jaremal think is appropriate. I'm just not accustomed to spending so much time on the basics."

She grinned and motioned for him to follow. They headed into the settlement, making their way along the trampled path between several buildings. It looked as if the grasses had once been taller, overgrowing much of this clearing in the middle of the forest. The scent of the earth filled his nostrils, and blades of grass sprung up with each step. Gavin found it surprising that the grass hadn't died off.

The smell of smoke drifted out of each building they passed. Savory aromas of baked goods mingled with cinnamon, a hint of mint, a touch of clove, and even boselberry—something he had thought rare and had known when he was younger. As they moved farther away, he detected the smell of hot metal and heard the steady clang of steel.

Gavin still hadn't been able to determine if the settlement had always been active, or if it had become active when Anna had escorted him out of Yoran. He had thought she was leading him into the heart of the El'aras lands, but she had only guided him to the settlement. He knew the full El'aras territories were farther from here, deeper into the forest and beyond. As far as he could tell, he was only several weeks away from the border of the forest and from the edge of Yoran and other lands.

"Have you been able to detect anything around us?" Anna asked.

"What am I supposed to detect?"

Her question felt like a test, the same kind that Master Jaremal had been putting him through. With Anna, though, Gavin wasn't entirely sure if she was testing him or simply asking questions. It could be either. Or neither.

"I was hoping that perhaps you might recognize what others like you have been doing."

Gavin cast a sideways look at her. "Others like me?"

"You continue to feel as if you are not among the people."

"It's more that I don't feel like I belong." He wasn't sure how to explain it to her. These weren't his people. While he increasingly believed that he was truly El'aras, he wasn't one of them. It was about more than just being of the same bloodline. It was about who he was, which was something he was still figuring out.

She smiled again. "Would you prefer to go somewhere else?"

Gavin looked around. "I agreed to come here."

"You did."

"And I agreed that there's a benefit in me coming here. I agreed that I can learn."

"You can. The difference is whether or not you are willing to."

He let out a laugh. "Now both you and Master Jaremal are disappointed in my ability?"

"There is no disappointment," she said. "You must find your own path."

They paused in front of a tall building shaped like a pyramid, which looked to have once been covered by the grass and vines that reached out of the forest. These signs of nature had faded away, retreating rather than being scrubbed free. This was an El'aras temple, though Gavin didn't know what god or gods they worshipped. He knew next to nothing about their religion. Anna had claimed that they held his old friend Cyran in one of their temples until his escape. Was that one more thing she wanted Gavin to learn?

She paused in front of the entrance. "I must show you something." A note of indecision lingered in her voice, as though she wasn't quite convinced that she should be revealing this to him.

Gavin looked around. There weren't many people in this part of the settlement. Were they staying clear of the temple? Or of him and Anna? He smiled at that thought.

She was the Risen Shard, and he was the Champion. According to the prophecies the El'aras had learned of and believed, he and Anna were supposed to destroy each other. He had the feeling that some of the people expected the two of them to do battle, though Gavin had never felt any desire to harm her.

Quite the opposite, in fact.

Part of the reason he was here was because of his growing attraction to Anna, and the belief that if anyone could help him understand what he was supposed to be, it would be her. He didn't know if she felt the same way, but there were times when he caught her glancing in his direction, which made him think that maybe she did.

But Gavin was always aware that she had her own agenda as the Risen Shard. From the moment he'd met her, he had known that there were goals behind what she did, and behind who she was. She was a leader. He was a loner.

"Now who's the one to sound hesitant in what they need to do?" he teased.

Anna looked over to him, her deep-blue eyes softening. "I've questioned whether I should do this from the moment we came here," she said, her voice quiet, and she put her hands to the side. "It is the reason I chose this place. We called it Arashil. In the common tongue, I suppose it would mean—"

"Place of power," Gavin said. Anna arched an eyebrow at him, and he shrugged. "I've had a lot of time. I've been studying your language."

"You've managed to pick it up that quickly?"

He shrugged again. "Patterns," he said with a small chuckle, shaking his head. "I can only imagine what Wrenlow would think of that."

Remembering his old friend caused his chest to tighten, the way it often did. Wrenlow had traveled with Gavin for the better part of several years, only to stay behind in Yoran. Gavin had felt compelled to move on because he had known it was his time, much like it was finally Wrenlow's time to stay in one place, establish himself, and have a home.

"Very few have managed to master the El'aras language in such a short time," Anna said.

He furrowed his brow. "I don't know if I would call it mastery. Perhaps you could say recognition? I recognize there are patterns to the language, much like there patterns to everything you've been trying to teach me since I've come here." He glanced over to her, and he snorted at the frown on her face. "I would think that you would be pleased by this. Isn't that what you want me to do?"

She regarded him for a long moment before finally nodding. "I suppose that it is. I have wanted you to understand, and if it takes you learning the language..." She shook her head. "Perhaps he did better than he realized."

"He?" Gavin asked.

"Your old mentor. Perhaps he trained you even better than he knew."

"I didn't expect you to stand up for him."

"That's not what I'm doing. I'm recognizing the benefits of his training."

She took a step toward the temple, and she traced her hand across the surface of the flat stone. Pale-blue lines began to glow. Gavin had seen similar lines before, beneath Yoran. When he had been in the El'aras hall under the city, lines like these had shown him the prophecy, which led him to question what Anna might be able to show him here. This area was as old as Yoran, he suspected. Maybe even older. This place of power was sacred to these people.

Anna let energy flow out from her and into the door. "I hesitated to bring you here," she admitted. "And not because I fear you seeing this," she added, though it seemed almost like an afterthought, as if she wasn't sure whether she should acknowledge that. "But more because I did not know how you might react."

"Why?"

"Arashil is an ancient place to the El'aras. For a long time, it had been abandoned." She paused with her hand on the door, and she looked back, not at Gavin but behind her to the rest of the settlement. "As we retreated from the lands that humans claimed, we withdrew to the forest, to the mountains, and to other uninhabited spaces. We did so in order to preserve our heritage."

Gavin turned to look at the rest of the settlement with her. He had never really considered that before. This place wouldn't have been on the fringes of the El'aras home-lands back then, but rather deep within the heart of them.

At one point, Yoran had been an El'aras city, and there was evidence of it all throughout. Now, there was only the scattered remnants of anything more.

"What was here?" he asked.

"You're seeing what was here," Anna said. "Not much has changed. At least, not so much that you would be surprised by it." She turned to him and smiled. "This land has attempted to swallow Arashil, but it has not done so completely. I don't think it could."

"What was it?" Gavin could tell that she was trying to

keep something from him, like she was attempting to prevent him from learning about this place or about what secrets it contained.

He had been here for several months, working on trying to understand his magic and what it meant for him, so he felt as though he deserved to know what she was trying to keep from him. He believed there was something more going on, that this place had more meaning than Anna had revealed so far. It had to, as the El'aras didn't do anything without purpose. Gavin had seen that in every experience he'd had with them. He had not yet uncovered more, though.

But then, he was El'aras. Not the kind she was, as many among them had made clear. He suspected that was Master Jaremal's intention all along—he wanted Gavin to know he wasn't true El'aras, at least not the kind that he and the others were.

"Arashil was a place where the priests would gather," Anna explained.

"Like Yoran?"

She frowned, and though the blue lines continued to swirl in the surface of the stone, she had not opened the doorway. "Not quite like it. Within Yoran, there was an ancient hall, an archive of sorts. This was different, a place where those who had the ability to see beyond our limitations would come celebrate, commune, and plan."

"It was an important place to your priests, then."

"To my people," she said. "*Our* people."

He smiled at the hesitation in her correction, but he didn't acknowledge it any further. Gavin looked at the edge of the forest. He suspected that it would be a relatively easy task for the people to protect this area. It wouldn't even take all that much for them to defend it.

"Then why would they have abandoned it?" he asked.

"The people wanted to retreat as far away as possible. They thought it was necessary to do so. In fact, they thought they had no other choice."

"Why would they have abandoned someplace that was this important, though?"

"Ultimately, it was just a place," she said, smiling tightly. "Or, at least, that is what they told everyone. That all of our homes were just a place and did not represent the people."

"I see. They didn't want you to refuse to move."

She nodded. "Right. They feared that the fighting would persist if we remained close to the lands the humans claimed."

"Sorcerers, you mean," Gavin said.

"Fine." She smirked. "Sorcerers, but sorcerers who led the humans."

Finally, she pushed outward, and he could practically feel the magic coming from her, and a burst of power exploded from her hand. He tried to pay attention, wanting to see if there was anything to what she did that he might be able to identify. He strained to find anything that would help him know how she activated the door and the pattern that was used within it, but he couldn't see anything. Was she trying to distract him so that he wouldn't be able to pay attention?

He smiled to himself. "What's in here?"

"As I said, this was a place where our people came to gather. From all over."

Gavin had a feeling that she was being careful to say "our people" again, and he was starting to understand what she was trying to get at. There had been a time when the El'aras families were not fragmented. Not like they were now, where the families were so divided that it made it difficult for them to work together. Some wanted to reclaim lands long lost to them, whereas others wanted nothing more than to maintain the tentative peace they already had. He had always known that Anna supported peace and wanted nothing more than to make sure that their people—her people, much more than his—maintained that peace, if only because she knew what would happen if they did not. Therefore, she had done everything she could to ensure that peace.

"Is there another prophecy here?" Gavin asked.

"I don't know."

She walked forward into the temple, and Gavin followed. As soon as he stepped inside, the door sealed behind him. He didn't think Anna had done anything to cause it to close, but he couldn't be certain. She claimed it was similar to the kind of power he had access to, though he didn't know if that was true or not. And perhaps it didn't even matter.

He followed her forward. Stone rose on either side of him, coming to a point high over his head. The inside of the temple was dimly lit, but it didn't take long before the faint light began to glow softly, then brighter and brighter with every passing moment. The walls themselves seemed to take on a glowing, absorbing energy, and finally everything illuminated in a blazing light.

Anna stood in the middle of the space, which was smaller than Gavin had expected. Still, there was a sense of energy that existed within it that he could feel, though he wasn't entirely sure why that was. He didn't know if it was something within himself, something within the temple, or something Anna had done that made him feel that.

"They gathered here," she said, her voice low, as if she was afraid to speak too loudly in this place. "There was once a massive table made out of the bralinath trees, which had given themselves to our people."

Gavin frowned. "The trees gave themselves?"

"One does not simply cut down a bralinath tree, Gavin Lorren."

"I didn't know."

She smiled, nodding to him. "I know you did not. And I know that you mean nothing by it. The idea that a bralinath tree would be chopped down at the hands of one of the people is dangerous, though."

"Why?"

"Because to do so would be a huge sacrifice, and it would do a great injustice not only to the tree but to the people."

"I'm guessing there is something about the trees that I don't really understand. I'm having a hard time wrapping my head around why this would be some sort of injustice to the people."

"Because the trees would never let us forget," she said.

Gavin waited for her to say more, but she did not. He frowned at her. "They wouldn't let you forget?"

"Not an offense like that. And we would not expect them to." She motioned around her. "But that is not why I had you come here. We can talk about the bralinath trees and their significance to the people another time. As you are now with us, you must understand why they are important, especially so that you do not make a mistake with them."

Gavin thought that she might be making a joke, but she didn't seem like it. "I suppose I would like that."

She nodded, as if that answered everything. "As I said, this is a place that once was powerful. Perhaps it still is. We are not entirely sure."

"What changed?"

"The power came from the place, but it also came from the people who were here, Gavin Lorren. The greatest and most powerful among the people would come, and they would meet here so that they could help lead the people."

She headed to one of the walls that sloped upward and angled into a point overhead. When she touched it, the wall itself started to glow softly. He had seen something similar in Yoran when they had been in the hall, learning about the El'aras and the prophecy there.

"You will see some of the oldest writings around the base here," Anna said. "They are some of the earliest from when Arashil was first founded and when the temple was built. As you make your way along the base, you can feel the power and the knowledge of those who preceded us."

Gavin joined her at the edge of the temple, looking at

the stone working up from the ground. The blue light that glowed all around him seemed to emanate from the stone floor, working its way up the walls, though it didn't illuminate any of the letters. It wasn't until Anna started to trace a pattern onto the wall that the letters took shape. He suspected that she was doing something to cause that, though he didn't know if it came from some power she had or if it was a specific pattern she used.

"This is what you wanted me to see," Gavin said.

"This is what I have feared showing you, but it's what you need to see." She turned to him. The light cast a strange shadow across her face, and a darkness glittered in her eyes. Gavin took an involuntary step back. He had never seen that from her before, and witnessing it from her now unsettled him.

"When your mentor mentioned another prophecy, I knew where we needed to go," she explained. "I did not want to bring you here, but I also knew I had little choice if we wanted to get answers. You need to understand that which is a part of you, no different than your heart or your lungs."

Gavin smiled at the comment. "I'm working on it."

"But there is something more here." She turned and traced her hand along the bottom row, where the letters were glittering, but she seemed afraid as she touched them. "This speaks of something more. A great shadow." Her tone suggested that the words were more than just words. As if they were a title. "It speaks of the people. And our destruction."

"How long ago was this written?" Gavin asked.

He still didn't understand why she was scared to share that with him, or what she worried about him finding, but if Anna felt the need to be careful with him, he would respect it.

"As I said, they are some of the earliest within Arashil. This settlement was founded thousands of years ago, when my people first began to spread beyond the forest, extending their reach."

He didn't make any comment about her saying "my people" rather than "our people" this time. He didn't want to correct her, especially since he wasn't exactly sure that he felt as though they were his people.

"There are other places within our lands where it speaks of the great shadow. Other places where there are warnings for us that talk about the dangers we might face." She looked down. "But none like this. None with such specific instructions on what we must do, and none with such specific signs that tell us why we must fear it."

"I'm not sure what you're saying."

"You faced one of the Sul'toral."

"That's not such a great shadow," Gavin said. He didn't want to fight somebody like that again, especially since he didn't know if he would come out on the right end of things, though he suspected that he could. "Certainly evil and dangerous, and I know that they serve some other being."

"They do," she said. "And even that is not the great shadow."

"It's not?" Gavin had half expected that Anna had been leading him to that conclusion, but if what she feared most wasn't this Sarenoth—which he had learned that the Sul'toral served—then what could be worse than that? They hadn't even faced Sarenoth.

"He is but one. A herald of something worse."

"And what is that?"

"I don't know. Only that the temple speaks of the herald returning, and what will come after."

"The great shadow," Gavin said.

She looked up, then nodded. "That is my fear."

"Well, considering that Sarenoth is still not freed and that we simply have to defeat the Sul'toral, then it should be a simple matter."

"Sarenoth is only one part of it, only one of the heralds. And that is what I fear your mentor meant." She turned her attention back to the walls of the temple, taking a deep breath and letting it out slowly. "And that is why you must understand your power."

"Because I'm the Champion?"

"Because we must all be a part of this. Perhaps you most of all, Gavin Lorren."

CHAPTER THREE

Gavin stood on the edge of a small valley, overlooking a stream that cut through the forest. The water burbled below him. He was tempted to jump down, splash in the water and take a drink, but he was moving carefully, tracking any signs of movement through the forest. He needed the escape.

Anna's words weighed on him.

This wasn't what he had trained to do. At least, not what he thought he had trained to do. He had no idea what Tristan had wanted from him, only that his mentor certainly must have had some goal in mind. He guessed that, in Tristan's mind, Gavin would become the Champion and then defeat the Shard.

But now that he'd learned that this wasn't all that he was meant to do, Gavin didn't know what more he could —or should—be involved in.

Stopping some great shadow? That wasn't for him. That was for the El'aras to do. Especially if Anna feared that this great shadow would destroy her people.

No matter how she tried to correct herself and call them both her and Gavin's people, they were *her* people, not his. They might be his by blood, but not by how he had been raised. Gavin didn't have a people. He was without a home. A nomad. And that did not bother him. He had come to terms with his role in the world and was content with that. At least, as content as one could be given those circumstances.

The trees nearby shook slightly, trembling from a soft breeze.

Or something else.

He frowned and crept forward, following the wind and the shaking of the trees. One of the branches on a small oak quivered. Many of the bralinath trees were surrounded by others, like the oaks and pine with occasional elm trees. Did the trees have to surround the bralinath trees to support them? Either that or they were offering up some celebration to the trees.

The branch was swaying unnaturally, though. Something had moved through here.

Gavin's training kicked in. He followed the swaying of the branch, treading carefully. As he meandered through the forest, he watched for anything that was out of place: shaking tree limbs, footsteps, the crack of a branch on the ground. Anything that would suggest that something had come through here.

He had gone only another dozen paces when he came across a small shrub that trembled slightly. Gavin reached for his sword and caught sight of a flash of green fabric.

El'aras.

He removed his hand from the hilt of his weapon. He wasn't going to attack one of the El'aras with him. At the same time, he didn't know if this was a scout or somebody coming to test him. He wouldn't be surprised if Master Jaremal had sent someone into the trees after him to test his abilities.

Gavin started to call on his core reserves, feeling for that power deep within him. As he did, he moved ever so carefully forward. He didn't feel anything, though he started to think that perhaps he had imagined what he had seen. The El'aras fabrics blended into the forest almost perfectly, far better than his own cloaks did. He kept waiting for Anna to offer him an El'aras cloak, but perhaps he just needed to ask.

He followed the occasional swaying of branches—the promise that there was somebody here—and still didn't come across anything more. Once he reached the stream, he crouched down, running his hand through the cool water.

A cough from behind him disrupted the silence.

Gavin jumped, spinning, already starting to move through one of his fighting patterns.

"Brandon," he said, withdrawing. He landed in a crouch and twisted back.

Brandon was unique among the El'aras. Not only was he shorter than most, but he also had dark hair rather than the golden hair more commonly found. His eyes were not quite as blue either, taking on a bit of the green of the forest. Were Gavin to see Brandon outside of this context, he would never know that he was El'aras.

"It took you long enough," Brandon said, shaking his head. "I swear, they keep talking about you as if you're some godlike figure, but you let me sneak up on you that way?"

"No one calls me that," Gavin said.

"Fine. Maybe not godlike, but certainly special." Brandon snorted, and he glanced at Gavin's hand, which remained near the hilt of his sword. "Were you thinking to spar? Or was it because you were scared?" A hint of a smile curled his lips.

Gavin shrugged. "I'm always open to spar."

And it wouldn't be the first time he had done so with Brandon. The man was skilled like all of the El'aras were, though he was less fluid than many of the others, and more brutal. Gavin found that he enjoyed their sessions more than any of the other ones. He could use his core reserves to enchant himself and gain the agility that the El'aras possessed, but the brutality was something else. It was harder to compensate for, which made Brandon a far more entertaining person to practice with.

"That's not why you grabbed for your sword, though," Brandon said, chuckling again. "I caught you. I told you I would."

Gavin nodded. "You caught me. Now, what are you doing out here?"

"Oh, you know. They only entrust the most important

people to be out on patrol." He winked at Gavin, and he chuckled. "I was lucky enough to be sent out here. Thomas likes to believe we'll find some of your people, the ones who have come after us and will maybe even attack, and he wanted us to be prepared for that."

"Some of my people?"

"They aren't your people? Well, you could've fooled me. You sure dress like them." Brandon leaned forward, wrinkling his nose. "And you smell like them too."

"I don't smell like anything."

"You smell like…" Brandon wrinkled his brow, frowning even more deeply. "I don't know. Meat? Copper? Maybe a hint of lightning on a storm." He grinned, flashing his teeth. "I like the last one, though. I wish I smelled like that."

Gavin imitated him, leaning and breathing in deeply. "And you smell like a hog farm."

"Is that good? I think that has to be good. Hogs are beautiful and graceful creatures. Quite intelligent, from what I understand."

"It's not the hogs. It's more the…" Gavin waved his hand, dropping the rest of his insult. Either Brandon wouldn't get it, or he would find some way of twisting it to be a compliment. "How long were you following me?"

It would be good to have a sense of how unskilled he was at navigating through the forest.

"Not long. Only since you left the settlement."

Gavin shook his head. "Just that long?"

"Well, I tried to follow you through the buildings, but I

couldn't get close enough to you. Besides, you're spending so much time with *her*." He winked as he said it. "I didn't want to interrupt. A man has needs, doesn't he?" He frowned. "I think that's one of your sayings."

"And you don't have those needs?"

"Why, I'm a graceful and delicate member of the El'aras society," Brandon said, sweeping his hands down and gesturing at his body. "Why would I have those needs?"

Gavin chuckled. "Care to walk with me?"

"I'm not so sure I would be able to spot anything dangerous if I walked with the great Gavin Lorren. I mean, the Chain Breaker?" He gave an exaggerated shrug. "Or do you prefer Champion?"

"Maybe none of them."

"I still don't know why you dislike your titles."

"I'm not sure that any of them are titles. The first one is my name. The other is a nickname that I was given when I was training. And the last is part of some made-up prophecy."

"The Champion isn't just a part of the prophecy with the Risen Shard," Brandon said, shaking his head. "It's more than that. I figured you would know that by now. There are references to the Champion in all different prophecies. Not that I get much into that. I wouldn't want you to get too big of a head. I mean, your head is already big enough, and you have such terrible hair."

"Now I have terrible hair?"

"It's too dark."

"And yours isn't?" Gavin asked, eyebrow arched.

Brandon ran his fingers through his hair. "Mine is a delicate shade of brown, almost as if the bralinath trees themselves have gifted me with a hint of their essence. And yours is a pale imitation, almost as if the hogs that you claim I smell like left their shit smeared all over your face."

Gavin barked out a laugh. "There you go."

"That one was good?" Brandon asked, beaming.

"That was a pretty good one. Though, I *was* trying to say that you smelled like that."

"I know you were. And then you gave up. You're too afraid of me."

"Not so much that I'm afraid of you as…"

Brandon chuckled. "First, I manage to sneak up on you, and now I have the great Champion scared. I'm having quite the day."

"You *are* having quite the day."

"Where did you want me to follow you? I can protect you as you make your way through the forest. It seems you need somebody to do that, don't you?"

"That's exactly what I asked from you," Gavin said.

"I figured. Where did you want to go?"

"I wanted to explore more of the area around the settlement."

"Most of it is patrolled by the El'aras. Thomas has us circling it. He's afraid that we might get caught off guard again."

"Again?"

"Well, I wasn't there when you were in the city, and he was caught unaware. I wasn't one of those who made the mistake of letting the other family attack."

"I don't think Thomas cared for that," Gavin said.

"He didn't. And I think it shames him." Brandon shook his head. "Not that it should... The families have been far too violent for my liking."

"I thought you enjoyed a little violence."

"Not among the families." All humor faded from his voice. "We need to be unified. The families have dealt with enough over the years, and for us to battle one another puts us in a precarious situation. If the sorcerers were to target us, there is a very real possibility that we would not be able to defend against them without working together."

These sentiments were too close to what Theren had told Gavin he believed.

"Thankfully, it is unusual for the families to be at odds," Brandon continued. "Most of the time, we work together. It's why I am here. And why you are too. The great Champion. I suspect everyone expects you to make sure that we have peace once more."

"I'm not going to be the one who can make that happen."

"No?" Brandon smiled. "Not that I can blame you. I can't imagine what it must be like. I know they have been trying to force you to take on some role. I wouldn't want anything like that."

Gavin shook his head. "It's not a matter of whether I want the role. It's that I'm not sure that I am what they believe me to be." The prophecy had been a fabrication of the Sul'toral. Gavin couldn't do anything with that other than fight what they wanted him to be. "According to Anna and Master Jaremal, I need to spend all my time training, trying to understand how to use that power so that I can become what they think I need to become."

"You do have some deficiencies," Brandon said, "though they haven't held you back much. It seems like even with those, you've managed quite well. You should be proud of yourself."

"Thanks."

He eyed Gavin and pursed his lips. "Are you not proud of yourself?"

"Are you going to come with me or not?"

"Now I see. All of this was really about you needing my protection."

"We already agreed it was."

"Good. Come on. I'll show you where you need to go," Brandon said with a laugh.

They started off, making their way through the forest. The water splashed softly, and Gavin tried to listen for other sounds around them, but he didn't hear anything. Brandon moved silently enough that he scarcely made a noise. Gavin considered himself relatively skillful at sneaking and navigating quietly but had learned that there were others who were far more capable than he was. Even those without El'aras abilities. Brandon made it seem easy.

"Have you seen signs of anything out here?" Gavin whispered.

Brandon shook his head quickly. "There's been nothing. I know Thomas and the others like to think we have to be worried about the possibility of an attack, but so far, we haven't come across anything. We're far removed from the cities of humans and from any places that they would even know about. They wouldn't come out here."

"It's not just them," Gavin said.

"You know something I don't?"

"Well…"

Brandon looked over to him, and his dark eyes narrowed for just a moment. "They shared the temple with you, didn't they?"

Gavin nodded. "You knew?"

"That's the story about this place."

"You don't believe it?"

Brandon shrugged. "Can't say that I do. I'm not a priest, and I'm not the Risen Shard"—he waved his hand as if dismissing the idea that the Risen Shard was an important title—"and I'm certainly not the Champion. Though I *have* scared him today, and I managed to sneak up on him, so maybe I'm better than him?" He frowned, scratching his chin in an exaggerated motion like he was trying to decide. "Either way, the elders have long tried to claim that we're under some great threat that will destroy our people." He chuckled. "No one has ever seen any sign of that threat, and other than the sorcerers who decided to try to attack our people, we haven't experienced any real danger. So I think it's more just a way to scare the children."

"It seems that some of the adult El'aras are still afraid of it."

"And they were afraid of *you*, too," he said, then grinned. "And you see where that got them, don't you?"

Gavin laughed as he paused at the stream's edge. "I see exactly where that got them."

Brandon motioned for him to cross the stream. "This is the narrowest part of it. We go across here, then I can show you to the edge of our perimeter, but we really shouldn't go much beyond that. I don't want to be the one to allow the great Champion to escape."

"I didn't realize I was a prisoner."

"No? I thought we were holding you here. Mostly for your safety." He winked.

Gavin jumped across the stream, borrowing from his core reserves to make it easier. He landed on the other side, then watched Brandon jump. He cleared it just as easily and with a bit more grace, though he landed closer to the stream than Gavin did.

"I almost got you on that one," Brandon said.

"I didn't realize it was a competition."

"Why shouldn't it be?"

They made their way even farther through the forest, with Brandon leading. They hadn't gone far before he stopped near one of the bralinath trees. Gavin made his way toward the tree, but Brandon caught his wrist and shook his head.

"Not so close to him," he hissed.

"The tree is a him?"

"Of course. But not so close. He won't like it."

"What am I not understanding about these trees?"

"Probably a lot," Brandon said. "But seeing as how there are many things about our people that you still don't understand, I think you can be forgiven." He chuckled, waving his hand. "Don't tell anyone else I said that. They would rather see you as a pariah, blame you for all of the wrongs we have suffered, and try to tell you that you will bring the great darkness down upon us."

"I thought it was the great shadow."

"Shadow. Darkness. Aren't they the same thing?"

Gavin crept forward, and Brandon stayed even with him.

"They have us patrolling all the way out here," Brandon said. "And it does give us quite the perimeter around Arashil, but can you believe they think we need to come all the way out here?" He shook his head. "I certainly can't. We have chased away anything that might come, to the point where there are no wolves, foxes, or even anything interesting like brisalt or igaral."

"I have seen the igaral recently," Gavin said. The massive cats prowled through the forest, though they were generally scarce. Despite being skilled hunters and dangerous predators, they generally left people alone. "But I would think you would be more interested in chasing dark creatures."

He looked over to Brandon, wondering if he had any experience with that. When Gavin had last spoken to Jayna, she had mentioned dealing with dark creatures, so he suspected that they were spreading out farther. Nelar was close to the southern edge of El'aras lands, and she was fighting dark creatures there.

"That's not the kind of fun I want," Brandon replied.

"What kind of fun would you have, exactly?"

"I don't know. In my homeland, we like to wrestle the ocelarn and ride them. They can be a little ornery, though."

"I'm not familiar with those."

"Well, they're bigger than cows, with hides thicker than any tree, and they get mean, especially when you try to climb onto them."

"So you just wrestle them?"

"We don't want to hurt them. It's more just for sport."

"So you aren't from the trees." He thought of Theren, who hadn't been from the forest either, and who had essentially betrayed everyone in his desire to return to a different time.

"Not the trees. My people come from the plains. We don't like all the tall trees scattered around us. Feels a little oppressive, if you know what I mean."

"And your family—"

"Oh, don't worry about that. We get along just fine with the Risen Shard. I'm not trying to overthrow her power or anything like that."

"I wasn't suggesting you were."

"I could see it in your eyes, Champion." He grinned. "But if I wanted to overthrow her, you know I'm strong enough. I mean, I scared the Champion. How could I not scare the Risen Shard as well?"

"I would not doubt your ability."

"Good. But don't tell her I said that."

Gavin chuckled to himself. Brandon was interesting, he couldn't deny that. But there was a part of him that found it difficult to trust the man, especially lately. He would have to be careful with him.

What he wouldn't give to have his team here with him. It had taken a long time for him to find others that he was comfortable working with and to trust them. Not just Wrenlow, but Gaspar and Imogen too. Thinking of them made him consider attempting to use his enchantment again to try to reach them, but it had not been effective last time. He wondered if Anna had prevented him from being able to communicate with them, but he didn't know with any certainty. Either that, or the enchantments around Yoran were interfering.

Besides, Wrenlow was busy with Olivia, Gaspar no longer needed Gavin, and Imogen planned to leave to chase down her own demons.

Gavin tore himself away from those thoughts. "What's beyond here?"

"Well, the trees start to thin, and the bralinath aren't found quite as often, if at all. That's part of the reason they don't want us to go any farther. The bralinath trees give us a different measure of protection, one that the people can't offer on their own."

"What do the trees do?"

"Have you ever spoken to one?"

"I didn't realize I could," Gavin said, glancing over to the tallest tree near him. The enormous bralinath had irregular bark, with branches arching high above his head.

Massive leaves unfurled, as if awaiting the warmth of the sun. The air smelled of their sharp fragrance, something that seemed familiar to him, though he didn't know why. The idea that it was a male tree, and that he could speak to it, seemed strangely foreign to him.

It was just one more aspect of everything he had been doing with the El'aras that reminded him of how out of place he was here. When he had agreed to come with Anna, he had done so because he wanted to understand the power he possessed and to learn whether there was anything he might be able to use it for. The more he began to learn about the El'aras and about himself, the more he began to question whether he had made the right decision. Gavin simply didn't know.

"Of course you can speak to them," Brandon said. "The real problem is that they don't always speak back."

"Always?"

Brandon shrugged. "Well, occasionally they do, but you have to really listen hard. I can't say I know too many people who have the ability or who can do it well, so they can't hear the bralinath. When you do, though, you can find answers."

"Why can you find them from the trees?"

"The trees are connected to each other," he said simply. "And they know secrets."

Gavin arched a brow at him. Though it was similar to what Anna had said, he found it difficult to believe that there were any real secrets found within the trees. Then again, he couldn't reject the idea out of hand. There was always the possibility that the El'aras truly could talk to them.

"What sorts of secrets?" he asked.

"I can't tell the bralinath secrets to you—not if you can't speak to them yourself. You have to find out on your own. And if they start to tell you their secrets, maybe you'll share with me what you learn?"

Gavin chuckled and shook his head. "We should..."

He trailed off as he spotted something deeper in the forest, on the other side of the bralinath tree. He started forward, shaking Brandon off when he grabbed Gavin's arm. Gavin wasn't sure what he saw, but there was enough to it that had him curious.

"Champion? Gavin?"

Gavin waved his hand. "There's something over here."

When he stepped past the bralinath tree, a strange tingling sensation worked along his skin, leaving his arms feeling as if he'd been in the sun all day long. The heat flared, faded briefly, then surged once more before disappearing altogether.

Once he reached the other side of what he imagined to be a boundary, the air took on a different quality. It was slightly more humid, but it was more than just the humidity in the air that Gavin detected. There was a change in the odor of the forest, as if the forest was trying to tell him something—a warning, perhaps. He moved forward carefully, hand hovering near his sword.

"Do you see anything?" Brandon whispered.

Gavin raised his hand, motioning for him to be quiet.

He crept carefully, and then he realized what was bothering him.

A pillar of rock stood before him. The structure seemed out of place, though he wasn't exactly sure why that was. The pillar, made of a faded yellow stone, looked to be about chest height. As Gavin approached it, he swept his gaze around him to search for anything else in the forest, but he didn't see anything more. Just the stone.

Gavin hurried toward it, and as he approached the pillar, he quickly glanced back. Brandon lingered near the bralinath tree, but he stood far enough apart from it that he looked like he was trying to give it space out of fear of getting too close.

Gavin turned back to the stone, moving carefully, and he frowned as he neared it. Why would something like this exist out here? The structure seemed as if it didn't belong.

He held his hand up to touch it once he approached, but froze with hand outstretched. Everything within him went cold at the sight of a symbol etched into the stone. Though almost burned and blackened, it had a familiar shape.

Gavin had seen that symbol before—the same one that was burned onto his foot through an accident when he'd been much younger. A series of interlocked triangles that he'd seen enough that he'd never forget.

Tristan's mark.

Why would it be out here, though? And what was Tristan trying to tell him?

He approached the stone, and as he looked around

again, he searched for any sign of Tristan. The fact that he left his mark here suggested that he knew where Gavin was. What was Tristan hoping to tell him?

The last time they had seen each other, Tristan had warned that there was something worse coming. Was this another warning?

"Gavin?" Brandon's voice was soft, hushed, but it carried through the air.

"You can come out here."

Brandon started forward, moving hesitantly. When he reached Gavin, he pursed his lips. "That wasn't here last time I was on patrol."

"You would have remembered?"

He looked over to Gavin and rolled his eyes. "I am not a fool, Gavin Lorren. When I take my patrol, I do as I'm asked."

"I wasn't saying you're a fool. I was just—"

"It wasn't here the last time I patrolled the area." He crouched, looking at the mark. "And what is this? What do you think that means?"

"I know what it means," Gavin said, looking all around him. "But what I don't know is why it's here."

"What does it mean?"

"It means that the man who trained me was here."

"Then what did he hope to accomplish?"

Gavin shook his head. "That is what we need to understand."

Brandon stepped forward, resting his hand on the stone. He traced a quick pattern, then the stone started to tremble. "There's nothing to it." He glanced over to

Gavin. "It's just this. Is that what your mentor would do?"

"I don't know. It's his mark, but I'm not exactly sure why it's here."

"We should—"

Brandon stiffened, eyes wide, and he jerked his head behind him.

"What is it?" Gavin asked.

"An attack."

CHAPTER FOUR

They raced through the trees. Brandon had the training of all El'aras who worked with their abilities their entire life, practically gliding along the forest floor. He leapt across the stream, jumped up the embankment, and bounded through the forest. Gavin had to call on his core reserves as he ran, immediately aware of just how much power he was summoning. There had to be a way to do so as a slow trickle rather than a burst of power the way he did it, but if so, he wasn't familiar with it.

He strained, but he was able to keep up with Brandon. "What kind of attack?"

Brandon shook his head, keeping his face neutral. He moved quickly and raced through the trees, forcing Gavin to concentrate more than he usually would as he navigated the forest. At least he knew where he was heading, though.

"I didn't get that alert," Brandon replied. "Just that there was an attack."

"Have you seen signs of anything unusual?"

Brandon glanced over at Gavin briefly before turning his attention back ahead of him. "On the patrols? No. We've been warned, though, and have feared there might be something, but we haven't come across anything." He clenched his jaw. "I shouldn't have been so far away."

"You said you were on patrol, and that—"

"I was on patrol, and with you, Champion, but I should have been closer."

"Would it have made a difference?"

"I don't know," he muttered, irritation palpable.

They reached the settlement, and Gavin didn't see signs that there was anything wrong. El'aras mingled in the city and moved through the streets, and there was no sound of fighting. But Brandon raced forward. Gavin kept pace with him, and as they neared the northern side of the settlement, Brandon unsheathed his sword.

Gavin did the same, and he focused on the power of the ring, letting that energy begin to sweep through him. If there was danger here, he wanted to be as prepared as possible, and the best way to do that was to call on the energy of the ring and use it to defend himself and the settlement.

As soon as they reached the far side and the trees again, the sounds of fighting rang out. The feeling of powerful magic began to build, pushing against him in an overwhelming pressure that reverberated. The magic seemed as if it were trying to press against his awareness and force itself upon him.

Brandon staggered, stumbling, and Gavin was able to catch him and help him to his feet.

"Come on," Gavin muttered.

"How can you withstand this?" Brandon asked.

"Come on."

He called on more power through the ring, dragging Brandon with him. The other man had turned pale, yet he clenched his jaw, squeezed his sword, and nodded to Gavin. They had only gone about another dozen paces before Gavin felt another surge of power within him.

Brandon stumbled and fell. Gavin grabbed for him, but Brandon shook his head, waving him off.

"You need to get up," Gavin said.

"Can't," Brandon said, gritting his teeth.

The pressure against Gavin was too much, and he was quickly becoming overcome by it. He was using every-thing within him, everything he could call on through his core reserves and through the ring, and he united the two powers as he attempted to push against it.

And still it intensified.

If he continued to hold on to this power, he would be spent, with no strength remaining. Without sh'rasn powder, the magical El'aras substance that allowed him to tap into some greater store of energy, Gavin wouldn't be able to withstand it.

Since traveling with Anna, he hadn't needed to take sh'rasn powder. There'd been a time when he had been forced to use the sh'rasn many times to defend himself and the El'aras, but since traveling out here, they had been safe.

Until now.

And whatever was coming was powerful.

Gavin took another step, and the energy continued to build upon him. Brandon remained on the ground, seeming unable to stand. As Gavin staggered forward, he tried to fight through the power pushing against him.

Some part of him questioned whether Master Jaremal was testing him again, but this wasn't the kind of thing he would do. He wouldn't have created a test that would torment other El'aras. Gavin looked back at Brandon, who was lying on the ground with his eyes wide and his face pale. If Gavin didn't have access to his core reserves and to his ring, he wasn't sure that he would be able to defend against this.

A darkened figure appeared between the trees and moved toward Brandon. They wore an all-black robe and held a blade that matched, made of a completely black material. Their movements were fluid, like an El'aras, but even more powerful than most.

The figure rose their sword high above Brandon.

"No!" Gavin darted forward while calling on the ring's power.

As he neared the attacker, his blade clanged off of another sword.

He wasn't fast enough without power. It was almost as if…

As if whatever this was wanted to force him to use his core reserves.

Gavin released the power, and it washed out of him. He could suddenly move, like he was unencumbered.

He didn't need to summon the power within him—the power of the El'aras—the way the other El'aras did. Gavin didn't have to draw on that power all the time.

He faced the robed figure. There were various fighting styles he could use, but one in particular came to him first. It was one that his friend Imogen had taught him, the fighting style of her people, one that few outside of the Leier knew.

Gavin fell into it easily. The power in the patterns allowed him to flow and glide forward. He brought his blade up as he crashed his body against the figure. Gavin spun, then stabbed, catching them in the chest.

They collapsed forward, but Gavin wasn't finished. He instinctively began to draw on his core reserves, before feeling the immediate resistance on him, making that attack difficult. He ripped the blade out, withdrawing from his attempt to call on the magic within him. He had to focus on only his patterns.

If Brandon weren't lying helpless behind him, Gavin wondered if he might enjoy this. There were so few times when he was able to face an opponent without needing to use his core reserves. There were so few times when he let himself fight.

He spun, and two other attackers emerged from the darkness of the forest. Like his first opponent, they were cloaked in black and had matching blades... that were dripping with blood.

That meant the El'aras were down.

How many?

Gavin pushed those thoughts out of his head. He could help here.

He darted forward, using a part of his mind to avoid calling on his core reserves. If he did, he would risk drawing on more power than he needed. Suppressing that desire, he raced forward and crashed into the nearest of the attackers, sweeping his blade up in a sharp arc, and he cut their arm clean off. They crumpled, sword dropping to the ground near Gavin.

With how powerful his El'aras blade was, Gavin might not need to use his core reserves.

A whistle caught his attention, and he instinctively ducked and rolled to the side. His reaction, honed through decades of training, helped him identify that threat.

He didn't need just his sword-fighting skill. In fact, that was probably his weakest fighting technique. But he could use a combination of his abilities.

He popped back up, not enhanced by his core reserves like he normally would be when fighting, and he brought his blade around, jabbing toward the dark-robed attacker. They twisted out of the way, clearly unencumbered by the pressure pushing on Gavin—the pressure that made him refuse to use his own magic.

Gavin shifted the blade in hand. He couldn't see their face, but he was curious what they would look like in death.

"Thought you could sneak in here and suppress the El'aras, did you?"

The figure started toward him, sweeping their blade around, then twisting with a regularity to his motions. Gavin didn't recognize the fighting style, but there was an aspect to it that reminded him of the Leier technique. One that carried power with it.

Could that be what they were using? Did they draw magic through the pattern itself? Until meeting Imogen, Gavin hadn't thought something like that was possible, and he would never have considered using anything like that.

But he could counter it.

He flowed, something that the Leier techniques taught him. The fluidity to his movements allowed him to understand how to hold on to the power of the patterns themselves. And Gavin had long since learned those patterns. They weren't ingrained in him the way others were, but enough that he could use their power.

He darted forward, carving his blade through his opponent's shoulder and leg, then stabbed them in the back.

Gavin glanced over to Brandon, who still hadn't moved. Whatever pressure was pushing down on him remained. Gavin didn't dare draw on his intrinsic magic or that of the ring, not if they were somehow pushing on him.

He could protect Brandon. But maybe he needed to do more than that. He had to help the other El'aras too. If there were other attackers in the trees, he had to find them.

He paused, listening. If he could find where the other

El'aras were, he could help them. The blood on the blades of these strange attackers left little doubt that there were El'aras in need of rescuing. They might not be able to fight. He might be the only one who could rescue them.

He followed the shadows of the forest. A pair of darkened figures came toward him.

Gavin flowed toward the nearest one and stayed in the Leier technique, gliding forward. When he reached them, they seemed almost surprised he could move that way.

He cut the first attacker down before they even realized he was there. He spun and found two more near him. They worked as a unit, which meant that they understood he posed a real threat.

Gavin darted toward the first. He got past their black blade, reached the next, and spun, driving forward with his weapon. He jabbed into the chest of one, and then into the side of another.

As he fought, he recognized that he was getting pushed deeper into the forest, but the pressure around him hadn't eased. Whatever strange force they were using against him, whatever strange magic they had that separated him from his core reserves, had not let up.

Gavin moved carefully, gliding forward, and he continued to flow within the Leier patterns.

A body lay on the ground.

There was one, then another, and then a third. A green cloak stained with blood. No movement from their chest, nothing rising or falling to suggest that they were alive.

He kept onward. Gavin twisted and turned through the trees, trying to find where he could go next, what he needed to do. Every step seemed to guide him away from Arashil, but he thought that he needed to fight back, that he needed to push. Why would they want to keep him out of the settlement?

Unless this was simply meant to target those who could fight back and to lure them away.

Gavin spun, racing back toward Arashil. He reached Brandon and glanced down at him, but Gavin made his way past and didn't help. As far as he knew, Brandon didn't need any help and may not be in any danger at all. It was possible that the attackers had tried to drive them out, weakening the El'aras, and then…

A scream pierced the air.

It came from within Arashil.

Gavin darted forward. He paused at the edge of the settlement and saw no movement—but he could *feel* something. That same strange energy pushed down on him, as if trying to squeeze through him and separate him from his core reserves to make it so that he couldn't use that part of himself.

He struggled to tamp down his temptation to use that magic. For so long, Gavin had attempted to reach it, to call it through himself, wanting nothing more than to feel that power and to know how it would work. But this time, he felt as if he needed to avoid using it. Instead of drawing on the core reserves, he had to abandon them altogether.

He raced ahead, ducking between a pair of buildings. Two dark-cloaked attackers stood there, facing away from him. Gavin jabbed his blade into the back of one and moved on to the next before they were even aware of his presence.

A figure lunged toward him like a snake. The blade was a flicker of movement so fast that he could scarcely follow it. Gavin brought his blade around, cutting through one block, then another, until he finally caught them off guard. He thrust his sword, but the cloak seemed to fold around the blade and squeeze.

No human could survive a strike like that, not with Gavin driving the blade right through his stomach.

What was this?

Could this be the kind of presence that Anna had warned him about? She had said there was some other power, but he had not expected it to be quite this significant.

He stepped forward again and brought the blade down, trying to catch them by surprise. But they once again seemed to fold, the shadows somehow sweeping around Gavin as if they were collapsing in on him.

Gavin jerked back, resisting the urge to call on his core reserves. He had a feeling that was exactly what this opponent wanted.

Fighting styles came to him instinctively. Inril. Bongan. Vutharin. Cislish. He had trained in all of them when he was much younger, and they were all a part of how he had learned to fight when working with Tristan.

His opponent countered each of them with a blade that moved in a blur, matching Gavin blow for blow, almost impossibly fast. He switched to one of the Leier techniques, and it was the first time the figure didn't seem to have a counter for what Gavin used.

A deep, dark laughter echoed around them. "You are as skilled as you were promised to be."

Gavin darted toward him, but his blows were blocked. He continued focusing on the Leier techniques, which seemed as if they would be his most effective ones. The man either didn't know the fighting style, or he didn't have any way of blocking it.

"He taught you well," the man said.

Gavin hesitated.

In that moment of uncertainty, the attacker sped toward him, bringing his blade up. Gavin matched him and raised his sword, thrusting it forward, but he wasn't quick enough. The other man countered his charge.

"Who are you?" Gavin asked.

"He didn't tell you about me. I'm not surprised."

He was doing what the man wanted of him, he knew, but that didn't change the fact that his curiosity was winning. Gavin needed to know. He had a sneaking suspicion that this attacker knew Tristan.

It was more than just that, though. This man knew Tristan's fighting style, and that was what worried Gavin the most.

"So disappointing," his opponent said. "I thought that after all the time he and I spent together, I would've meant more to him than that." He chuckled, but there was no amusement in it. "He never was one for such sympathy, though." He dove toward Gavin.

The suddenness of his movement suggested that he was enchanted.

Enchantments.

Gavin hadn't even tried that. Ever since coming to the settlement, studying with Master Jaremal, and working with Anna, he had not felt the need to use any enchantments.

He jumped out of the way, slipping his hand into his pocket and grabbing a bracelet. He had it on him at all times, more as a reminder of who he had been and where he had come from than anything else.

This enchantment gave him speed, and he had another one, if he could reach it.

He fished into his other pocket, but the suddenness of the next attack caught him off guard. Gavin twisted, spinning out of the way, thankful that the enchantment still worked the way it should've. He didn't feel the same pressure on him with using the enchantment as he did when trying to draw on his core reserves.

He blocked the next few attacks, buying enough time to reach into his pocket again and slip a ring onto his middle finger. The construction was different than the ring that granted him greater access to his El'aras abilities. The one he wore now was an enchantment made by one of the most skilled enchanters in Yoran. It granted him hardened skin, as if he were made of steel. Gavin hoped that it would work well enough to protect him against these attacks.

He twisted to the side, deflecting the next attack, and the next. Each time he turned, he felt the power within the enchantment begin to fade. The magic in each enchantment was limited. If Anna had made it, he was certain that it would've been effective for much longer.

Gavin blocked another attack. The hardened skin protected him from one blow, but he still felt it like a boulder slamming into his arm. He spun to face the attacker and glanced around him as he did. He didn't see anything other than the row of buildings around him. No other El'aras.

How many had been killed already?

Had Anna died? Had Master Jaremal?

The attacker stepped forward. "Enchantments? That's a lesson he tries to beat out of his disciples."

"It didn't take," Gavin said.

The man chuckled. "Obviously. Otherwise, you would not have dared use that on me."

"I figured I needed to level the playing field. If you're using enchantments, then I should as well."

"I am using no enchantment," he said, laughing again.

"You could have fooled me."

"It won't be the last time."

Gavin snorted. "Arrogance. You must've been quite popular with him, then."

Increasingly, Gavin believed that this man understood Tristan and had trained with him, and he realized he was at a disadvantage. He knew people who had trained with Tristan at the same time he had been there, but not anybody who might have done so before him. It was possible—likely, even—that Tristan had mentored other students before Gavin had begun working with him.

"Perhaps," the man said, "though I suspect he would call me something else."

He darted forward, moving impossibly fast—faster than Gavin's enchantment allowed him to react. Gavin was thankful for the hardened skin, but its power continued to fade.

"What would he call you?" he asked, blocking a few thrusts.

"A failure."

Gavin had no choice but to try one more thing. It wasn't what he intended to do, and he wasn't sure if it would even make a difference, especially not against somebody like this, but he had to try.

He had the El'aras ring. He had the blade.

And stopping somebody like this required more than what he could do on his own.

Gavin summoned the power through the ring. As soon as he started to call on that energy, something weighed down on him. But he didn't need indefinite magic now. He had a strong feeling that this man and his attacks were the last he would have to face, that he was the leader of this group. Which meant that if Gavin could stop him, he had a better chance of stopping the attack altogether.

He simply had to get past him, find some sh'rasn powder, and finish the rest.

The man moved in a shadowy blur, but Gavin channeled the energy of the ring. He had already seen that he could use it despite any attempt to try to suppress it. It might take everything within him to summon all of the power he wanted, but he knew he could do that now.

He had no other choice.

The power of the ring filled him and surged not only through him but through the sword itself. His blade began to glow, first a faint blue, but increasingly brighter. Gavin became ablaze with light, and the power exploded outward, slamming toward his attacker.

A weight seemed to lift from Gavin. His core reserves were no longer suppressed the way they had been.

He lunged, and as his blade struck his opponent, the shadows around the man folded the way they had before, like they were trying to collapse along the sword. Enough power filled Gavin and poured out of him that he no longer worried about this man overwhelming his control. All he needed was to blast through what this attacker was doing. All he needed was to carve through him. All he needed was to destroy.

But he didn't have the chance.

The man disappeared, and Gavin was left holding his blade, staring at the emptiness.

Only questions remained.

CHAPTER FIVE

Gavin hurried through the settlement, fear of what he might find coursing through him. Given how the attack had taken place and the level of brutality, how many El'aras had fallen and died? He hadn't gotten to know the people here all that well, but they had stayed in Arashil because of Anna. And she had stayed because of him.

He hadn't gone far before he found the first.

A young woman named Moira lay with an open wound across her chest, her eyes glassy in death. He had come to know her during his journey. Her hands were empty, no weapon to be found. She was not a fighter. She would've had her El'aras abilities, until these attackers had suppressed them and stolen whatever power the El'aras needed to defend themselves.

Gavin traced his hand across her pallid skin, feeling a

moment of remorse, then moved on to the next fallen El'aras.

Robert had been a fighter, and his sword rested near him. Given the way Brandon had been subdued, though, Gavin suspected that Robert had struggled the same way. So many had fallen without the ability to fight.

Gavin had seen brutality during his days. He couldn't train with someone like Tristan and not be exposed to it. But staying with the El'aras had left him thinking that he would have a measure of safety and calm, yet that was not to be.

There was no safety here. There was only death.

Still, in all the years that he had trained and fought, Gavin had never seen El'aras fall so easily. Even when he had faced them, he had struggled. What kind of opponent could do this?

He hurried through the streets and found far too many bodies.

Finally, he came across the first survivor.

Gowaneth was an older El'aras—a priest, Gavin suspected, though Anna had never called him that. He had long, flowing hair that was kept bound back in a length of colorful silk. His flowing green robes were a different style than the forest-green cloaks that many of the El'aras bore. A symbol on the chain at his neck seemed to glow, as if he had pushed power through it.

Gavin reached for him, but Gowaneth jerked his head back like he was trying to move away from him. "I'm just trying to help," Gavin said.

The priest looked up at him, blinking for a moment. "I don't know what happened. I could not reach for that part of myself. It was as though I could no longer breathe."

"They had some way of suppressing El'aras power."

"Such a thing should not be possible."

Gavin extended his hand again, and this time, Gowaneth accepted assistance and allowed himself to be helped to his feet. The man clasped his hands together with eyes closed and stood motionless, looking deep in contemplation. Then he opened his eyes, glanced over at Gavin, and met his gaze for a long moment.

"How did you withstand it?" Gowaneth asked.

"I don't need my core reserves to fight."

"How do you withstand that?" This time, the nature of the question was different. There was more of an edge of disdain in it, the same way other El'aras spoke when it came to talking about living without access to his power.

Gavin let out a small chuckle. "Well, seeing as how it is all I've ever known until recently, fairly easily. I can't hold on to my power constantly the way you do."

"And these soldiers?"

Gavin snorted. "They weren't soldiers." He needed to investigate more, but he was certain that they weren't soldiers. He didn't know what exactly they were, though he felt as if others here would. Perhaps Master Jaremal. Maybe even Anna. The answers would be found within the encampment.

"They slaughtered so many. I tried to protect our people, but there was only so much I could do. I

attempted to defend myself, and others, but I was limited."
He looked up at Gavin, his eyes wide, sadness within
them.

"I'm sure you did as well as you could, but they had
some way of suppressing your abilities." He felt as if he
needed to repeat that, hoping that perhaps Gowaneth
would have some answers about why that happened, but
he didn't acknowledge it. "Where is Anna?"

"The Risen Shard, along with others, retreated to the
temple."

Gavin turned toward the structure. "Why don't you
check on others who may need assistance. I'm going to
make sure that Anna is…"

He wasn't sure what else to say. All he could think of
was that if Anna had died, the one connection he really
had to the El'aras would be gone. He had come here
because of her. Because of his attraction to her, if he was
being honest with himself. But it was more than that.
There was something that bonded him as the Champion
to her as the Risen Shard, and Gavin needed to understand what that was and what it meant for him.

He hurried off, leaving Gowaneth behind, though he
did glance back to make sure that Gowaneth was checking
on others. The man still seemed stunned, but Gavin
understood. He had seen plenty of others react in much
the same way after battles. They struggled with the attack,
then struggled to deal with the aftermath, especially if
they weren't trained to fight. So many of the El'aras were
not. In a place of power like Arashil, Gavin doubted that

there would be too many who could fight. There were those who had come with Anna, but that was about it.

He reached the temple. The door was closed, but he remembered what Anna had done and how she had managed to open it. Gavin pressed his hand against the door, tracing the patterns he recalled her making. He didn't know them well, but he remembered them well enough after seeing them only once. He didn't have to understand them in order to replicate them.

Gavin formed the patterns and pushed out a hint of power from his core reserves into each one he generated. The door began to glow softly, but then it fizzled out.

He decided to try something else. Rather than drawing on his core reserves, he called on the power of the ring. As he placed the ring's energy into the patterns he had traced, the blue lines began to glow more brightly. This time, they didn't fizzle out. Gavin continued to send power out through him and into the patterns, until the door finally came open.

A force like a boulder slammed into his chest. He staggered back and braced himself, instinctively strengthening his body with his core reserves. Briefly, he realized he was still wearing the ring that granted him hardened skin, which he had put on to defend himself against the attackers in the settlement. Had he not, the blow might've been more than he could handle. With the enchantment, he could at least tolerate it, though with difficulty.

"It's Gavin," he said, hurrying back to the door while rubbing his chest. "Whoever is inside can come out. The threat is neutralized."

The face that appeared before him was not the one he expected.

Thomas had his sword unsheathed. He eyed Gavin before sweeping his gaze past him, out into the rest of the settlement. "What happened?"

He was one of the few El'aras who looked old, something that Gavin knew better than to ask him about. But given that the El'aras could live for centuries, he remained impossibly curious about how old Thomas really was. Tristan was supposedly several centuries old, which meant that Thomas might be twice that. His navy-blue cloak, which was slung over his shoulders, fell slightly askew as he sheathed his sword.

"Well, I was about to ask you, or perhaps anyone who might know something about this—"

"We could barely do anything," Thomas said, and Gavin sensed the irritation within him. "The Risen Shard defended us, deflecting some of the attack, but she warned that we needed to get to safety."

That made sense. Gavin had been able to use his power through his ring, though it had strained him considerably. Anna used something similar with her connection to the shard, and it didn't surprise him that she would've been able to tap into her own power, using that against the attack.

"How many fell?" Thomas asked.

Gavin shook his head. "I'm not sure. Gowaneth is sweeping through Arashil to see how many survived."

"How many attackers were there?"

"I brought down half a dozen. And there was one more who escaped."

Thomas pressed his lips together in a tight frown and sighed. He glanced around him, and when he looked back at Gavin, there was a flicker of emotion in his eyes that Gavin couldn't quite read. Was it fear?

"How were you able to withstand it?" Thomas said.

"I fought without my... well, my El'aras side."

Thomas nodded. He stepped back, and Gavin wondered for a second if he was supposed to follow him, but then Anna emerged from the temple. Her hair hung loose, and some dirt had stained her dress, but she looked otherwise unharmed. She wore no weapon, though he knew that she was capable of fighting. It was probably for the best, though. He had no idea how she would've fared if she'd tried to face their attackers.

"You live," she whispered.

"You don't have to sound so surprised."

"You weren't in the settlement when the attack came, so I didn't know. We weren't sure where you were."

"I was out with Brandon, wandering around the perimeter of Arashil." Gavin shrugged at her arched brow. "I needed to get out, after our conversation."

She looked behind her and said something quickly in the El'aras tongue, though Gavin didn't understand it. Though he'd been studying how to read their language and knew some of the words, understanding their speech was something else entirely, especially with how fluid it sounded when they spoke.

"What did you say?" he asked.

"I told Master Jaremal that he could come forward. He has been concerned."

"He couldn't defend you?"

"He is powerful, Gavin Lorren, but he has limitations at his age."

For Anna to acknowledge his age suggested that he was incredibly old. Gavin had been questioning how old Thomas might be, but Master Jaremal had to be even older. Ancient, even by the El'aras standards. He had no idea that the El'aras had any limitations with age. If he were to live that long, would he end up having similar ones? Perhaps the better question was whether he *wanted* to live a prolonged life. He had long ago prepared for the idea of an early death, but meeting Anna and learning the truth about himself meant that he might live far longer than he had ever expected.

"What did they do?" he asked.

Anna shook her head. "I have not seen anything like it."

"Could it be—"

She raised a hand, cutting him off, and looked at him with a sharpness that suggested he not say anything.

"At least tell me what you know about how they were able to suppress the power," he said.

Gavin thought that he was going to have to know what was done, mostly because he had a feeling that it wouldn't be the last time he faced something similar. He had never experienced anything like it before.

When he had trained as a young man, he had learned how to use his core reserves to help him fight. He believed that Tristan had been preparing him to use his magic, even if that wasn't the way Tristan had ever phrased it. But what if there was something else? What if Tristan had been training Gavin to fight without his core reserves for a very different reason?

"Is there a reason that would be important?" Anna asked.

He shook his head. "I think that the lead attacker knew Tristan."

Master Jaremal emerged from the temple, and he frowned at him. "You survived. I suppose that shouldn't be surprising. You are so inconsistently connected."

"I survived *because* of that," Gavin said. "And because I'm able to control how much of that connection I use." He knew that he shouldn't be arguing with him, but the fact that Master Jaremal was antagonizing him now, of all times, rubbed him the wrong way. "It was only because of that separation, along with this"—he held up the ring—"that I was able to withstand the attack. I don't suppose you can tell me anything about it."

"You were there. Perhaps more than I was. I imagine that you needed to use some of the techniques I was demonstrating to you. They are useful, aren't they?"

"I couldn't use any of your techniques," Gavin said, "so no, they were not useful. And I suspect that anybody else who would've tried to use them would fail."

Master Jaremal furrowed his brow. "I heard you say that you believe this attacker knew your instructor."

"He did."

"Then we must speak with the Order."

Gavin glanced over to Anna. "I thought you didn't care for the Order."

"It's not my choice," she said.

He turned to Master Jaremal. "You recall that the Order was the reason that the Shard survived her attack."

"And I also understand who leads the Order."

"Led," Gavin corrected. As far as he knew, Tristan no longer guided the Order.

He followed Anna and Master Jaremal through Arashil, making their way to the more dilapidated part of the old settlement. The Order had been assigned this area, which made it clear where they stood within the hierarchy of the El'aras. Given how much help they had offered, Gavin found this disappointing.

As they walked through the settlement, he looked over to Anna. "How much were you restricted?"

She shook her head. "More than I could have ever imagined possible. I have never felt anything quite like that. They should not have been able to suppress my connection quite as significantly as they did."

"Can other El'aras do that?"

"Not that I know of."

She glanced over to Master Jaremal, frowning for a moment, and said nothing more. She didn't need to.

They reached the outskirts of the settlement. For the most part, Gavin knew that the Order spent their time training, preparing, and readying for danger that only they truly believed existed.

Rayena led the Order of Notharin, assassins for the El'aras. The rest of the people viewed them with disdain.

Though Gavin hadn't spent much time with the Order since arriving at Arashil, he understood that they viewed themselves as important in ensuring the safety of some aspect of the El'aras life. Tristan had trained them, which was even more reason for Gavin to go to them now.

Rayena crouched over a body near the edge of the settlement, brushing golden hair back from the person's brow. Blood stained the ground near them. She looked up as they approached.

"What happened here?" he asked.

She glanced over to him. She was tall for an El'aras, and she had a hardened edge to her that was likely the result of the training she had received to serve the Order. "You know exactly what happened here, Gavin."

"Well, actually, I don't. All I can say with any certainty is that the settlement was attacked, whoever came had some horrible ability, and they managed to nearly destroy all the El'aras."

"That was not their goal," Rayena said, straightening.

Gavin looked down at the man she had been crouched next to. Bross had been easygoing and skilled with a blade, and he had fought alongside many of the other El'aras in Yoran.

"What was the goal, then?" Anna asked.

Next to her, Master Jaremal wore a sour expression. Gavin had previously noticed that there were some issues between him and the Order, likely because he didn't approve of the line of work they had selected for themselves. Gavin wasn't sure if that was all there was to it, or maybe it was more about how the Order had abandoned the rest of the El'aras to fight sorcerers. Some, like Anna and those who worked with her, wanted peace with sorcerers, but it wasn't as if the Order had gone after the Sorcerers' Society as a whole. Rayena had gone after specific ones—the Sul'toral.

"Why do you think we chose this structure as our headquarters?" Rayena asked.

Anna frowned at the question. "You didn't choose. We assigned you here."

Rayena snorted. "Assigned. We only allowed you to think that you did. We wanted to be here."

Gavin regarded the unassuming stone building behind her, wondering why they'd chosen it. Most structures within Arashil were similarly plain. The only buildings that were larger than the rest were the temple and several of the ones Master Jaremal used, located in the center of the settlement.

"What were you protecting here?" Gavin asked.

"They weren't protecting anything," Master Jaremal said.

Gavin ignored him and held his gaze on Rayena.

"We don't know," she said.

Master Jaremal scoffed, and he spun away, heading out into the rest of the settlement.

"You can go with him," Gavin said to Anna.

She shook her head. "If they were defending something here—"

"They don't know what they were defending." Gavin knew there was more to it than Rayena was letting on.

"Go with Master Jaremal," he told Anna. "See what else you might be able to uncover."

She regarded him, and it looked as if she wanted to say something, but she refrained. He noted a question in her eyes, one that he couldn't quite read. Was it worry? Maybe fear, much like Thomas had.

She left, leaving Gavin with Rayena.

"How many of the Order were lost?" he asked.

"I am the only one who survived," Rayena whispered.

There had been nearly a dozen of them, all of them incredibly skilled sword fighters. They would've been helpless.

She hung her head. "They came and slaughtered everyone. We could do nothing." She flicked her gaze down to the fallen El'aras on the ground, then turned to the building behind her.

A sense of regret filled Gavin. He hadn't spent much time with the Order, but he should have, especially knowing that they somehow viewed him as important.

"Do you think you were the target?" he asked.

Rayena breathed out heavily. "I do not think so. We chose this building because of this mark." She stepped toward the structure and gestured to a small, faded mark on the stone.

Gavin crouched down in front of it, studying it. It was difficult for him to read, though not impossible. He traced his finger along the surface, reminded of the symbol he'd seen on the stone pillar outside the borders of Arashil.

Tristan's mark.

"Has he been here?" he asked.

"He would have been at some point, at least once."

"Why didn't you tell me?"

"I..." Rayena turned away.

Gavin got to his feet and hurried over to her. "Why wouldn't you tell me?"

"I worried about how you might react, Champion."

"You knew this was his, and you knew that I trained with him, so I should have known about it."

"I do not disagree," she said, her voice soft. "But I was instructed not to facilitate your journey."

Gavin snorted. "Even now, he thinks to try to test me?" He couldn't believe that Tristan would try that now, here, and with everything that had happened.

"What did you find?"

"Nothing," Gavin said.

He glanced at the doorway again, but he didn't see any marks on it other than Tristan's. Gavin had been around that symbol for most of his life and easily recognized its triangular shape and the distinct irregularity around it. He might call it a rune, but not one that had any power. As far as he could tell, it also didn't represent any form of El'aras writing.

He stepped inside the building. The air was still, quiet, and it stunk of death. He pulled on his core reserves, sending energy through him and out from the sword he carried. The blade burst with a pale-blue light, illuminating the room.

From the entryway, he saw bodies littered all around him. They had died brutally. But at least they'd died quickly. Some of them looked as if they hadn't even attempted to fight. Given what he had seen from Brandon and how the infiltrators had incapacitated him in a heartbeat, Gavin wasn't surprised that these Order members wouldn't have been able to defend themselves. How could they, if the attackers had some way of neutralizing El'aras abilities?

"Were you able to resist the pressure?" he asked, glancing back to Rayena, who hadn't entered the room.

She swallowed hard. "I was not."

"How did you survive, then?" He turned a suspicious gaze upon her. He knew that members of the Order had worked with Tristan, which meant that they had a tie to him, but so did the attackers. It wasn't that far of a leap to question whether the attackers had infiltrated the Order.

"I couldn't move," Rayena said, her voice slow, halting. She nodded to the far part of the room. "I was in the back. Unfortunately, when the attack came, I felt it quickly. I suspect they came from the perimeter and looped around the building, so I was affected first." She shook her head, her eyes wide as she recounted the events. If it was an act, it was an impressive and convincing one. "I tried to move, but I couldn't. My body simply didn't work for me. I've never experienced anything like that. I've trained to fight my entire life, and I've learned to use all of my essence when I do, but this was something else."

"I think that's how they incapacitated you," Gavin said softly. "They have some way of suppressing El'aras magic."

"The nihilar." Her voice came out as little more than a whisper. Rayena took a step back, her eyes even wider than they had been. She retreated, continuing to shake her head. "I had not thought it real," she muttered.

Gavin had never seen Rayena unsettled like this. He had fought alongside her, and she had managed to deal with terrible powers, ones that were more dangerous than he had seen previously. She hunted Sul'toral, so she was not someone who scared easily.

"What is the nihilar?" he asked.

She paced around the room, never looking in his direction, and she ran one finger along the hilt of her sword. She seemed ready to draw it and attack at any moment.

Finally, she turned in his direction, and her eyes settled a bit. "I should not speak of it."

"Why?"

"Doing so is said to draw its attention."

What sort of superstition was this? It surprised him that Rayena, of all people, would believe something like that.

He shook his head. "Speaking of a thing does not call its attention to you."

"It does with this. You can't understand."

"Because I'm not one of the El'aras?"

She didn't answer, and Gavin sighed as he looked around the room. He took a mental image of the way the bodies were positioned. Had they been hiding or protecting anything? If attackers had focused their sights enough to come here, then perhaps there was something to find—or perhaps it was simply about revenge.

He knew that a staircase led down into the pitch black,

but a door blocked access to it. A feeling of darkness filled this place with a strange and twisted energy.

Gavin watched her. "I need to know what you know."

"I only know that it's a type of power," Rayena said. "A dark one, like so many others. It is said to strike terror into the hearts of the most valiant warriors."

He snorted, and she jerked her head up, meeting his gaze.

"I wasn't dismissing it," Gavin said. "But this wasn't about striking terror into the hearts of the most valiant warriors. This was about suppressing power. There is something magical about it."

And even with his paltry training with Master Jaremal and others who had magic, Gavin understood some aspects of power. Perhaps not this, but he grasped enough to know that if something had a magical origin, there had to be some way to counter it. He might not always have the ability himself, but he had to think it would take little more than the right focus.

"Magical," Rayena said, nodding slowly. "Of course there is something magical. Something terrible too. We encountered evidence of it while hunting the Sul'toral. We tried to avoid it, but there were some within the Order who thought we should try to pursue understanding. There is no understanding this, though."

"Why wouldn't you want to?"

"Do you chase death?"

Gavin grunted. "I don't chase it, but I don't run from it either."

That wasn't entirely true. There had been a time when

he'd barely considered death, but that was because he had nothing to live for. So much had changed for him. *He* had changed. At this point, he wanted to live so that he could learn more about what he was supposed to do, and that meant he would have to fight with every ounce of his ability to stay alive.

"We recognize the danger it posed. Those who went after it never returned. Those who avoided it lived." She shrugged. "It was as simple as that. We began to realize that we could not chase it."

Gavin noticed that she did not say the word "nihilar," which told him all he needed to know about her fears.

He started moving toward the door as she continued.

"And we had other purposes. I chose to chase them, rather than it. *It* is violence. It is the darkness. It is death."

He froze and looked over to Rayena. She stood in the sunlight just beyond the doorway, and her eyes were still shadowed somehow, as if the fear about what had happened here had consumed her in ways he couldn't quite explain.

"What did you say?" he asked.

She blinked, looking up at him. "You heard me."

It couldn't be a coincidence that she would refer to something as the darkness, especially after what Anna had said about her people's beliefs.

He hurried over to her. "Seal off this building. Gather whatever you need and then close it. They came here for a purpose. Until we know what that is, this place shouldn't be left open."

"You fear *it* as well."

Gavin shook his head. "Not the way you do. But I understand the superstitions of your people." He might not share them, but he at least acknowledged them.

He strode forward, making his way through the mostly empty settlement. He had no idea how many El'aras had died, but it was far too many. And for what? This wasn't an attack to target them specifically; it wasn't some vengeful strike. There was some other focus here. Why else would they have risked it?

Then again, would it have been a risk for them at all? Had Gavin not been here, the attackers would have been able to move through all of Arashil, slaughtering anyone and everyone without difficulty.

He couldn't shake the feeling that there had been something here they were after. Not the Order's building, though. He had to get to the temple.

The door stood closed and unguarded. He strode forward, immediately drawing power through the ring, and traced the patterns necessary to activate the doorway. As he pushed that power out, Anna approached him.

"Have you heard the term 'nihilar'?" Gavin asked without turning to look at her. Anna's soft gasp told him all he needed to know. "Why did you not mention it?"

"Where did you hear it?"

"Apparently, Rayena thinks that's what attacked."

Anna rested her hand on the wall, as though she wanted to try to prevent him from entering the temple.

"Anna?"

"It is a name we don't speak of," she said finally. "And I have not kept it from you," she quickly added.

"You obviously have."

"It is something that only the elders knew. And now, because I'm the Risen Shard, I was brought in to understand it."

"What about me? Since I am the Risen Champion, shouldn't I be aware of things like that as well?"

"Perhaps," Anna said, then shook her head. "It is a dark and deadly power, and one that no one has ever controlled before. Many have tried to reach it, but they have all failed, or were destroyed."

"Are there any prophecies about the nihilar?"

She stiffened as he mentioned the word again, and he suspected that she believed in the same superstition Rayena did, though Anna at least understood that there was no point in countering him and his willingness to say it. Gavin doubted he would be drawing any attention to some power by uttering the word. And if he did, perhaps that wasn't the worst thing in the world. If they could attract the nihilar, maybe they could learn about it and come up with a plan about how to deal with it.

"There are prophecies about the great shadow." She motioned for him to follow, and he stepped into the temple after her. "Most believe that the great shadow is tied to the nihilar in some way, but not all do." Anna didn't close the door this time, and as the light began to glow around her, she illuminated the writing along the base of the temple. "There was a time when there were old gods, powers that filled the world. All the magic you know today stems from those old gods."

"If you believe in such things," Gavin said.

She looked over to him. "I do."

"Then what happened?"

"The old gods fought. They died. Some left magical remnants of themselves in the world, which can be found all over. From the sorcerers you have encountered, to the enchanters, to the—"

"The El'aras," Gavin said.

"The El'aras, along with others. There are the Porapeth, the ogaran, the beselik, the—"

"I get it. There are other beings with magic."

"Powerful ones. And there are those who use corrupted versions of it."

"Like the Sul'toral."

"The Sul'toral were not always dark magic. There are some who are, but there are others who seek understanding and try to protect from the corrupted ones."

He supposed that was true. He had seen that himself, and he had come to understand that Jayna and some of those who served Sul'toral like she did certainly didn't chase dark power the same way. She didn't seem interested in that so much as she was in preventing those with the wrong kind of power from using it against the helpless.

"What are you going to do?" he asked.

Anna released some of the hold she had on the power circling around her, and the lettering along the walls began to fade. "We have suffered a great defeat." She shook her head. "And Arashil is no longer safe."

"You're going to leave."

"It's time for you to continue your training somewhere else."

Arashil wasn't as comfortable as Yoran had become for him, though he had stayed in Yoran far longer than he had in many places over the course of his life. It had become home, if such a thing were even possible for him. Arashil, on the other hand, was just a place.

But now Anna wanted to take him away. It was strange for him to feel that he didn't want to go. It was why he was with her, after all.

"You want me to go deeper into the El'aras lands."

She locked eyes with him. "That is why you came."

"It is, but…"

He hadn't expected that there would be infiltrators who had the ability to suppress El'aras power. What if they continued to attack? They obviously weren't afraid of confronting the El'aras. They would've slaughtered everyone. Anna might've died. She was the Risen Shard, and given that she had a kind of power similar to Gavin's, she might've been able to overwhelm whatever these attackers had managed to do against her. But perhaps not.

"I can't go with you," he said.

"Gavin Lorren—"

He held his hand up. "I want to understand what I can do, and I'm not saying that I won't continue my training. Master Jaremal would be disappointed." The man would undoubtedly make a point of admonishing Gavin for his failings. "But I saw what happened. I need to understand more about all of this so that we can know what they were after."

"If they serve it—"

"You can say the word," Gavin said.

Anna inhaled slowly, nodding. "If they serve the nihilar, then they seek destruction."

That was the sense he had from them as well. And maybe they simply wanted to destroy, or maybe they had come after him because he was the Champion... or maybe there was something else. They had gone after the Order first. Everything else seemed to be a distraction.

He couldn't shake the feeling that this was tied to Tristan in some way. His former mentor knew him, and the Order had been targeted. How could it be a coincidence?

Tristan had mentioned another prophecy. Could everything be tied to that?

Gavin knew so little. He had been kept in the dark, shielded from something—either his destiny or learning more about the El'aras. And now he didn't have answers.

"No. They were after something," he said, "and I need to understand what it was."

It meant that he would have to leave before he'd intended to.

There was a hint of disappointment in Anna's eyes, and he hated being the cause.

"I plan on returning," he told her.

"You will know how to find me." The enchantment she had long ago given him began to vibrate softly in his pocket.

He smiled at that. "I'm sorry."

"No," she said, shaking her head. "I don't think you are.

CHAPTER SIX

Gavin's cloak was heavy, all of the enchantments he'd brought with him from Yoran filling his pockets and weighing them down. There was a time when he would never have embraced using enchantments, but having them now provided him a measure of reassurance, especially since he wasn't sure that he would've survived the last attack without them.

He reached the perimeter, pausing at the bralinath tree. As he looked at it, he thought about what Anna had told him regarding the various types of magic that had existed in the world at one time. All of those powers made a different sort of sense now, and he couldn't help but wonder if perhaps the tree had been gifted the same kind of power as all of those beings Anna had mentioned.

He strode forward until he approached the stone pillar. He made a circle around it, studying Tristan's mark. Gavin wasn't sure why the mark was here, but he had to understand it. He pressed his hand out and ran it along the symbol, then began to focus on power.

A shuffling sound came from behind, and Gavin spun to find Brandon chuckling at him.

"I almost had you this time," he said, a grin plastered on his face. "Though I did have to give you a little bit of a warning. I wasn't going to scare you."

Gavin hadn't spent much time talking to Brandon since the attack, which he now realized was a mistake. "I'm leaving," he said softly.

"I know. The Shard said that you were. Others were going to return to the trees. They feel it will be safer. Master Jaremal was muttering about how you know too little and will probably end up dead because of it, but I had a sense that the Shard wants you to go."

That wasn't the feeling Gavin had from Anna, but perhaps it didn't matter at this point. He needed to be here, and he needed to go after this.

Brandon tilted his head. "Why do you keep staring at this rock?"

"Because it's more than just a rock."

Gavin got to his feet and circled the pillar, making note of how the grasses around it were trampled down. Why would Tristan have made a mark on this pillar? He was no closer to understanding the reason.

What if it hadn't been Tristan, though? Given what Gavin knew of the lead attacker and how he had some connection to Tristan, there was a real possibility that he had been the one responsible for this mark. If so, for what purpose?

"You think the attackers knew your mentor?" Brandon's tone had turned serious, and Gavin glanced over to him. He had on a deep-green cloak, and the paleness to his complexion following the attack had disappeared, leaving his skin practically glowing with a golden hue.

"They did. And I think they wanted to make sure I knew they knew him."

"Why?"

"That is what I need to find." Gavin stopped in front of the symbol again. "Either they left this, or Tristan did. And either way, I have to understand why it's here."

"Why wouldn't your mentor just come out and reveal himself, if he knows something?"

That troubled Gavin as well. Tristan had no reason not to. He had certainly made sure to train the Order, but he hadn't done anything else, as far as Gavin knew.

He pursed his lips in thought. "I don't know. Maybe he has some history with the El'aras leaders that makes him afraid." That didn't fit with Gavin's understanding of Tristan either, but he couldn't think of many reasons for Tristan's behavior.

"There are quite a few who have difficulty with the elders," Brandon said. "The elders have their view about how things need to be, and if you don't follow it... Unfortunately, it's all too easy to get exiled. If you say the wrong thing, do the wrong thing, be the wrong thing..." He shrugged.

Gavin looked over, curiosity rising within him. "What happened to you?"

"Oh, nothing in particular. Just that my people aren't

always what they like to consider the 'right' kind of people." Brandon shook his head. "Can't say that I care too much about that. It isn't anything that tears me down."

Gavin regarded him for a moment. His experience with Theren had made him leery of other El'aras who might have similar issues with their leadership. He knew that he should consider each person independently and that it didn't seem as though Brandon was anything like Theren, but there was a part of him that remained cautious. He had to be.

"Why are you with them?" Gavin asked, nodding toward the settlement.

"I can fight. I like to fight. And thankfully, there was a need." He shrugged again. "Besides, my father is awfully friendly with the Shard's father."

Gavin relaxed slightly at the fact there was a connection between them. "I have to decide what I'm going to do about this pillar."

"Why do you have to do something about it?"

"Because I need to know if there is anything to it."

He paused in front of the symbol again. This time, he held his hand out, and he started to push power out from himself. He needed to know if Tristan had placed some sort of danger here, and he wasn't going to understand until he tested to see what Tristan might have done.

That was assuming it *was* Tristan. The possibility remained that it wasn't him at all but might have been those who had attacked. And if it was, then he had even more reason to seek to understand what this was about. There had to be something more here.

Gavin focused on his core reserves, and he used the energy the way Master Jaremal had instructed. As he let the power flow out through his entire body, he tried to hold it lightly, ever so lightly, as he had been instructed to, so that he could feel it reaching beyond himself. In this case, he pressed outward so he could let that energy fill him and flow through his fingertips, and then he used a hint of power to trace an outline.

"You've gotten better," Brandon said.

Gavin resisted the urge to look up. "Shouldn't I have?"

"Well, to hear Master Jaremal speak of it, you're little more than a bumbling child."

Gavin grunted, continuing to trace a pattern across the top of the stone. "That's what he makes a point of telling me, as well."

"I think he tells everybody that. Whether or not it's true is another matter, and I can't say with any certainty if you really are a bumbling child, but you have some control. It took me several years to get to that point."

"Several years?"

"We do learn how to work with the power within us from an early age. It's just a part of us."

"No different than breathing," Gavin muttered.

"That's right. There you go. Now you just have to learn to breathe more regularly. Right now, it's almost as if you're gasping, and then when you let it out, your power flows out of you."

"But at least I can hold my breath."

"Is that what you did?" Brandon whispered.

Gavin glanced up at that. Even though his power filled

his fingertips and he was tracing letters on the stone, preparing to try to understand what had happened here, he suspected that this was an important conversation that had to take place. Brandon needed to understand what Gavin had done and how he had managed to deflect the attack.

"I don't use the power continuously," he explained. "More now than I had before, but not continuously."

"And you can simply hold back?"

"Like I said, I never learned to use it the same way you did."

Brandon's frown deepened. "That would be useful. I suppose that if I could learn to hold my breath, maybe I wouldn't have to worry about attacks like this."

"If you're going back with Anna, I doubt you have to be concerned about similar attacks again."

"And what about you?"

"I need to figure out why all of this is happening."

"Why you?"

It was the same sort of question Anna had asked, though with Brandon, there was less of a plea and more of a curiosity to it.

"Because I'm not sure who else can do it, and because I think it's tied to me in some way."

"It doesn't have anything to do with running from who you're supposed to be?"

Gavin looked over to him. "And who am I supposed to be?"

"Well, you were the Chain Breaker. Then you became the Champion. I don't know what you want to be now."

"I don't know either," Gavin said, shaking his head.

Brandon chuckled. "It's late in life for you to be starting to understand yourself."

"I had a friend who told me the same thing."

"Then they were a good friend."

Gavin breathed out slowly, staring at the symbol again, and he nodded. "One of the best I've ever had."

He resumed tracing the symbols around the pillar. Perhaps he should bring Master Jaremal out here to help him understand what energy had been spilled into the stone, but right now, Gavin didn't feel anything dangerous.

"Can you tell me if you can detect anything here?"

Brandon joined Gavin at the pillar and regarded it. "I'm not sure I'm going to figure out anything more than you did."

"You have more experience using your abilities than I do."

"Oh, so now you need me again? I really have had a pretty good week. First, I scared the Chain Breaker, and now he needs me."

"You also almost died."

Brandon waved that away as if it were not a concern of his. "I didn't. I was defending the Champion."

Gavin arched a brow and was met with a grin. "Just tell me what you feel here."

Brandon pressed his hands on either side of the stone, which came up to his chest as well. He cupped his hands around the top of the pillar like he was going to grab it, but he never did. He held his hands outward, with elbows at his sides, and then began to move his fingers slowly. It was different from any of the techniques Gavin had learned from Master Jaremal. It was a pattern, though, and Gavin instinctively began to copy it, realizing he had seen Anna using something similar. Pale-blue lines began to form, coalescing from his hands and spreading around the top of the tower. The lines spiraled downward, and the pillar itself started to glow softly. The energy around it began to crackle with blue sparks as the magic worked its way down.

Brandon took a step back, frowning. "That's as much as I can do. I've never seen anything like it. It's almost as if this power is filling the entirety of the stone. I'm trying to push through it to see if there's a way to probe for some part of it, but…" He shook his head. "I can't find it. Maybe you can, Champion."

Gavin almost laughed at the comment, but perhaps there was something to it. Maybe there was a way for him to do more.

The magic surrounding the pillar had to be El'aras, or something along that line. It likely couldn't be from the attackers because they had not used any power like that.

Gavin stood back, regarding the structure for another moment.

"What are you going to do?" Brandon asked.

"I think I need to see what's inside."

"What makes you think there's anything inside?"

"The power I feel."

Gavin traced the pattern, but he didn't need to. After the way Brandon had placed power around it, Gavin could see the energy working along it. He didn't need anything else to be done. And now, as he saw it, he began to feel as if there was something more to it. He couldn't help but wonder what he needed to do here.

Get through the magic.

It was not a simple kind, though. If it were, he would be able to figure out some way through it, but as he continued to trace the few patterns he knew—mostly probing ones he had learned from Anna, not from Master Jaremal—he was unable to find the key to what he had to do. He would have to find another way.

After several moments, Gavin realized that it wasn't a matter of just probing through it. Increasingly, he was certain that it had to be Tristan. No one else would've placed anything like this. No one else would've thought that Gavin needed to solve it.

And if it was Tristan, then he had to figure out what his old mentor wanted from him.

"Champion?" Brandon said.

"Gavin," he replied absently.

"You're just standing there. You're watching the stone as if it's going to change. Now, I know of other El'aras who have done that over the years, but they all go mad if they wait for too long. Stone does change, but it takes decades. Or centuries. If you intend to sit here until then, we might want to get some food, and perhaps make some other preparations."

Gavin glanced over, unsure whether Brandon was making a joke or not. "I'm just trying to decide what to do about it."

"You don't need to do anything about it. It is beyond us."

"It is."

"Do you want me to bring Master Jaremal? I imagine he has some way of trying to break through these things."

"Break?" Gavin said, arching a brow.

"Well, that would be one way to disrupt the spell. That's what you're getting at, isn't it?"

Gavin nodded slowly, continuing to study the pillar. "It is."

"Then how would you go about it?"

"I *am* the Chain Breaker."

And Tristan knew that.

Getting Master Jaremal might not be enough. Tristan would know that there'd be El'aras with specific abilities here, ones who had more power, more control, and more knowledge than he did. He would have anticipated that. Which meant Gavin might be the only one able to do this.

He smiled at the thought. He was the Chain Breaker. Why shouldn't he be the breaker of other things? He had proved that he was the breaker of magic and the breaker of spells. Now he would be the breaker of stone.

It would take more than his core reserves. He would need to use his ring.

Gavin began to focus on his connection to the ring, feeling the power building within him. Though slow and steady at first, it continuously increased, and he let that energy course through him until it reached the ring, where it suddenly amplified.

"You might want to stand back," he said, without looking back at Brandon.

He continued to focus. The energy crackled within him.

There were times when he let himself draw on this power that he felt, as if he were tapping into some deep river of energy. Most of the time, the core reserves were like a pool of power within him, one that he once thought was some hidden part of him that he could access when needed during fights. But now that he recognized that his core reserves tied him to the magic he possessed as someone who was at least part El'aras, he understood that the power he could connect to was something else.

And the ring changed all of that, turning the pool into something much deeper. A lake. An ocean. It gave him access to that power, with the only limitation being his own strength to hold on to it. That and the knowledge he possessed to be able to use it correctly.

Gavin realized he needed to focus the energy, to target Tristan's mark. He had to harness that power within him, unleash it on the stone, and shatter it.

Because he had fought the attackers, he was more tired than he normally would've been, and some of his energy had diminished. But Gavin still had access to more than enough for what he thought he needed to do.

He crossed his wrists and forced power out through them, into the mark. The stone cracked where struck, then exploded in a massive burst of debris and dust.

Gavin was thrown back, and he slammed into the ground behind Brandon. For his part, Brandon seemed to have prepared for it. He had his hands held in front of him, locked into something that reminded Gavin of the triangular pose Master Jaremal had used. A light-blue glowing ball of energy surrounded him.

"You could've warned me," Gavin muttered.

"Warned you? I thought you knew what you were doing."

"I knew what I needed to do, but that was about it."

"Looks like you broke it." Brandon grinned. "I assume that's what you wanted?"

"I think it was the only option."

Gavin made his way toward the fallen stone. The top half had come clean off and was broken into fragments that lay scattered all around them. The bottom had cracked but was still partially intact. As he approached, he realized there was another mark situated in the center of the top of the stone that was now at about waist height.

Tristan's mark again.

This *was* all part of some plan of his.

Gavin repeated the same technique, though he didn't push out nearly as much power as he had before. He focused it on the symbol, letting it course into the stone and increasing it until the stone cracked. The pillar began to split and peel back like an onion, with layers of stone falling off, until only the mark was left untouched. That began to crackle, and then it turned to dust.

Where the stone had been, a metal box now rested on the ground. Gavin reached for the container.

"Are you sure you should do that?" Brandon said.

Gavin looked over to him. "This is meant for me."

"Or it's meant as a trap for you."

"Maybe."

He didn't think that was the case, though. If Tristan wanted to trap him, there were other ways he could do it. Why something like this? And increasingly, Gavin no longer felt as if Tristan were trying to harm him, which meant that he might be trying to help.

He picked up the silver box, which felt light in his hands, and moved away from where the pillar had been. Tristan's mark adorned the surface of the lid, one more sign that it was something his old mentor wanted him to have. Had Tristan intended to harm him, he wouldn't have marked the box, or the pillar, quite so distinctly.

Gavin braced himself and finally pulled the lid open.

His mind had gone through various possibilities about what Tristan would've left for him, but he wasn't sure what to expect. A letter. A book. Some item of power, possibly.

A small, leatherbound ledger rested inside the box. He'd seen Tristan carrying it before, though the last time had been long ago.

Brandon leaned over his shoulder, looking down into the box. "What is that?"

"A message."

Brandon chuckled and reached for the book, but Gavin twisted so that he couldn't grab it. He pulled it out himself, and as he opened the cover, a little figurine tumbled out.

Gavin picked it up and examined the black stone, which felt perfectly smooth. The shape resembled a man, though one with oversized arms and legs, and ears that were curved and pointed at the ends. The head also seemed too large. This was a smaller replica of a figurine Gavin had once stolen for Tristan.

"What kind of message is that?" Brandon asked softly.

"He's telling me where to find him."

CHAPTER SEVEN

The air was heavy and still in the small clearing of trees, which fit Gavin's mood. A sense of urgency filled him. He needed to get moving, and couldn't help but feel as if he finally had a destination.

Nihilar.

That thought stayed with him.

He hadn't mentioned anything to Brandon, though, who had followed him to this clearing in the forest. The El'aras moved beyond the perimeter that Thomas and the others had marked, and he seemed unmindful of the fact that Gavin intended to leave.

As Gavin reached into his pouch, pulling out one of the stone enchantments he had brought from Yoran, Brandon moved closer to him. "What are you doing now?"

Gavin tapped on the enchantment, pushing just a hint of his core reserves into the stone. While it wasn't necessary for him to use his power to activate the enchantment, doing so allowed him to connect to something within the enchantment more effectively than he could otherwise, and it always reacted to him better that way.

He had a strange connection to the stone wolf that was now life-size, and it was more than just the fact that he had used him as often as he had. He had the sense that some part of the wolf responded to him. Gavin felt the same way about the paper dragon, though he had avoided using that enchantment lately, not wanting to expose that much power unless necessary.

As he crouched next to the enchantment, he ran his hand along the stone fur, which felt almost real. He could imagine what it might have been like when Mekel had created the enchantment. There was an energy, a power, that he detected within the creature.

"You should go with the others back to the El'aras lands. It's going to be safer," Gavin said.

"And you?" Brandon looked at the stone wolf, seeming to consider it for a long moment. "How do you think you are going to find those responsible for the attack?"

"I know where to begin. And that's enough."

He climbed onto the enchantment and tapped on the stone wolf's side. Even though he knew it was just an enchantment, Gavin always felt impressed by this one and Mekel's other creations. Something left him feeling as if the enchantments were more than just stone.

"Then I'm coming with you," Brandon said. "Well, I will if you have more of those. Unless you want us to ride double. That thing doesn't look nearly large enough for both of us, but maybe you can make it bigger? I don't know how other kinds of enchantments work. The ones we use are nothing like that."

Gavin snorted. "What would Anna think?"

"She would tell me to do what I thought I needed in order to find my own journey, which is part of the reason I'm here in the first place."

"Why is it that so many of the El'aras working with Anna are looking for some purpose?"

Brandon shrugged. "How can I know? I just came here to learn what I could so I could help protect our people. And seeing what you've shown me so far, I think heading this way is how I'm going to best protect them. If I can understand what you know about holding your breath, as you called it"—he flashed a smile—"then maybe I can help teach others, in case we are ever attacked by the same people."

Gavin sighed as he looked over to him. "The last time we were attacked by the nihilar, you weren't able to do anything. I don't want you to risk yourself like that."

"I want to. Besides, if this is as dangerous as you say, you can't go alone."

"I have done so many times before."

"You might've, but you don't need to this time. Besides, it would give me a chance to surprise the Champion again." He grinned at Gavin.

There was a time when Gavin would have refused. He would've simply ridden off and done things on his own. Even now, there was a part of him that hesitated, despite everything that he had gone through lately and how he had needed help to succeed. But his time in Yoran had taught him that working alone was actually a detriment. Working with others strengthened him. That was a lesson that Tristan had never learned, though these days, Gavin no longer knew how much of what had happened to him was because of a lesson Tristan wanted him to know.

"You can come, but I won't be responsible for the repercussions," Gavin said, shaking his head.

"You aren't going to feel bad if I die?"

"Those aren't the repercussions I'm talking about. I'm not going to be responsible for what Anna does to you for leaving."

Brandon chuckled. "Do you have another one of those?"

Gavin reached into his pouch and thumbed through the various enchantments he had on him. Before leaving Yoran, he had made certain to bring dozens of different types of enchantments. Some were more useful than others. In addition to the stone creatures, he had enchantments that would enable speed, strength, improved eyesight, and impervious skin. He hadn't expected to need them while studying with the El'aras, but he also hadn't expected to leave the El'aras so soon either.

"I'm not sure you're going to like this one," Gavin said.

"Why not?"

He climbed down from the stone wolf, set the figurine on the ground, and activated it. As the enchantment stretched, it elongated into a strange lizard that slithered along the ground.

"You're giving me the ungalt?"

"Is that what it's called?"

Brandon stared at him as if Gavin was making a joke. "Of course. We have these creatures on the border of my land. Violent, a little dangerous, not hard to wrestle down."

"Then you should be right at home."

"I'd rather have a hog."

"I don't know that I have one of those," Gavin said.

"Well, I told you they were beautiful creatures."

Gavin climbed back onto the wolf again and looked over to Brandon. "They move quickly, and we're going to go as fast as possible so we can reach the city before it gets too late."

"What city are we going to?"

"Hester."

Although Gavin hadn't been there in years, he remembered that it was to the east and slightly to the south. It surprised him that Tristan was guiding him to Hester, though perhaps it shouldn't. One of the last jobs he'd done for Tristan had been there, stealing a dark figurine from an impossible-to-reach temple. The artisans there used great care and immense skill to carve those figurines, which were each made of volcanic rock found around the city. This one that Tristan had left for him was one of the most skillfully made that Gavin had ever seen. He couldn't imagine how much it cost to produce. What he didn't know was whether there was magic mixed within it, though.

"I've not been there," Brandon said. "Sounds fun."

"You might think differently once we get there."

They started off. The stone wolf moved in a steady,

pounding rhythm, one that was powerful and also jarring. While it was unpleasant to ride the wolf, he did appreciate the speed with which they could travel, and he braced himself so that he wasn't miserable as the enchantment barreled across the ground.

They hadn't been journeying long before he began to feel a stir in his pocket, and it took a moment to realize what it was: one of his enchantments was vibrating. He pulled out the culprit and examined it, recognizing it as the one Anna had given him.

Gavin slowed his mount. They were in a thinner part of the forest, having headed south quickly through the trees and moving well beyond the ability to see the settlement. Once they left the forest altogether, they would be able to travel at a faster pace. At this point, Gavin wanted answers, and he was not about to wait behind in order to get them.

"What is it?" Brandon asked.

"Anna is summoning me."

But it didn't seem to quite be a summons—it was more a steady vibration. When he turned the stone wolf, he didn't feel the vibration change at all. It was almost as if she wanted him to wait.

Could Anna have decided to come with me?

He tried not to get his hopes up. She had other responsibilities, and he wouldn't take her from them, much like she hadn't tried to take him from what he had felt he needed to do. There would have to be another reason for the enchantment, then.

They didn't have to wait long for a figure to appear in

the trees. They were dressed in a long, forest-green cloak, but the height wasn't right for Anna.

"Rayena," Gavin said.

She approached, eyeing the two stone golems quickly before meeting his gaze. "If you're going after them, I will go with you."

"You don't have to do this."

She pressed her lips together in a tight frown. "The Order has been mostly destroyed. I need to go."

Gavin glanced behind Rayena. He didn't see any other movement, but he wondered if there were other El'aras who had accompanied her. Maybe she didn't feel comfortable staying in Arashil.

"You know what I'm going after," he said.

She inhaled deeply, and her jaw clenched for a moment. "I do. And I want you to know that I'm not afraid."

"I would never accuse you of that."

"You don't need to."

She made her way over to Brandon and nodded to him. "Slide over."

He glanced over to Gavin and winked. He moved back, and Rayena climbed in front of him. Brandon wrapped his arms around her waist, earning him a sharp elbow to his chest.

Brandon gave Gavin another wink.

Gavin sighed. This was going to be his team.

At least they were both capable. They were each skilled with a sword and had their own sort of magic, which should protect them. Under any other circumstance,

Gavin would have been pleased with this group, regardless of whether or not he trusted them. But it was about more than trust—it was about safety. With neither Rayena nor Brandon having any way of suppressing their El'aras magic, Gavin knew they would need to be careful in case they encountered more of the nihilar.

"Let's get going," Gavin said.

"Where to?" she asked.

"Hester," Brandon replied, grinning.

Rayena said nothing for a long moment, but there was tension in her hands and a hint of a twitch around the corners of her eyes. "I've been there before."

"Oh? How is it?"

She breathed out slowly, almost like she was trying to force the tension out of her. "Horrible."

She'd had her own experience with Tristan, and Gavin couldn't help but wonder what it might've been like for her, but now was not the time to press that issue. It would be, soon enough.

They started off, their stone golems racing across the ground, far faster than they'd be able to travel otherwise. The ungalt moved in a strange, slithery manner and practically wiggled as it worked its way forward, though it was faster than the wolf Gavin rode. Still, he preferred the wolf because of the connection he felt to the creature, even if that was only his imagination.

They traveled through the day. The forest led to a rolling grassland. When darkness fell, they camped and hurriedly made a small fire. All of this reminded Gavin too much of when he had traveled with Theren and how he had been betrayed by another El'aras. He pushed those thoughts out of his mind.

Rayena stared at the crackling flames. She had been quiet for the most part, and Gavin thought that he understood: she wasn't sure what to make of what they were doing or her role in all of it. Tristan had pulled her into this as well.

It was Brandon that Gavin wasn't exactly sure about.

"Can you teach us?" Brandon asked.

Gavin blinked and looked over to him, pulling himself away from the thoughts he'd been lost in. "Teach you what?"

Brandon grinned. "The way you can withstand the attack. If we have to face the nihilar again, don't you think we should know what to do? You obviously have some technique. Teach us, Chain Breaker."

Gavin stared at the crackling flames. The air was calm, damp, and the steady buzz of insects carried to him. He had found that insects sounded different all throughout the world, and this place sounded strangely familiar to him, though he had been to Hester before.

"I don't know if I can teach you how to separate yourselves from your power. I have my own, and for the longest time, I didn't know it was El'aras magic. It has always stayed pooled within me. I have to push it out in order to use it." An idea came to him. "It's possible that you might be able to tamp yours down."

"You want us to withdraw from ourselves?" Rayena asked.

Gavin shrugged. "Again, I'm not exactly sure. You have

to find whatever connection you have to your power, pull it back, and store it so they can't influence it. If you can't..."

He didn't need to describe what would happen if they couldn't. They had seen it. Too many had died.

As the others talked quietly, he fell silent, staring at the flames. Tristan had sent him on this journey, and all because of what? What did he hope Gavin would find?

Every so often, Brandon grunted or Rayena muttered to herself, but Gavin suspected they were trying to figure out some way of keeping their El'aras abilities from flowing through them naturally the way they'd been taught.

He looked at the book, remembering the first time he'd seen it. He had been young, barely twelve, but even then, Tristan had been protective of it. The symbols across the cover were difficult for him to interpret, though they seemed to create a pattern on their own. He leaned back, opened the book, and started to flip through it. He didn't recognize any of the writing. Diagrams filled several pages, and others had more writing. The faint ink was almost gray and had faded into the pages, making it almost impossible for him to see. Answers *should* be there, but he found nothing he could read or interpret. How could Tristan? Or *could* he, even?

"Can you tell anything from it?" Brandon asked, coming over to him.

"I can't."

"Let me have a look," Rayena said. She sank down next to Gavin, and she peered down at where he had the book propped open on his lap. "I don't recognize the language."

"Neither do I."

"Are you a linguist, then?" Brandon chuckled. "So many different nicknames for you. I mean, first we have Chain Breaker, and we have Champion, and now we have—"

"Nothing more," Gavin said. He positioned himself to keep Rayena from grabbing the book, since he was getting the feeling that she intended to. Tristan wanted him to have it, maybe to protect it? He closed it and slipped it into his pouch. "We should rest. We can reach Hester later in the day tomorrow."

Gavin found a spot to lie down next to the stone wolf and slept. When daylight broke, he quickly cleaned up the campsite, and the others joined him.

The stone enchantments sped along, and they passed into a much thinner forest with scattered trees. Everything seemed quiet here, giving the air a sense of anticipation, though it didn't feel quite as potent as it had near Arashil.

None of them spoke much, though Gavin could tell that Brandon was practicing suppressing his El'aras abilities as they rode. They hadn't made it far before he started to feel a slight tension along his skin.

Magic.

He motioned to the others to slow. Brandon tightened his grip on the back of the ungalt, likely avoiding making the mistake of wrapping his arms around Rayena again. They both looked over to Gavin.

"There's something here," he said.

"Nihilar?" Rayena asked. Despite her denial, there was an edge to her that suggested that she was more uncomfortable than she let on.

Gavin shook his head. "Not them. This is magic. Traditional magic."

"Sorcery." Her hand went to the hilt of her sword.

"We're not cutting through sorcerers. I just wanted you to be aware of what I detected."

"How is it that you were able to sense this so soon?"

"I feel a certain tension when magic is used around me." Gavin wasn't exactly sure how to describe it any other way. He also didn't know if this was tied only to him or to all of the El'aras. Given their reaction, he suspected the former.

And if it was only him, he didn't know if it was because of the ring and his role as Champion, or because of the experience he had dealing with sorcerers in the past. Perhaps his time around them had taught him to understand how magic was used in a different way.

They moved the stone creatures forward carefully. The landscape had shifted dramatically ever since they'd left the forest. The rolling hillside wasn't as vibrant or grassy as the ones found farther to the north. This was dried and rough, almost as if the landscape around him had started to suffer, and it was left with little more than a sense of decay and death. Maybe that was only his imagination, though.

It was probably more that he just didn't care to travel in this direction, and that he feared what he might encounter more than anything else. Gavin had been through these lands before, and he knew them. He couldn't shake the feeling that there was something here, some niggling sensation that power existed, a threat to him and to those with him. The others didn't seem to notice it.

Hester was straight south from here. They would eventually hook up with a road that would guide them into the city, but for now, he wanted to keep heading directly south.

Gavin tapped on the stone wolf, leaning close. "Have you detected anything?"

He didn't expect the wolf to respond to him. It was more his discomfort that motivated him to ask, but he still felt as if he needed to try to communicate the enchantment.

Brandon glanced over. "Does it talk?"

Gavin patted the side of the wolf before sitting upright. "No."

Brandon smiled, but the expression faded quickly when Gavin didn't react. "Why talk to it, then?"

How could he explain his reasons? He knew that it was a ridiculous thing to do, speaking to an enchantment that had no way of communicating back to him, only there were times when it felt like the wolf did understand him and knew what he wanted, even if unable to speak back. The same was true with the paper dragon. Gavin didn't know if it was because he had used them more often, or if there was anything that had truly connected him to the enchantment.

"We should be ready—"

The ground rippled beneath them.

What Gavin had thought was a mound of rocky ground stretching in front of them was not that at all. Only a golem could cause that. An impossibly large one.

It suddenly separated from the ground and stood upright. Enormous arms of stone spun, swatting toward them. The enchantments they rode responded, jumping and bounding out of the way.

Gavin considered his options. He could ignore this monstrosity. That was certainly one possibility, to leave the stone golem alone and ride past it. He wasn't sure it could harm him.

But if he left it, others might come across it.

He let out a frustrated grumble. "We need to destroy it."

Rayena nodded.

"I'm not so sure that you need to," Brandon said. "We could just leave it."

"I think we have to," Gavin said. "We don't know who placed it or why, but it's entirely possible that whoever is responsible for it has already disappeared."

When he had dealt with the Sul'toral outside of Yoran, there had been many similar enchantments left behind. Gavin worried about what would take place if somebody who didn't have the ability to deal with them accidentally encountered them. What might happen to them? Would they be targeted? Would they be attacked?

"Why would they leave it behind?" Brandon asked.

Gavin shook his head. "I can't really say."

Gavin raced over toward it, but how was he going to stop an attack like this? There had to be some pattern controlling it. As the creature spun away from him, he jumped onto its back and hurriedly scrambled up, like he was climbing a mountain that was alive.

He clung to the creature. Somewhere down below, Brandon and Rayena shouted at him. He ignored them both as he searched for the enchantment that activated it.

And then he saw it—a mark on top of the creature's head.

Gavin grabbed for it, but the golem twisted violently. He had only a few moments here. He pressed his hand on top of the golem's head and traced the pattern.

As much as he wanted to figure out how to add some part of himself to the enchantment to gain control, there didn't seem to be any way to do so. He was too ignorant, too untrained, as the El'aras made a point of telling him. And he didn't have the time.

He brought his sword up in one hand as he held on with the other, and he stabbed down toward the enchantment on the golem's head. The blade bounced off the stone.

Gavin brought his sword up again, gripped the golem's head with his other hand, then jabbed downward. As the blade neared the ring, he poured all of the power of his core reserves through the ring and into the weapon. With a loud shriek and a crack, the stone composing the creature's body exploded outward.

Gavin was tossed into the air. He tried to twist as he was thrown free, wanting to land gracefully, but the force of the blast was too much. He hit the ground awkwardly, one knee slamming into it and his sword nearly ripped from his hand.

He looked up at where the golem had been, and only pieces of stone were left. Brandon emerged from the dust of the debris, grinning widely as he approached Gavin. Rayena followed him, her sword still clutched in hand, sweeping her head from side to side while looking for additional threats.

"So, you really are the Stone Breaker, aren't you?" Brandon asked.

Gavin grunted. He tried to get up, but his knee throbbed. How badly was he hurt?

He didn't need an injury to slow him down, with everything else they had going on. He would recover, he knew that, but it would still take time even though he generally healed quickly.

"What took you so long?" Rayena asked.

Gavin scoffed. "You could just say thanks."

"Thanks. But what took you so long?"

Gavin hesitated to answer, feeling foolish to acknowledge what he had intended, especially because Rayena had said he couldn't do it.

"I wanted to try to take control over the enchantment."

"You would need to know the person who held it," Brandon said. Rayena looked over to him, and he shrugged. "I'm not saying it can actually be done, I'm just saying that you would need to know who controlled it, and then you would need to understand the pattern and the power involved so you could overrule it. Even that might not be enough. Some enchantments, especially those made by sorcerers, are quite sophisticated."

"So it is possible?" Gavin asked.

"I'm saying that it's feasible, not that it would be easy. Maybe for the Champion," he said with a grin. "But possible."

Gavin looked at the remains of the golem. It was something he would need to work on. Maybe not now, and maybe not ever, unfortunately. As much as he wanted to learn that aspect of himself, to better understand his magic in this regard, it was possible that he just would not have the time to do so.

He let out a long sigh, patting the wolf on his side. They had to move on.

It was time to reach Hester. It was time to find Tristan.

CHAPTER EIGHT

Hester was large for a city in the south. Many of them were on the smaller side, mostly because the land was difficult to travel between, but Hester had an advantage that others didn't. People could get to it by road, the way Gavin and the others had, but they could also reach it by sea. The ships moving in and out of the active ports spoke of the vibrancy here.

In the distance, a massive mountain loomed along the shoreline, glowing softly. The volcano was not active for the most part, though every so often it was rumored to erupt, spewing lava into the ocean and causing steam to spill outward. These events were exciting for the artisans of Hester. They would race outside and collect the lava rock for their sculptures, much like the one Gavin now had in his pocket.

"This is it?" Brandon asked, eyes wide as he looked around. He had been excitable during the rest of the journey, asking all sorts of questions about enchantments that Gavin didn't have answers to. They were questions he had as well. Who was responsible? Why would someone have left them there? Why *those* enchantments?

And unfortunately, Gavin hadn't been able to figure out any reason behind them. He had no idea what would have compelled those enchantments to be there.

"We should head to town, grab rooms for the night, and then—"

"You want to stay overnight?" Rayena asked. "I thought your plan was to get this over with as quickly as possible."

"Well, it is. But we need to be careful here."

"What are you afraid of?"

Gavin reached into his pocket and pulled out the sculpture Tristan had left him. "What am I afraid of? Him." He nodded to Rayena. "When did you last see him?"

She held his gaze for a long moment, saying nothing.

"I thought so. He trained you, but then he left you, didn't he?"

"He trained all of us within the Order," she whispered.

"You didn't question why?"

"We knew the reason behind our mission. We understood what we were tasked with doing. We had purpose. We understood, and we agreed to it."

Gavin sighed. "I didn't agree to what I was forced to do."

"Did you resent it?" Brandon asked.

"There was a time when I did."

"What changed?"

"I don't know," Gavin admitted. "Maybe me."

He stuffed the sculpture back into his pocket. He knew where he was going to lead them and how he was supposed to use the sculpture to find Tristan. They would have to visit a place where he had trained with Tristan all those years ago, one that he knew was significant. Gavin didn't know why it was important to him, though.

There were reasons behind everything his old mentor had done. Training Gavin the way he had, helping him understand how to reach his core reserves so he could use that magic when he needed to, manipulating him into stopping dangerous creatures in Yoran, coercing him into taking on the mantle of Champion—all of it was tied to some plot Tristan had laid out. His old mentor had intended all of this for Gavin, but he'd also kept his entire plan from him.

"We should settle in," Gavin suggested. "Maybe a tavern or somewhere else to lodge for the night. I can look into anyplace Tristan might have been."

"He won't be here," Rayena said softly as he started forward.

Gavin glanced over to her. She knew Tristan in ways he did not. She would've known Tristan as the leader of the Order of Notharin, which would've been much different than Gavin's experience.

"Why do you say that?" he asked.

"This would not be a place he would stay. It's too likely he would be caught unaware."

"There are ways to escape here," Gavin said. "He could go by sea or by ground, but he could also—"

She shook her head. "He could not escape easily."

Rayena had been around Tristan more recently, and there was no telling how much he had changed in the time since Gavin had trained with him. He found himself bothered by the slight twinge of jealousy bubbling up, one he knew he should not feel.

As they meandered down the road and headed toward the city, Gavin climbed off the stone wolf, pushed power into the enchantment that activated it, and watched as it shrank down into little more than a palm-sized sculpture. He stuffed that into his pocket next to the obsidian sculpture Tristan had left for him. The others climbed down from the ungalt and Gavin deactivated it, then placed it into his pocket with the others.

"Why can't we ride them into the city?" Brandon asked.

"We would draw the wrong kind of attention," Rayena said, glancing over to Gavin.

"She's right," he said. "It's more than just enchantments. You have the wrong dress for this place as well."

"We need to get rid of our clothing?" Brandon asked.

"There aren't too many people who would know and identify you as El'aras, and those who would—"

"Would attack us," Rayena said.

Gavin shrugged. Ever since they had left Arashil, something within her had started to change, it seemed. She had regained some of her confidence. He approved of that, especially as he would need a self-assured warrior, not the hesitant person who was afraid of the darkness.

He stared at the city as they approached. The buildings were all made of heavy stone, typically lava rock, making them all black so that they blended in with the night.

Everything around Hester had a sulfuric stench to it, and when the lava flowed, a thick haze hung around the city. A thin layer lingered, not as dense as it could be.

The tall buildings along the outskirts were filled with a soft, glowing orange light, likely from lanterns, or perhaps sorcery. The people of Hester were not afraid of enchantments, and certainly traded in them happily. The streets were mostly empty, with only several people out. As they passed through, very few cast glances in their direction. Given Hester's location and this part of the world, it wasn't uncommon for people to travel through, even those who were dressed like El'aras.

"You know any taverns here?" he asked.

"I'm not sure what's still here. I haven't been here in a while," Rayena said.

Gavin nodded. "The last time I was here was a few decades ago. Tristan brought me here for the same reason he often brought me places. A test."

He could easily remember that time. The test hadn't been all that difficult, at least compared to some of the things Tristan had asked of him at that point in his training. When he had been tasked with finding where the sculpture was, breaking in, and stealing it, he had thought it to be an odd choice. In hindsight, everything Tristan had made Gavin do had been either a test or something tied to Tristan's search for power. Or perhaps because he had been searching for the Champion.

Gavin didn't think Rayena had been tested the same way, but he didn't actually know everything the Order had been through during their time with Tristan. Perhaps she had experienced much of the same tests he had.

Gavin watched her. "How did you get to know Tristan?"

"He trained me, as you know," she said.

"How did you come to work with him, though?"

"You need to know that now?"

"I probably should've asked a while ago. Especially since it plays into my view on Tristan. At this point, I'm still not sure how to feel about him."

"He trained me," she said, this time with more force but no louder than it had been before.

"Right. He trained me as well, but some of the ways he trained me were not ways I would have used," Gavin said.

She glanced over to him. They passed by what seemed to be a bakery, the fading daylight making it difficult for Gavin to make out the sign, though the smells from within were a promise of the sweetness of bread.

"Do you regret what you learned?" Rayena asked.

"I knew nothing about myself when I was younger," Gavin said. "I knew I had been saved from... something. I still don't know what it was. My parents were gone. I don't know how, I don't know why. All I know is that Tristan took me away, and then he worked with me. He turned me into a fighter."

"What would you have done otherwise?" Brandon asked.

Gavin glanced up, but it was Rayena who held his attention as she watched him. Her pale-blue eyes were not as dark as some within the El'aras, but there was a fierce intensity to them.

"I never knew who I was supposed to be," he replied. "I never knew what I was supposed to be. And I didn't even know that I was like you until I was much older."

"He should not have kept that from you," Rayena said. She turned away.

"Why won't you talk about it?"

"Because I do not know what I am to share with you."

"You were perfectly willing to work with me," Gavin said.

"I was. I am. You are the Champion. I believe that. I have been trained to serve the Champion, as have all within the Order..." Something in the way her voice trailed off suggested that she was more bothered than she let on.

"Why does that trouble you as much as it does?"

"Because the Order is gone. At least, in its previous incarnation. Now..." Rayena shook her head, her eyes closing, and Gavin had to grab her arm to pull her away from buildings she nearly crashed into. Her eyes flew open. "I don't know what I am to do. I was taught to serve the Champion. I was taught to serve the needs of the Order. And perhaps that is what I still must do."

"What were the needs of the Order?" Gavin asked.

She held his gaze for a long moment before tearing it away, and she shook her head. "It doesn't matter."

"It does. It seems to me that the Order wanted you to accomplish something."

Learning what the Order wanted would help Rayena

know what she should do, and it would help Gavin understand Tristan and his motivations. He still didn't feel as if he grasped everything that his old mentor had been after.

"It is nothing," she said, marching ahead.

Gavin started to follow, but Brandon grabbed his arm. "That one is having a hard time reassimilating with the El'aras," Brandon said. "I think she came with you as an opportunity to try, but that doesn't mean she feels any more comfortable. The Order has always existed on the fringes of the El'aras." He shrugged, and he nodded to Rayena's figure as she walked away. "I've tried to tell her that I don't see her that way."

"You don't?"

"What do I care what she does? It is not my decision. Besides, after meeting you and learning about the Shard, I can't help but think that the purpose of the Order was reasonable. Others don't necessarily see it that way, and I'm sure you understand that."

Gavin nodded. He did understand, but he wasn't sure what he could do about it. Maybe nothing. He was caught up in a prophecy that he truly had no part in, but that seemed to speak to who Tristan wanted him to be—something Tristan had believed Gavin *could* be.

"I can keep an eye on her for you, if you'd like."

Gavin didn't know if he could trust Brandon, either, so said nothing.

As they made their way through the city, Gavin followed Rayena. When he had first met her, she had agreed to follow him willingly. It was only after he had decided to leave Yoran, to go with Anna and the other

El'aras, that something had changed in her. It was almost as if some part of her had suddenly shifted, becoming more uneasy than it had before. Like she had realized that everything she had done in service of the Order would come to a head. Then they had gone to the settlement, where she and the other members of the Order were treated differently. And he hadn't done anything about it.

Gavin let out a slow sigh. That had to be the cause of her agitation, not that he could blame her. He should have done more for her. For the others. And now there was no opportunity for him to fix it. They were gone, and she was the last of the Order.

Perhaps there was no reason for the Order any longer. Now that both the Champion and the Shard had risen, maybe there was no purpose for the Order to exist.

He found Rayena stopped in front of a building, the sounds of voices and music drifting out of the door.

She nodded to the sign. "This place," she said curtly.

"Do you know it?" Brandon asked.

"I know *of* it."

Gavin could use a tavern. After their travels and all the time he had spent with the El'aras, there was a part of him that longed for the normalcy of a tavern. Something about that felt right.

They walked inside, and Gavin found a table in the middle. He nodded to one of the servers making their way through, and the man approached, wiping his hands on a white apron that was surprisingly clean for someone who worked in a place like this. The man was barely in his twenties, with a scruff of beard and long brown hair pulled back into a ponytail.

"Just the three of you?" the man asked as the others took a seat next to Gavin.

Rayena looked up at the server with suspicion, and Brandon simply grinned.

"Just the three of us," Gavin said.

"We're busy tonight. I need you to eat, drink, and leave."

Gavin nodded. "You look it," he said, sweeping his gaze around. There were still several tables open, so he was surprised that the server would push back the way he had, but perhaps they were anticipating getting busier.

"What do you have?" Brandon asked.

The server shook his head. "Look at the board. You don't need me to spell it out for you, do you?"

"Let's start with ales for the table," Gavin said, glancing at the others with him.

The server frowned. "You have coin to pay?"

"I do."

The man lingered at the table, as if waiting for Gavin to flash his coin, but then he sidled away.

"That is unusual," Rayena said. "When I was here before, most taverns were more accommodating of visitors."

"Maybe the enchantments outside the city have something to do with it," Brandon said.

It was possible, Gavin conceded to himself. If there had been sorcery here, they might recognize that the El'aras had some access to magic, and perhaps the people of Hester felt similar to how Yoran had viewed magic in the past. There were other places in the world that outlawed magic, but not nearly as many had gone so far as to banish it altogether like Yoran had. And this place had not felt this way when Gavin had been here before.

"I don't really care for a place like this, anyway," Brandon said. "It makes you start to question why anyone would ever come here."

"Maybe this place isn't all bad," Rayena said.

The server returned, carrying three mugs of ale. He set them down in front of them and started tapping his foot.

Gavin looked up and realized the server was waiting for them to order. "You need to give us more time. We haven't even had a chance to look at your menu."

"Gods," the man said. "Your kind are all alike." He spun, storming away.

Gavin frowned. "Our kind?" He looked over to Rayena, who also had a frown on her face. "He knows we're El'aras."

"When I was here last, there was no sign of the people."

"At that time," Gavin said. "But something changed."

"The families have been moving," Brandon said. "When the Shard called to them, it sent a signal to the others. Maybe that's what we are starting to see." He took a long drink of his ale, his nose wrinkling as he did. "It's possible one of the families has decided to come here. It's not all bad for a city. If it has taverns, places to dance, music, and the water…" He trailed off as he said it, and he glanced up at Gavin. "There are certain families that like those things."

"Yours?" Gavin asked.

"Not the water," Brandon said, shaking his head. "But the taverns. The dancing. The women." He glanced over to Rayena and winked. "We like all of those things."

"You liked wrestling hogs as well, I seem to remember," Gavin said.

Brandon gasped in mock surprise, and he leaned back in his chair, placing his hand over his heart. "I can't believe that you would accuse my people of such things."

"You probably also kiss them," Rayena said.

"Now you too? I thought I would have someone on my side, especially a lady as lovely as yourself."

This statement elicited a glare from Rayena, and Gavin chuckled. He looked around the tavern, watching the people. The longer he did, the more he started to realize that eyes were on them. Not just glancing in their direction but looking at them with suspicion. There was more at play here than he had realized.

"I don't know that we should stay here," Gavin said in a lowered voice.

"I haven't even finished my drink," Brandon groused.

"Finish it, then maybe we get going."

A group of muscular men at a table near the hearth all got up at once. With their tattoos, low-cut shirts, and the foul stench of fish that emanated from them, Gavin guessed that they were fishermen. They approached slowly.

Gavin glanced up. "What can we do for you, friends?"

The one who was likely the leader spat on the ground at Gavin's feet. His eyes were dark, matching his hair, and his skin was deeply tanned. A tattoo worked its way around his neck, the ink in a style Gavin wasn't familiar with. He didn't think it was from Hester.

"Your kind aren't welcome here," the man growled.

Gavin looked at the other two. "My kind?"

The man glared at him. "Your kind." He nodded to Rayena. "Your kind." He stared at Brandon the longest. "And your kind."

Gavin took a drink of his ale, looking as casual as he could. He'd never faced El'aras discrimination before—and had no idea how the man had identified him as one. Had he changed during his time training with them?

"Is that right?" Gavan asked. "I didn't realize my kind were anyone you needed to fear."

The man spat again and took another step toward him. Brandon stiffened, and the others behind the leader shuffled forward. Gavin glanced to Brandon and shook his head briefly. He didn't need anyone to cause trouble, but at this point, it seemed entirely possible that they would have trouble regardless.

"We're just here for a little food and drink, and then we plan to be on our way," Gavin said with a shrug.

"No," the man replied.

Gavin snorted. "I didn't realize we were asking for permission."

"Well, you don't have it."

"I didn't ask."

The man took a step toward Gavin, who jumped to his feet. Gavin swept his leg out in a quick hook, his hand curling into another, and he jabbed his palm at the man's throat, forcing him back. The others started toward Gavin, and he drove his fist into the nearest man's stomach, caught the next one with a heel to the groin, and glared at the last, sending him staggering backward.

The large man lay motionless on the ground.

Gavin looked down at him. "I think we *will* stay and eat."

"Your kind aren't welcome here."

He had to give the man credit. Despite having been easily handled, he still reacted with more calm than expected. Which meant he had reason to be calm.

Gavin turned. The rest of the people in the tavern had gotten to their feet. He scoffed, shaking his head. "It's like that, is it?"

No one moved. Certainly not close enough to come toward him, but they watched him. In a city like this, there was a real possibility that some of these people ignored the law to avoid magic and had enchantments on them.

He looked at those watching him. "Tell me. Do you think you have to take me on?"

"There are at least twenty of us," the man on the ground said.

Gavin chuckled. "Twenty. Twenty isn't going to be enough."

"Gavin," Brandon warned.

"If they want to play, we can let them," he said with a shrug. He glanced to the bar, where the server watched him with irritation. "But I don't intend to do so inside. When I'm done with all of you, I'm going to have a seat, finish my ale, and enjoy my food. And you lot are going to pay for it."

The leader laughed as he started to get to his feet. "If you survive, we'll treat all of you."

Gavin grinned. "It's a deal."

CHAPTER NINE

G avin rubbed his knuckles while working on the mug of ale in front of him. He was only a little sore, and he suspected that ache wouldn't linger long. It never did these days. Now that he understood his core reserves better, there was no reason for him to suffer as he once had. His body had always recovered rapidly, easily, and it seemed that this was tied to his own magic.

Rayena leaned toward him. "Do you really intend to stay here and finish your food?"

"Why? Because they might want a rematch?"

He looked over to where the leader had been sitting. He had vomited after the second blow.

Gavin hadn't even needed to use any of his core reserves. There was something exhilarating about fighting like that. Twenty men would've been an incredible challenge for him once, but these men were not trained and he'd been fighting those with magic for far too long.

Dealing with them was little more than a distraction, along with a way to get their meal paid for. He'd been lying when he'd told the server he had coin on him.

"What if they go after others?" Rayena asked.

"They can go after anybody else they want." He made a point of raising his voice loud enough for them to hear. The others had seen how he'd fought, a combination of precision, skill, and mastery of dozens of different fighting styles.

Gavin had even enjoyed it. Other than his sore hands and the still-throbbing knee from when he had fought the stone golem, he'd had very little difficulty with them. They weren't accustomed to fighting together, which would've been a greater challenge. Twenty men in a coordinated attack…

No. What he had faced was no more than two or three trying to come at him at one time. A relatively easy fight.

"Finish your food," he told the other two.

"I'm not hungry," Rayena said.

Brandon laughed. "I am. I didn't expect to have so much fun in a city like this. Did you ever figure out why they don't like our kind?"

Gavin shook his head. "No. I think we're going to have a few words with our friend over there at the bar so we can get answers."

"What do you think he knows?" Rayena asked. She had become even more sullen.

Why did she seem so perturbed by all of this?

"I'm not sure, but I want to know his reasons for their reaction to the presence of El'aras in the city," Gavin said.

He waited until the server came over to their table, and as soon as he did, he gestured to an empty chair. "Have a seat."

"No." The server started backing away.

Gavin held his gaze. "It wasn't a request."

The man froze. Slowly, he took a step toward them and grabbed the remaining chair at the table. He sat perched at the front of it, looking ready to run at any moment.

"You said you have some experience with our kind," Gavin said.

The man glowered at him. "If you want to beat on me like you did the others, go ahead."

"Did I say I was going to?"

"You didn't say you weren't."

Gavin snorted, and he leaned toward the man, who slid back in his chair. "No, I did not. Now, I want to know what you know of our kind."

"We've seen you. Gathering in the shadows to the west of the city, you do. Stealing. Causing trouble. Using that —" He shook his head, as if he realized that he was about to say something he would regret, and instead looked up and held Gavin's gaze. "Eat and be gone. You've already done enough damage."

"I think my new friends were more than happy to pay for our meals."

The server looked as if he wanted to open his mouth and say something more, but he bit it back.

"Where to the west?" Gavin said.

"What?"

"Where. To. The. West?"

The man blinked and glanced around at the others in the tavern, but nobody came to his aid. No one would be willing to do so now, not after seeing the way Gavin had dispatched them as easily as he had.

It was almost enough to make Gavin smile. Almost.

"I told you. West. Near the harbor."

Gavin nodded. "There. That's all I needed."

The server tensed. "I can go?"

"Go."

Gavin finished the rest of his food, which consisted of a slab of overly cooked fish and some mushy onions and carrots, but they did fill him and settle his stomach. He couldn't be certain that the server hadn't spit in his food, but given the man's hesitance, Gavin suspected he would have been too afraid to out of fear that Gavin might find out.

"We didn't learn anything," Rayena said, leaning toward him.

Gavin arched an eyebrow. "Are you sure?"

"What do you think you uncovered?"

"I know where the sculpture leads us, and if this is going to bring us someplace similar..."

"The rumors?"

Gavin nodded. "The rumors. I'm not exactly sure what to make of them, but it's significant." He sat back, finished his ale, and wiped his sleeve across his mouth. "How about the two of you? Are you done?"

Brandon had long ago finished his food, now picking at the remains and grinning as he looked around. As

Gavin had fought, he'd stayed to the side and laughed. What would Brandon have done if Gavin had started to lose? Luckily, they hadn't had the opportunity to find out.

Gavin still didn't know if he could trust him. He had made that mistake once before, though he didn't have the same feeling from Brandon as he had with Theren. Brandon's was more of a reckless abandon, something Gavin had seen in others before, though he was surprised to find it in one of the El'aras.

"I'm done," Rayena said.

"Then we can go. I wasn't going to go after Tristan tonight, but perhaps we need to."

"And them?" she asked, nodding to the other men gathered around.

"They aren't going to follow us," Gavin said.

"Are you sure? You made quick work of them, and men don't like to be treated like that."

"No, but they were treated the way they deserved."

Gavin got to his feet, and no one stood to challenge him. Not that he really expected them to. Rayena wasn't wrong, though. There was a real possibility that the moment they walked out of the tavern, they would be forced to fight. Given that Gavin had not revealed his additional abilities, he wasn't concerned. If they brought even twice what they had before, he'd be able to dispatch them. He didn't want to kill them, though, and had been careful to only beat them until they fell, not harm them in any way that would leave them permanently injured.

At the door, he looked around the tavern, meeting each

person's gaze and daring them to come after him. Everyone kept their eyes down.

Gavin stepped out into the darkness and waited until the others joined him. The air stunk of fish, seaweed, and a hint of salt, the briny odor lingering in his nostrils. They passed a supply store, with netting and fishing lines and other supplies dangling in the window display. A fish-monger stood nearby, where most of the stink seemed to emanate from. The city needed a good breeze to carry it away, but there was none.

"How long before they come back?" Rayena asked.

Gavin breathed out in the hazy air. "I don't know. And it doesn't matter. I know a way from here."

He guided them onward, and they hadn't gone all that far before he paused to check for anyone who might be trailing after him. He didn't think they would make that mistake, but he didn't really know.

"Where would Tristan have hidden here?" he asked.

"An ancient temple," Rayena said without hesitation.

Gavin looked over. He hadn't been sure that she would know. "That's right."

"Have you been there?"

"Only once."

He glanced behind him toward the volcano. Occasional trembles came from it, making him think that it might erupt at any moment. When he had snuck into the artist entrance on the job Tristan sent him on, he had found it illuminated with a strange glowing light that left him wondering if the volcano was more active than Tristan had believed.

"What's so special about this place?" Rayena asked.

"It's not that special," Gavin said. "It's a place he used."

"Then why do you think he wanted you to come here?"

"That's what I need to find out."

Rayena eyed him skeptically. "And that's going to somehow help you understand what you need to do?"

"It's going to help me understand why he sent that message."

"What do you think that has to do with what we experienced in the tavern?"

Gavin frowned. That had been bothering him more than he had let on to the others. When it came to the El'aras, and reactions to them, he found himself conflicted. He had his own feelings about the El'aras and what they meant to him, but finding that others were suspicious of them seemed surprising, at least in a place so far removed from them. How would they even have identified them as El'aras? Gavin had certainly moved through the world without anyone identifying him as one.

"I don't know," he replied. "Perhaps it's one of the families that hasn't aligned itself with the Shard." Maybe he would have to reach out and warn Anna.

"She might not have known," Rayena said, shrugging when Brandon and Gavin both looked in her direction. "When I was traveling outside the lands, I saw evidence of other families. There are plenty out in the world, some of them more active, and some of them more open to revealing their presence."

"I saw families too," Gavin said. "And they wanted power."

"It's not about that."

"I know what it was about."

Rayena shook her head. "No. What you experienced was not a pursuit of power."

Gavin frowned. "When I dealt with Theren—"

"He was not after power."

"His pursuit of that Toral ring could have fooled me, then."

"He was after a means of destroying sorcery," she said. "That is a very different thing than chasing down power, especially for one of our kind. There are many El'aras who would have understood what Theren was after. They may not have agreed with what he did to accomplish that goal, but they would have understood him. I know that my family would have. We had our own struggles with sorcerers."

"Did you ever consider hunting them?" Gavin asked.

Rayena held his gaze. "No. There was no point in pursuing that fight. Our people had retreated. We have our own lands now, those that are not touched by the foulness of sorcery. I only meant that others would understand where he came from."

As Gavin watched her, he realized that she meant it. What was stranger for him was the fact that he didn't know if he could even understand. There were times like these when he was acutely aware that he was not one of the El'aras. Not really. He might share their bloodline, but being raised outside their society made it so that he didn't understand them nearly as well as he wished he could.

"Do you think there are any families like that here?" Gavin asked.

Rayena shook her head. "I would've heard about it."

"When were you last here?"

"It's been a while," she said.

They reached a point in the road where it started to slope downward, leading toward the water. Gavin went by memory. When he had last been here, he still hadn't branched off from Tristan. He'd stayed with his old mentor, thinking that he needed to be with him so he could learn different fighting styles, learn what Tristan wanted him to do, and learn what it meant for him to be the fighter he was destined to be.

And he had been tested. But he remembered the temple, which had been part of the test—one he was expected to pass.

He glanced over to Rayena. "Do you think it's the same?"

"I don't know."

Brandon glanced between the two of them. "What's the same?"

"That," Gavin said, gesturing to the temple in front of them. Much like many other things in the city, the structure was made of obsidian. At one point, it would've been impressive, though time had caused it to fall into disrepair.

At least, that's what it looked like from the outside.

Gavin knew differently. The temple held various protective layers both inside and out, all of them designed to keep any intruders from getting too close to the temple itself or too far inside if they managed to enter. He only knew of a few of them directly. It was entirely possible that Tristan had placed other protections that would make it incredibly difficult to get all the way inside. Gavin was going to have to be fully prepared for the dangers he would have to face. Then again, he had anticipated that it would be risky when he'd decided to come here.

He made his way slowly forward, and something began trembling. A beam streaked across the ground, shooting from one building to the next. Gavin unsheathed his sword in a heartbeat, jumped forward, and brought the blade down on top of the mechanism controlling it. The beam would've torn through them.

"What was that?" Brandon asked.

"One of his protections," Gavin said.

"That was a protection?"

Rayena nodded. "One of many. There will be more."

"Why do we need to go in there?" Brandon's voice sounded wary.

"We need to get in there to see why Tristan summoned me to this place," Gavin replied.

He was increasingly certain that they had indeed been summons. Tristan didn't do anything simply. If Gavin wanted answers, he was going to have to find them the hard way. Which meant that he would have to fight through whatever protections Tristan had.

"So he had a beam. What other dangerous things will he have?"

"There will be different types," Gavin said, thinking through what he had seen in the past. "There will be certain layers of protection for those who have been here before, and unless they have the appropriate key, they won't be permitted access. For newcomers, there will be different safeguards to prevent them from even getting close."

"What about those who have been here before but are supposed to come back?" Brandon asked, glancing from Gavin to Rayena.

Gavin frowned. "You wouldn't be able to get far inside. Maybe five steps?"

Rayena shrugged. "Perhaps four. It depends on what kind of mood he was in when he activated them."

"That's true. It does depend on his mood, along with whether he was worried about what was to come."

Given what they knew about the potential within the city, Gavin suspected that they had to be careful here. If there were others in Hester who were also irritated by the presence of El'aras, there was a real possibility that Tristan had activated his stoutest defenses in order to defend against those people. He looked over to Rayena, and her tight expression showed that she was feeling the same way.

Gavin started forward, and a faint stir caused him to jump. Spikes shot upward from the ground, then quickly retreated. He landed, but doing so seemed to have activated something else. He twisted and flipped in the air, barely dodging another bolt that shot across the narrow street leading toward the temple.

He reached the doorway, and it started to squeeze in on him. He hurriedly traced a pattern on either side of it, then pushed his core reserves through that power and deactivated the energy.

He breathed heavily, knowing this was just the beginning.

Gavin glanced back to the others, who were picking their way forward carefully. He had intentionally gone ahead, activating as many of the protections as he could to allow the two to move without running the risk of disturbing the other traps. Rayena knew the dangers and maneuvered around them, but Brandon simply weaved through them as if unconcerned. Perhaps he didn't have to be. He had never been here before, and there was nothing here that he would necessarily activate.

Gavin remained on edge, prepared to react and try to protect them from anything else that might be triggered, but thankfully did not need to.

"What now?" Brandon asked when they reached him.

"Now we open the door and see what treats are inside," Gavin said.

He pressed his hand on the door. He expected some sort of enchantment or dangerous reaction, but he didn't feel anything. The night was dark, and he needed some light to illuminate the door. With his El'aras dagger in hand, he pushed a hint of his core reserves into it and waited as the blade started to glow softly.

"What are you looking for?" Rayena asked.

"Tristan placed his mark on everything he left me."

"You think this will be the same?"

Gavin shrugged. "Maybe he doesn't want us to break down his protections. Maybe he only wants us to open it."

"Will you be able to do that?"

"I have no idea. Quite a bit has changed since I last spent any real time with Tristan. I might have needed to break down the door back then, but now…"

He swept his blade across the door, searching for any evidence of Tristan's mark, but he didn't see it. He stepped back, and immediately wished he hadn't.

A trapdoor threatened to drop down on them. Gavin reached up to stop it, and spikes from overhead pierced the meat of each thumb.

"I could use some help here," he said, wincing and gritting his teeth.

"He's kind of an ass, isn't he?" Brandon said.

Gavin clenched his jaw. "He's very much an ass. Now help me."

Brandon and Rayena helped force the trapdoor upward, each of them jabbing a dagger into opposite sides to lock it into place. Gavin held his breath and waited, worried that it wasn't going to hold.

"You didn't know about that one?" Brandon asked.

"I probably shouldn't have stepped back," Gavin said. "It would have been there to prevent our escape."

"Then he doesn't want you to leave?"

"I don't know whether it's for me or somebody else."

Either way, there had to be some reason for it. Tristan didn't do things for nothing.

Gavin swept his gaze along the door, double-checking that he didn't miss any sign of the mark. He wanted to take it in more slowly, but he was afraid to linger.

Maybe there wasn't a mark here.

"What are you doing?" Rayena asked as he stepped forward. "You aren't going to—"

Power exploded from Gavin through his ring and into the doorknob. He half expected the knob to shatter and the door to pop open, but neither happened. Instead, the door started to glow softly, revealing Tristan's mark.

"He might be getting cleverer in his old age," Gavin muttered.

"How much power did you put into that?" Rayena asked.

"Nearly everything I could."

"So you won't be able to break it open."

He shrugged. "Maybe not."

"Does he intend for you to get inside, or was this all to draw you into a trap?" Brandon asked.

Gavin frowned. He believed that Tristan wanted him to be here, but there was the distinct possibility that it might be a trap. Then again, there might be another way, one that Tristan had left only for him, much like the pillar had been.

He focused on the handle, pushing power out from himself, but nothing else changed. What else could he do? He didn't want to break the door or destroy it. What he needed was to find a way of activating whatever enchantment Tristan had placed. It wasn't just about pouring power into it. With Tristan, things weren't always so simple.

It had to be some pattern. What if Tristan's was the one Gavin needed to make?

He started to etch that pattern across from the one that

was in the door, began to fill that with the power of his core reserves, then added what he could of the ring. The new pattern started to glow, at first softly, and then with an increased vibrancy.

"Keep going," Rayena urged. "I have seen him do something like that before. I did not know what he did, though, because he always hid it."

Could it be so simple? If so, then why had Gavin wasted his time breaking through the stone pillar? He could have simply activated it a different way.

He continued to push power outward until he felt something shift.

The door clicked open.

Gavin stood motionless for a long moment. "Be ready," he said to the others.

He took a step inside Tristan's old temple. As he did, he immediately began to feel something strange. He wasn't sure what it was, not at first, but they were not alone. The temple itself was quiet, dark, and it had an empty feel to it. He knew there were rooms that could be used for sleeping quarters or for training, but there was not much else.

Gavin paused just inside the doorway and looked around, but everything was impossibly dark. He waited for a sign of anyone else's presence and continued to feel as if there was something more here. He just didn't know what it was.

"There is—"

Shadows suddenly seemed to move toward them, and

a weight began to press down on Gavin. He had felt something like that before.

"Stay behind me," he said. He immediately released his connection to his core reserves and to the ring, and he grabbed his sword instead.

This was going to be a fight, but this was going to be *his* fight.

If the nihilar were here, or those who sought to use that power, then he was going to be ready.

But why were they in Tristan's temple?

CHAPTER TEN

Gavin prepared himself. Having fought these attackers before, he was ready. It had been a simple matter to take them on last time.

But he quickly realized that they must've learned new tricks after the assault on Arashil. Now, as the attackers pressed forward with a flurry of techniques, Gavin was put on the defensive immediately and forced back toward the doorway.

And toward Tristan's defenses.

Gavin lashed out and kicked, risking the danger of exposing himself, but he needed to give Brandon and Rayena a chance to regroup.

"I don't know how many are here," he said, shouting at them. "But—"

An attacker surged toward him. Gavin hurriedly reached into his pocket, grabbing for one of his enchantments. He only wished that he had taken the opportunity to purchase more, especially knowing that the enchantments might be the only way to defeat these people. They didn't seem to be prepared for the possibility that Gavin would come bearing other enchantments. They were likely expecting his El'aras abilities, along with the sword and ring, but they didn't know he could do more.

He managed to get the enchantment for speed onto his wrist, but its use would be limited. Without being recharged, the enchantment would not have nearly the same strength as it had when he had first faced them. It put him at a disadvantage, but he thought that with enough speed and quickness, it wouldn't matter.

A blade blurred over his head. Gavin darted forward and ducked inside its reach. His own sword was forgotten as fighting styles flashed into his mind, and he fell into them instinctively.

He grabbed the man's wrist, twisting and snapping with the quick hold of the Karan style. Then he kicked, sweeping the man's legs out from underneath him with the Tiliant techniques. Gavin dropped and used a simple grappling maneuver, then slammed his fist into the attacker's face over and over until he didn't move.

He glanced up as Rayena approached. "Bind him. We need to question him."

"What about you?" she asked.

Gavin sprung to his feet. The pressure on him still hadn't eased, and he suspected that it hadn't eased for the others either. They were managing better than they had in Arashil, which suggested that either the power pushing on them was not nearly as much as it had been before, or perhaps there was only one attacker.

The idea that there might only be one of them didn't make any sense, though. The timing was suspect. Why now? Why here?

Gavin moved deeper inside. The entrance of the temple was made of darkened stone. Lanterns were set on either side of the wall, leading the way farther in, remnants of a time when people had worshipped a different god. There was something almost suffocating about the temple, but he ignored that, instead hurrying forward. Though they had only seen one attacker, he suspected there might be more.

"I'm here," Brandon said from behind him.

"Not so sure you should be," Gavin said, without taking his attention off of the path in front of him.

He slid one foot after another, moving as carefully as he could in the dim light. He suspected that the darkness was natural, but there was always the possibility that one of these attackers had used the strange shadows they seemed to command and darkened it even more.

"You need me, Champion," Brandon said. "Can't have you going off on your own and ending up injured. I've seen it too many times."

"You have?"

"Well, I've seen how you need me."

Gavin shook his head. "Stay behind me. If there's any pressure..." He frowned. "Have you learned how to hold your breath?"

Brandon chuckled. "I've been trying. You said I have to separate myself from it."

"Something like that."

He wasn't entirely sure how to describe it in any other way, only that separating it from oneself seemed to be fitting and sounded like it made the most sense. In Gavin's case, it was merely a matter of dividing himself from his core reserves and his power until he was ready. But the El'aras who had lived their entire lives using that ability needed some instruction on how to do it. He hesitated, glancing down the hall as Rayena joined them.

"He's tied up," she said. "Securely. And I made it so that he can't move at all. I bound his arms and legs with a bit of enchanted rope. It's connected to me, so he won't be able to release it. It would take somebody more powerful. I also may have tied him up so that he's in an uncomfortable position."

Gavin frowned. That was more brutal than he would've expected from Rayena. She was a member of the Order, though, so perhaps that should not be surprising.

"I was talking to Brandon about suppressing the El'aras magic inside yourself," Gavin said, keeping his words low.

The inside of the faded temple felt oppressive, compelling him to keep his voice quiet so that he didn't draw the attention of anything or anyone else. Least of all, he didn't want to draw the attention of more nihilar attackers.

"Why would I want to suppress it?" she asked.

"If you want to fight, and if you want to have a chance

of defeating these opponents, you might need to." He waited until they leaned closer, and though he could only make out the faint outlines of their faces, he could guess that Rayena's brow was furrowed. "Brandon has described it as holding his breath, and I think that's a reasonable description. You have learned to hold on to that power and have access to that magic inside of you from a very young age. It is part of you, no different than breathing."

"It should be part of you as well," she said.

"It should be, but it's not. My connection to these abilities is different. I have to intentionally use them, unlike you. And because of that, it gives me a slight advantage over you in this scenario."

He waited for her to refute that, but she said nothing. "You need to find a way to trap that part of you and push it down."

Gavin had no idea what that would involve for them. If using their magic was no different than breathing for them, it would be like holding back some piece of themselves. Or maybe it was more like trying to stop the blood flowing through their veins.

"I don't have a good answer as to how to do it," he continued. "I don't know how you hold on to the power within yourself." He felt foolish about describing this to two full-blooded El'aras—who had grown up among their people and knew the power they had, how to draw on it, and how to use their ability—but that was where he was. "When I use it, I feel a pool deep within me. It's faint, but it's there. And then I can pull it up. Anna taught me how to draw the magic up through my body, out into every part of my being. And from there, I'm supposed to be able to control it."

Supposed to be. He could to an extent, but it was incomplete at best. Despite how much he wanted to have complete control over it, he still struggled.

"It flows through me. I don't know if I can push it back." Rayena's voice was hesitant.

"Treat it like wringing out a rag," Brandon said. She looked over to him, and he shrugged. Even though Gavin couldn't see his face well enough, he imagined Brandon winking. "You have to squeeze it out. I think that I can pull it through my fists, and once I do that, I think... Oh."

"What happened?" she asked.

"I can feel it being drawn away." Brandon glanced over to Gavin. "I don't know if it's like that for you."

"Probably not. When I use that ability, I have to push it out into the rest of my body. I have to make an effort of using it. And there are limits."

"Maybe that's why you're the Champion. You can call on it at will, whereas we have a steady state, and what power we have is the power we have. You can shift and change yours."

It was the first time anybody had described how he used his ability in that way, but it was probably true. He could call on his at will. And he had managed to use it to overwhelm El'aras. The El'aras were skilled fighters, but even in that, Gavin had still managed to defeat many of them.

But being able to access his core reserves—something that coursed through him and could be sent out into every part of his being—gave him an advantage that the El'aras didn't have because he could focus it more than they could.

"Just try to wring it out in your hands."

"Not so much holding your breath as it is drying a towel," Brandon muttered.

"If it works, that's all that matters," Gavin said.

The pressure on him still hadn't shifted. He didn't dare reach for his core reserves, but he didn't know that he needed to. If he focused on that pressure, he might be able to feel something, but it was a matter of trying to grab it and fully master it.

"I don't know if I can do it," Rayena said. Some of her bravado was missing, and her eyes had widened enough that Gavin could see the whites of them.

He understood her concern. He was asking them to push away some part of themselves that they believed necessary. He was asking them to ignore the El'aras magic within their being.

"Whatever you do is temporary," he reassured.

At least, for them it would be. For him, it was using the power that was temporary. He might be El'aras, but he did not have the same connection to his ability that they did.

"Are you ready to keep going?" Gavin asked.

He wasn't sure how much longer they could linger here, confident that there were still other attackers around. And, Gavin feared, there was still the leader. He didn't know anything about the man, only that he seemed to be after something, and Gavin needed to learn what it was. More than that, he needed to stop him.

"I'm ready," Brandon said.

Rayena nodded.

They walked deeper into the temple. Only hints of light glowed from the lanterns within it. The walls seemed to press inward, giving Gavin the sensation of pressure around him, though the feeling wasn't unpleasant, just persistent. Doors led off the hall into two rooms that Tristan had used for people to be able to stay, train, and isolate themselves.

"There weren't doors along these walls when I was here before," Rayena said softly.

"How could doors disappear?" Brandon asked, his voice too loud.

"I suspect it has more to do with the protections Tristan has placed here. He obviously has defended the temple."

"So we have to assume that somebody got here, they were making their way through, and… what?"

"I imagine that they have left someone to guard and watch this place to alert any others that are here," Gavin said.

"Which means this person knew about Hester and the temple?" Brandon asked.

Gavin frowned but nodded.

The darkness in the temple was difficult to navigate easily, yet, if he remembered correctly, they didn't have to go much farther before the hall ended. From there, it would open up into a larger chamber at the bottom of the stairs.

They reached a dead end.

air had a heaviness to it, seeming to carry some part of the energy of the temple, guiding them deeper into the earth. He found himself holding his own breath, not just his core reserves.

He waited at the top of the steps, anticipating another attack, but nothing happened. As a precautionary measure, he slipped on enchantments that granted him increased speed and hardened skin. Gavin started down the stairs and half expected to feel some pressure or something to suggest that an attack was coming from behind them. But every time he took a step forward, he found that there was nothing.

At the bottom of the stairs, a soft flutter of wind triggered his instincts. The breeze was enough to tell him that something was moving, and Gavin lunged back and kicked outward simultaneously. Something struck his boot, but because of the enchantment he wore, it only cut through his shoe and not his foot.

Rayena grunted, but Gavin didn't hear Brandon make any sound.

Gavin scrambled to the side, hoping his enchantments were going to be enough for whatever was to come. He lunged forward, sweeping his blade toward the attacker. As he crashed into them, they grabbed him. Gavin wrapped his arms around them, but they had impossible strength. Enchanted strength. He gritted his teeth and continued to squeeze, keeping his arms pressed tightly around them, using everything he could to knock them out.

He still had the enchantments. With the impervious

skin, he didn't worry about them stabbing him, but there was a point where the enchantment would fade if he drew on its power for too long. He tried to ignore that possibility and focused on fighting.

Gavin brought his knee up and connected with some part of his attacker, though he couldn't tell which. He spun, twisting his body around. With a sharp jab, he was rewarded with a gasp, allowing him to roll off to the side and break the grip.

He darted forward again and immediately began to feel something pushing against him. Magic, or perhaps an enchantment.

Somewhere distantly, he heard another grunt. Even though he couldn't see much, he could tell that Brandon and Rayena were fighting too. The pressure around him began to build even more like it was trying to suppress some part of himself.

"Hold your breath!" he shouted to them.

Distant laughter reached his ears. The man who'd attacked him in Arashil.

He had known about Hester. About the temple. Of course. He knew Tristan, after all.

Pressure weighed down on Gavin, and he knew that the others weren't going to be able to do anything. It would have to be him. He didn't need his core reserves. He didn't need anything other than the enchantments he had. He had a limited amount of time before the magic within them ran out, but for now, he could fight.

"You don't even know why you're here, do you?" the man said. That same angry voice from before.

sight." And the times that Gavin had tried to see what was written in its pages had been met with failure.

Much like now.

"He didn't fear anything," Rayena said.

Gavin peered through the open doorway. "He didn't fear anything, but he also understood protecting himself." If there was one thing he knew about Tristan, it was that he was skilled at ensuring his own safety. He had managed to escape before his own trainees overthrew him. Then again, maybe they hadn't actually tried. Everything Gavin had been told about that had come from Cyran, who had been after a different kind of power—far more than he should have been. "We have to assume that Tristan knew they were after him. And if he knew they were and he left this for me, it means I can somehow help."

"You are the Champion after all," Brandon said.

Gavin looked over to him, and he shook his head. "I'm not so sure this has anything to do with being the Champion. I wonder if this has more to do with being the Chain Breaker."

Gavin had acquired the nickname while working with Tristan, as he was first learning how to channel the power of his core reserves—the beginning of using his El'aras magic. Tristan would've known that that's what those core reserves were. Gavin felt increasingly certain of that, even if he hadn't had the opportunity to question him.

But in this case, it wasn't about his core reserves. He hadn't needed them, and in fact, they would have been a detriment against these attackers. Perhaps Tristan had known that as well.

"Let's see what he's hiding," Gavin said, taking a deep breath.

They walked through the doorway and entered the room. The space was little more than the size of a closet, only about five paces by five paces. The walls were lined with alcoves set directly into the stone.

And they were all empty.

Brandon raised an eyebrow. "He gave you the sculpture to find an empty room?"

"Apparently," Gavin muttered. Had all of this been for nothing? "He gave it to me to protect it, which means he believed that not only was it in danger, but that there was something here for me to protect."

And maybe not even something he had to protect, but something he had to keep others from acquiring. The nihilar had likely either known or suspected this and had come looking for it.

He took in the closet, glancing to the empty alcoves. "He wouldn't have given me this if there was nothing here," Gavin said to himself. "Unless this was all some game of his."

"And you're still willing to play?" Rayena asked.

"Tristan and I have a rocky relationship. There was a time when I revered him. Then a time when I hated him. That wasn't all that long ago. Now I don't know how to feel about him, only that I'm increasingly certain he knew things and was trying to prepare me."

"He knew about the Order."

"Of course he did, but it seems to me that there is more

than just the Order at play here," Gavin said. "And I need to understand just what Tristan was trying to show me."

He leaned back, his mind working. He had to try to think like Tristan, to come up with some way of knowing what he might have done in this place.

Brandon took a step forward. "What if he's not trying to show you anything? What if, to him, you were just the Chain Breaker?"

"Just," Rayena said, snorting.

"Well, that and the Champion. Although, at the time he trained you, did he even know that you were the Champion?"

"No, I don't think so," Gavin replied.

"There you go. Then maybe it's not about you. Maybe all of this is because of Rayena." He turned to her. "Now, since it's up to you, what would you have us do?"

Gavin shook his head, ignoring him and turning back to the alcoves. He held the sculpture and moved from place to place, curiosity rising within him. Whatever was happening had to be tied to the sculpture Tristan had given him. There was something to it, he was certain of it. He might not know what it was, he might not even know how to use it, but he was increasingly certain that was the reason Tristan had gifted it to him.

Brandon and Rayena continued talking quietly, with Brandon occasionally trying to get Rayena to open up, to tell him about her family, but she refused to answer those questions. Gavin found himself listening, curiosity filling him about her as well. She seemed to want to hide everything about her family. Maybe she felt ashamed, or perhaps she was concerned about how they might react.

Gavin shook his head, returning his focus to the task at hand and tuning them out. There had to be something within the alcoves.

He set the sculpture into various parts of the room, testing one spot after another. The first few alcoves had nothing. By the time he reached the bottom row, he started to think that perhaps this was a mistake and he'd been wrong about this. It was entirely possible that there wasn't anything here.

Then he noticed a mark on the center of the floor.

He set the sculpture down in the middle of the room, and as he did, the sculpture seemed to solidify in his hands and settle into place. The figurine rocked back and forth for a moment before sinking down into the stone.

Gavin held his breath, scarcely able to move. This was what Tristan had wanted for him to do. Now he had to understand why.

A small opening revealed another statue, much like the one Tristan had stored in the book. This one was substantially larger and had a strange warmth to it. It could be an enchantment, or it could be nothing more than a sacred sculpture to the people of Hester.

Gavin pulled it free, then sat back, resting on his heels. "This?" he asked, mostly to himself.

He turned the sculpture over in his hand, trying to figure out why this would be important enough for Tristan to leave behind. There had to be something more to it. He looked around at this space. Without the book and the small figurine, he would never have been able to reach this room or find the larger statue. Why send Gavin on a hunt for it?

Realization struck him, followed by irritation. "He didn't want me to protect it. He wanted me to bring it to him."

"Why do you say that?" Rayena asked.

"Because Tristan would've been able to come for this himself. He placed the pillar outside Arashil. He sent me here, knowing about the sculpture. And then this." He shook his head. "All of this is because Tristan wants me to bring it to him."

"Why not come himself?" Brandon said.

"Either he couldn't, or he feared them finding him." Gavin looked over to Rayena.

"It's possible," she said.

He pulled his satchel free and rearranged the items inside until he had room for the newly discovered sculpture. He stuffed the book into it as well. Then he looked at the other two. "It's time to go. I need to find Tristan, it seems, but I don't know where to do that. This was the only clue I had."

"Other than the book," Rayena said.

Gavin glanced down at his pouch. "If only I could read it."

"Do you know anyone who can?"

He had an idea of somebody who might be able to help him, but he didn't like it. "There might be someone who has that ability."

He hadn't wanted to return to Yoran so soon, and he

certainly didn't want to put anyone he cared about in danger, but if it meant getting answers, maybe it was time.

They made their way back through the temple. Gavin paused where they had fought the attackers and looked for the one they had faced. The fallen man remained bound.

Gavin nodded to Rayena. "Grab him. We need to question him."

He was surprised the man's companions would've left him behind—unless they weren't concerned about him sharing a secret, or they simply hadn't known that Gavin and the others had bound him.

They dragged the man to the entrance of the temple, and Rayena and Brandon retrieved their daggers that had kept the door open. As soon as they withdrew them, the door dropped, sealing the temple off.

No one would be able to enter, which Gavin suspected was for the best.

"Such security for a book," Brandon said with a sigh.

"Books have power. They are a way of acquiring knowledge," Rayena said. "Those in my family have always appreciated the truth that can be found in learning about the past. Sometimes those truths get rewritten over time, enough so that you lose track of what is true and what is not."

Gavin looked over and nodded. "I've heard others say the same thing."

They made their way carefully along the street leading from the temple, dodging the traps Tristan had placed and

"And for a long time," Rayena continued, "I wanted nothing more than to blame the sorcerers for what had happened. It was a time when many El'aras families lost to the sorcerers. How could we not fault them?"

They had reached the shoreline, and the water lapped along the shore, though it wasn't the only sound he heard. Rayena's soft breath. His pounding heart. And a distant humming.

She turned to him, meeting his gaze again. "You want to compare me to those you've dealt with before, go ahead. I feel much the same way. Or did. I'm not going to deny it. There is no point in telling you anything other than the truth. I felt that way. Then I found the Order."

"How did the Order help you?"

"I learned that not all sorcerers were responsible." She said it slowly, as if the words pained her to admit, but when she looked up at him, there was a measure of defiance in her expression. "Something I suspect even you can acknowledge."

"I can," Gavin said.

"And when we acknowledge that not all sorcerers are responsible, then you have to also acknowledge that not all El'aras are responsible."

"I have never blamed all of the El'aras."

"But you want to blame me."

"It's not you. All of it has to do with me—what I've gone through and what others have decided they want for me to be. And now if other El'aras families are involved, I'm concerned that this is moving beyond what I had anticipated." Maybe it was time for him to go back to Anna and bring her in on everything.

"I don't know the Woven family," Rayena said. "So if you want to worry about anyone in their trustworthiness, you should worry about Brandon."

"I am."

She frowned at him. "And what about the Shard?"

Anna was more complicated, and Gavin didn't have a good answer at the ready.

"Why did you want me to come with you? You challenge me to find out if I'm going to betray you?"

"Actually, I wanted you to come with me because I wanted to know if we could learn more about what's going on in the city."

He started making his way along the shoreline and hoped she would come with him. She eventually followed, and as they walked, she looked out over the water.

After several minutes of walking in silence, Rayena turned her attention back to him. "There aren't many who care for our kind."

Our kind.

No matter how often he heard references to that, it was still difficult for Gavin to acknowledge. He was one of the El'aras, even if he didn't necessarily feel like it.

"I've never really known that challenge," he said. He paused at the edge of the water where the bay started to curve again. A few ships bobbed in the waves, but their lights were darkened, making them difficult to see.

"If you were to fully return to the people, you would start to understand. It may take you a few years, maybe a decade, but you will feel how the rest of the world views us."

He looked over to her, but she had already started walking away from him. What was she trying to tell him?

He felt the energy of the waves crashing along the shore, seeming to press inward. There were answers here, Gavin was certain. He had no idea what was making him so sure, only that he couldn't help but feel like there was something going on.

"We could spend a long time searching here," he said, catching up to her.

She glanced over to him. "We could."

"And we may not find any answers."

Rumors. That was all they had to go on at this point. Rumors, and no explanation for them.

And he had the book, he reminded himself. Gavin suspected that he wasn't the only one after it, but finding the book was a different matter from understanding it and understanding what they were after. He didn't know why the attackers would be searching for the book, and until he did, he would have to keep looking for answers.

They wandered along the shoreline for a little while longer, and he listened to the waves as they crashed against the land. It was peaceful—or it would be if he didn't have such heavy thoughts.

"What job brought you to the city all those years ago?" Rayena asked.

"I told you. It was a test."

She snorted. "If you don't want to share with me, then you don't have to, but you don't need to hide it either."

Gavin turned away from the water. "It's not a matter of wanting to hide it from you. It's the truth. Most of the time, when I went anywhere with Tristan, there was some kind of test involved."

"Why did he continually feel the need to do that to you?"

"He was molding me."

It was a simple answer, and one that came to Gavin the easiest. He had always believed that Tristan was molding him into a better fighter, one who was more skilled and fearless. Somebody who was not afraid of death as he pulled the jobs Tristan had trained him for. Over time, he had become hardened. Not only his body and mind and his ability to recognize patterns and replicate them, but Gavin himself had become hardened to the ways that Tristan had wanted to train him. This was just one more test.

"I had to sneak into a building near the volcano," Gavin said. "There was a box there, and I had to take it." Within the box had been the sculpture that Tristan had now left for him.

"How long ago was it?" Rayena asked.

"I don't know. I was around twenty. Skilled at that point."

"I would've thought that you were always skilled, Chain Breaker. Are you less skilled now?"

He hesitated before answering. It seemed like an easy question, but there was something to it that gave him pause. "I think I was a more fearless fighter then."

"What changed?"

he started to question if perhaps that was also part of Tristan's plan for him.

Despite everything Gavin had gone through, there was a piece of him that still felt as if Tristan were trying to manipulate events so that Gavin would behave in predictable ways. He knew better than to fall for that.

Shouts rang out in the night, and Gavin looked up.

"What do you think that is?" Rayena asked.

"I suspect it might be our friends from the tavern."

"Then we won't be able to get through the city easily, unless you intend to fight everybody who comes at you."

"No. I most definitely do not."

"We have the ungalt, and you have that strange wolf creature," Brandon said. "I prefer the ungalt, if you ask me. Well, that and sitting alongside the lovely Rayena." She shot him a hard look, but he just chuckled.

Gavin didn't necessarily want to fight his way through the city. With what they had dealt with, there was a real possibility that they might need to do so if they tried to travel by ground. Thankfully, he had other enchantments.

"I might have another way."

"What?" Brandon asked. "Something better than the ungalt?"

Gavin nodded. He reached into his pocket, pulled out a folded piece of paper, and prepared to activate the enchantment within it. "How do you feel about flying?"

CHAPTER TWELVE

Soaring above the ground was almost peaceful. If they didn't have such a sense of urgency, Gavin might have tried to enjoy it. Brandon laughed behind him and Rayena remained motionless, seated to the right of Gavin.

He had ridden atop the paper dragon several times. The exquisitely made enchantment was formed from stiff paper, as if it were truly a dragon's leathery hide. There were no scales, like dragons supposedly had in stories he'd read as a child, and this one didn't breathe fire, which Gavin suspected would destroy it. But still there was something quite magical about it. Flying like this was freeing in a way that he would never have expected. He loved this enchantment more than any others he had used before.

They soared above the dark volcano that loomed over Hester, which had an odd haze surrounding it. As they circled, Gavin guided the paper dragon toward it and saw that parts of the volcano had started to crumble. Rock had sheared and separated, covering some of the sacred artisan buildings and leaving them in piles of rubble.

A troubling thought came to him. Could *that* be why the people of Hester didn't care for the El'aras? What if these nihilar had used their power to destroy parts of the city, much like they had with the temple? What would be their reason for doing so, though? The place was sacred to the people here, but as far as he knew, there wasn't any power in it.

The answer had to be in the book.

As they traveled, Gavin looked over the side of the dragon. The landscape below was a dark blur, though there were occasional dots of lantern light far below him that marked villages, distant cities, and even isolated homes here and there. Wind swirled around him, and he sucked in a deep breath and pulled at his cloak as the gusts whipped through his hair.

"What are you expecting to find?" Brandon hollered, leaning toward him.

"We know they're still out there."

"But do you think you can see them? Gods, I had a hard enough time seeing them when I was facing them in the tunnel."

Gavin couldn't necessarily see them, but he was curious if he could let his core reserves guide him. If he felt some pressure against him, he would know that he was getting close.

As the dragon flew high overhead, he held onto his core reserves.

"Why didn't we take this the first time?" Brandon shouted.

"Because I don't know how much power it has," Gavin replied. "The person who made it is what we call an enchanter. Not a sorcerer. Not El'aras."

Despite that, Alana was incredibly powerful. She was gifted in ways that few were. The same was also true of Mekel, who had made the stone creatures they had ridden. He was more powerful than most of the enchanters.

"You can always add more of your magic to it," Rayena said.

Gavin glanced back at her. She was gripping the dragon tightly and looking straight ahead. There was a stiffness to her, though it had been there ever since the attack in Arashil. She managed to cling to the paper dragon, and she had a powerful appearance and aura to her.

"I've tried that," Gavin said. "I have to help the dragon fly over great distances, but there's always the possibility that my own power will fade too."

"But it will return."

There were limits to his core reserves, and he worried about what would happen if he called on power beyond what they held. Death, possibly.

"It will," he conceded.

"How many of these do you have?" Brandon asked.

"She provided me with several, but I prefer this one," he said, patting the dragon on the side.

He wasn't sure why that was the case. The other dragons were fine. They were smaller, and because of that, they were probably less obvious to anybody watching from the ground. They might even use less power, but they wouldn't be able to carry as many people. The real reason that Gavin chose to use this one rather than the others, though, was that he felt as if he had a connection to it. Given that it was an enchantment and not something actually alive, he didn't know why he kept feeling drawn to this one. There were other enchantments that he could use, other paper dragons, but generally he went with the same one. It was also the case with the stone wolf. He wasn't sure why he felt that connection with some over others.

"I see something down below," Rayena said, tipping her head to the side of the paper dragon.

Gavin peeked his head over and looked down, frowning. "I see that as well."

A small campfire. If he was right, they weren't terribly far from Yoran. He focused on his core reserves, pushing power out, but he didn't feel the same suppression. They circled above the campfire for a moment. In the darkness of the night, no one would be aware of their presence. They would look like a cloud or a shadow, nothing more than that.

"It's not them," Rayena said.

Gavin nodded. "I don't think so either. If it was, I would feel something pushing against me."

"Agreed."

"I still think we should check it out, though."

Rayena didn't argue, and Brandon looked over without saying anything, appearing curious or perhaps puzzled by

Gavin's interest in seeing what this was. Gavin didn't have an explanation for why he was, only that something about the fire bothered him.

He tapped on the side of the paper dragon and pushed on his core reserves, connecting to the creature and feeling a surge of power that was shared between them. As he did, that energy burst. The dragon rapidly descended, diving toward the ground, only pulling up at the last second.

Gavin climbed down, but not fast enough. The ground rippled in a quick and unnatural way. As he watched, he tried to make sense of what he was seeing, and he recognized that there was power flowing from enchantments.

But why? What purpose would there be in keeping enchantments out here? Did they somehow know that he was coming through this way? Or were all of these residual enchantments from the last attack?

They were close enough to Yoran that he wanted to eliminate them.

He unsheathed his blade as he darted ahead. A strange stone monster lumbered toward him, and he slashed through it, carving through pieces of rock. He rolled to his side, avoiding another attack, and stabbed at the next twisted enchantment. This one looked like his stone wolf, though it was made out of mud. This creature didn't give off the same sense of power as the stone wolf, which Gavin suspected was for the best. He looked over, briefly checking on the others, and found Rayena and Brandon fighting back-to-back.

There came another burst of power. This time, Gavin felt something within it.

Magic.

His blade suddenly began to glow with a vibrant energy. The magic was coming from nearby, radiating toward him—a warning. He hurried over to where he detected it, saw a swirl of darkness, and thought it might be the same nihilar power that he had felt before, but that wasn't what this was. This was instead a dark, shadowy figure.

They turned toward him. Power surged, swirling from the ground all the way up to encircle Gavin's chest and constrict him. By the time he burst through it, the figure was gone.

"Where did they go?" Brandon asked, racing over to him.

Gavin shook his head. "I don't know what that was."

"Nihilar?" Rayena asked.

He didn't think so. If it had been, he would have felt the pressure on his core reserves, but he had not. Instead, he felt the same awareness he had whenever he was around sorcery.

"I don't know what it was," he said. "Not the same thing we dealt with before. When we get to Yoran, I might have to alert them of what is out here." He didn't like making somebody else deal with sorcery outside of the city, but he wasn't sure he needed to be handling it himself either. Not with everything they were working on now.

They climbed aboard the dragon again and took to the sky. When they neared Yoran, Gavin tapped on the dragon's side, and they began to quickly descend outside the city border.

Brandon leaned forward again. "Why aren't we going in?"

"Because the city has protections around it. Or it did when I was last here."

Once they reached it, he would learn whether those protections remained. He suspected that the constables and the enchanters had continued to maintain them, but he didn't know if those protections would limit him. Now that he was better able to draw on the power of the ring, those barriers might not hinder him.

But it was more than just that. He didn't want anyone to realize that he had returned. Most of them deserved the peace that came from believing that he was done with Yoran. These were his friends, and he had been gone for only a few months.

"You hesitate," Rayena said.

The dragon reached the ground before Gavin had an opportunity to answer. He pushed a hint of his core reserves into the paper creature and triggered the enchantment to shrink and fold in on itself once again.

Gavin looked over to Rayena, nodding. "I don't want to bring any more trouble to them. And unfortunately, with this," he said, patting the pouch with the obsidian figurine, "I fear it will only serve to endanger the city again. People I want to protect. People I care for."

He motioned for them to follow, and they headed toward the darkness of the city.

Given how late it was, he knew that entering Yoran at

this time of night would draw little attention, unless somebody was out there focusing on the use of magic and somehow able to pick up on his crossing the barricade. He wasn't exactly sure what it would feel like when he passed through the protections placed by the constables and the enchanters, but a strange energy washed over him. He felt a wave of relief knowing that the barrier was intact, and he surprised himself by worrying about the safety of the city, even in his absence.

They moved forward into the familiarity of Yoran. Gavin had spent much more time in this city over the last few years than he had in many other places. Not only that, but he had established relationships and connected to this place in ways he had never intended. There were the ever-familiar bells trees, many of which crowded buildings and forced everything around to make space for them. He recognized a series of shops that he used to pass frequently—a general store, a butcher, a baker, and many more he'd visited during his time here. A hint of music drifted toward him, likely coming from a tavern. Somewhere in the distance, a person shouted. All of it was as it should be.

The air smelled like he remembered too. The slightly pungent aroma of the bells tree flowers mixed with the stink of the city. Yoran was not nearly as detestable as so many places he had visited, and in some ways, it was almost pleasant. If nothing else, the city was familiar to him.

Gavin reached into his pocket, pulled out the communication enchantment Anna had made for him, and situated it into his ear. After he had left Yoran, he'd tried to reach Wrenlow and Gaspar a few times, but they'd failed to connect through the enchantment. Eventually, he had stopped trying, and he didn't know if Wrenlow would still have his on him.

The enchantment connected his ear to a metallic piece that allowed him to control the volume, and Gavin tapped on that to activate the device. "Wrenlow?"

There was no answer.

As they moved farther into the city, many of the store-fronts they passed were made of old stone, probably from when the El'aras still occupied the city. A strange under-current of energy had always filled this space, and knowing what he did of the El'aras and where they had lived before they'd been forced out by the sorcerers, Gavin questioned what it might've been like when they were here.

They neared an intersection. In the distance, Gavin could see the outline of a market, which was empty and quiet at this time of night. He could practically imagine the vibrancy and life that was there in the daytime as people moved through the square. He had shopped there many times, and he had also chased dangers through the market.

"Where did you stay when you were here?" Brandon asked.

"Several places," Gavin said. "The El'aras tunnels underground were what I used most recently."

"I heard there was a hall."

Gavin nodded. "There was an El'aras hall with the

prophecy, and I hope that you were told that the prophecy was a sham."

Brandon watched him with darkness in his eyes. "The stories of the Risen Shard and the Champion have long been a part of our people."

"Again, it was a story made up by a sorcerer."

"But there are other stories." Brandon looked over to Rayena. "You must've heard them. My homeland can't be so far away from the rest of the people that I hear stories others don't."

She stayed silent.

"What stories?" Gavin asked.

"About a way the Champion can defend the people."

"I'm not defending the people from the Risen Shard."

Brandon shook his head. "No, no, no. That never made much sense to me. The Risen Shard was meant to unite people, and the Champion was meant to defend the people, so it never really made sense that they would fight each other. They're *meant* to work together."

"That wasn't what I was taught," Rayena said softly.

"What were you taught?" Brandon asked her.

"That the Risen Shard would bring great stability. And there would come a time when the Champion would end that stability."

"Well, even that isn't the two battling each other. See?" Brandon said, then looked over to Gavin. "You were worried about what you'd have to do with Anna, and even the older prophecies don't speak of the two of you fighting."

"I don't know," Gavin said. "If she is to bring stability

and I am to destroy it, it does sort of sound like we are working against each other."

"It sounds like it, but it's not. Stability can mean many things. It doesn't have to mean the families coming together. It could be stability from violence. Or maybe you really are supposed to lead us back to our old homes."

Gavin grunted. "I'm no leader."

"And you don't really have to be one," Brandon said. When Rayena shot him a look, he shrugged. "What? He doesn't. He doesn't have to be the one to lead, but he may have to be the one to fight. That's a consistent message with the prophecy."

Gavin glanced over to him. They were getting closer to the Dragon, and he had to get his thoughts in order, especially if he was about to visit with his old friends. "The prophecy was made up by one of the Sul'toral, who used it to try to drive a wedge between the role of the Risen Shard and that of the Champion. We know that much, and we know that they would use that to their advantage. They want to drive even more division between us."

"But there are older elements to the prophecy," Brandon said, ignoring the way Gavin had challenged him. "I'm no elder, and certainly no scholar of these prophecies, but I have learned a few things in my years. So many people get caught up in the prophecies and don't pay attention to the truth behind them."

"And what is the truth of the prophecy?"

"Why, it's obvious, isn't it?" Brandon glanced from Gavin to Rayena. "Prophecies are full of shit."

Gavin stared at him for a moment. He'd expected something more profound, but that was all he had?

Rayena barked out a laugh. "He's not wrong," she muttered.

"I suppose he's not," Gavin said. It was the same way that he felt about prophecies, or *had*, until he'd ended up dealing with all of this.

The emptiness in the street reminded him of how late at night it was. They had not spent that much time in Hester, and maybe they should have stayed there instead of traveling to Yoran at such a late hour. Maybe no one was awake.

He tapped on the enchantment again and whispered, "Wrenlow."

The likelihood of Wrenlow answering at this point was low. It was probably too late for him to be up and paying attention to the enchantment.

The headset crackled, and Gavin halted in his tracks.

"Gavin?" The surprise in Wrenlow's voice was obvious. "It's me."

"Is everything... Wait. You have to be close enough for me to hear you. Are you back in Yoran?"

Gavin chuckled. "I'm here. I have something I need your help with."

"Gods, Gavin. Do you know what time it is?"

"Not really, but I've had a long day and have dealt with some pretty nasty people. I was hoping for a little safety and maybe a mug of ale, if the Dragon is still open."

"I don't know. Jessica might be disappointed to see you."

Gavin slowed as they approached the Dragon. He hadn't even thought about the idea that Jessica might not be willing to welcome him back. But he should have. He hadn't been around her in quite some time, and she had been angry with him when he'd left.

"I'm kidding, you know," Wrenlow said.

Gavin let out a relieved laugh. "Well, I actually didn't know."

"Who are you talking to?" Brandon asked, leaning his face close to him. "Oh. You have an enchantment. I hadn't even realized you put that in. I thought you were just talking to yourself. You know, prophecies speak of people who are a little bit off, if you know what I mean. But then, I'm sure you do know what I mean. You are the Champion, after all."

"I'm speaking to a friend of mine through this," Gavin said, pushing him away. "Anyway, Wrenlow, can we meet you at the Dragon?"

"We?"

"Anna's not with me, if that's what you're concerned about."

"Well, I wasn't the one concerned about it so much as being worried about Jessica's reaction. I will send word."

"And Gaspar?"

"I haven't seen him in—"

The enchantment crackled again, and then it went quiet.

Gavin tried listening and waited for a minute, but there was no further response. He knew that the enchantment's effectiveness would be limited, especially given the protections around the city that prevented magic from being used, but he'd thought that he might have a bit more time to speak to Wrenlow. At least Wrenlow knew he was here now.

And perhaps Gaspar would as well, but that was assuming that he had kept the enchantment on. Gaspar had rarely done so when Gavin had been in the city, so with Gavin being out of Yoran for as long as he had, Gaspar likely wouldn't have been willing to keep it on him.

"It's not much farther," he said to the others.

"Are you sure you can trust your people with whatever is in that book?" Brandon asked.

Gavin smiled to himself. He could trust Wrenlow far more than he could trust these two. "I have somebody who might be able to interpret this."

"And if they can't?"

"If he can't, we may have to keep digging."

"We could always go back," Rayena said.

Gavin nodded. Anna might have information about the writing, so it might come down to asking for her help to understand the book. But Gavin didn't want to bring that danger back to Anna or her people if he could avoid it.

He didn't really want it in Yoran either, but there were protections here that might limit what the attackers could do. Not only did the protections limit sorcery, but he hoped they would limit other kinds of magic, like whatever had been used to attack him and the others.

"Right," he said. "We could always go back. I might need to anyway, but I'm trying to avoid it."

He glanced around and didn't see any signs of constables patrolling the streets, which surprised him. Maybe they had fortified the protections around the city so much that they were unconcerned, or perhaps they had taken other steps to keep the city safe.

Gavin motioned for them to follow, and they reached the Roasted Dragon, a simple building in a row of others like it. He had always appreciated its unique door, which was made of stout oak, with a shape of a dragon worked into the wood. He traced his hand over it, right as the door jerked open.

Jessica stood with her hair pulled back and her eyes tight, but she smiled at him, and everything seemed all right. "Gavin Lorren. Showing up at my door in the middle of the night just like the first time I met you."

"It wasn't quite this late then," he said.

She chuckled. "I suppose it wasn't. What are you doing?"

"I assume Wrenlow sent word?"

She nodded carefully. "He did. I wasn't sure whether or not to believe him."

"I wasn't sure if you would welcome me."

For a moment, her eyes flickered, but then that faded. "Never banished you from my tavern, and I never would. You have always been welcome here, Gavin."

He had, and for that he was thankful. Even when things had become awkward between them, it was more because of his discomfort, not Jessica's.

Gavin glanced to the others with him. "This is Brandon and Rayena."

"Nice to meet you. Looks like Gavin has himself a new crew, doesn't he?"

"We're just along for the ride," Brandon said. "I hear you have ale?"

Jessica arched a brow and laughed. "He's not like the others, is he? You might as well come in."

She stepped aside, revealing a hearth that was already lit, and several lanterns glowed with a comfortable light. The inside of the Dragon looked mostly as Gavin remembered. Tables were situated neatly throughout the tavern, though there was no one else here. A stack of neatly folded napkins rested on a center table. A row of booths lined one wall, and the portraits that hung above the booths were new. Gavin wondered who those represented. Maybe Jessica's family? She had acquired the tavern from her aunt, though that had been long ago.

But the feel of the Dragon was the same. As strange as it was, it was comforting in a way that so few places in his life had ever been. It was almost like home. Well, it had been his home for quite some time—long enough that he had made a place for himself in the city.

"Have a seat," Jessica said. "You can even take your usual spot."

Gavin glanced over to Brandon than Rayena before shaking his head. "That doesn't feel quite right." Instead, he walked to a table in the center of the room, pulled a chair back, and sat down. This felt unfamiliar in a familiar place. He didn't care for it, but he wasn't intending for this to be a long stay.

Jessica drifted off to the kitchen, disappearing behind the door and leaving Gavin with the others.

"You seem uneasy," Rayena said.

"It looks like you didn't want to upset the proprietor." Brandon winked at him.

Gavin shook his head. "Don't."

Brandon opened his mouth as if to say something, then clamped it shut when the door to the tavern swung open.

Wrenlow strode in, his hair messier and his appearance more disheveled than last time Gavin had seen him. His build was surprisingly more muscular. Gavin frowned at the possibility that Wrenlow had been practicing without him. He figured Wrenlow would've stopped after Gavin had left, though there had always been a part of Wrenlow that wanted to learn how to defend himself.

"Gavin," he said, throwing himself down into a chair. He glanced up and seemed to just realize that Rayena and Brandon were there. "And two El'aras. Of course. I'm Wrenlow."

Brandon nodded at him. "Nice to meet you. The Champion speaks highly of your mind."

"Nice," Gavin muttered. He looked over to Wrenlow. "Though I did."

"That's why you're here?"

"I have a puzzle for you."

Wrenlow frowned at him. "Just a puzzle?"

Gavin wanted to tell his friend that he had missed him,

but for whatever reason, he stayed focused on his task. "I probably shouldn't have come back, but I need help from somebody who can decipher this."

"Well?" Wrenlow asked, leaning forward. He shifted his cloak and nodded to Jessica, who had emerged from the kitchen. "I tried to send word to Gaspar, but he's not available."

Jessica set several mugs of ale down in front of them, and Gavin took his, staring down at it for a moment. It felt so normal.

He shook his head, pulled the book out of his satchel, and slid it across the table to Wrenlow. "Tell me if you can figure anything out about this."

Wrenlow took the book, tracing his fingers along the leather surface. He murmured something under his breath, and Gavin couldn't tell what it was, only that Wrenlow seemed to be speaking to himself while lost in thought.

"It's old," Wrenlow said, "though I suspect you knew that. The binding is made from a strange leather, thicker than usual. I don't recognize the symbols on the cover." He didn't look up as he ran his fingers along the surface of the book, and he began to slowly turn the pages, mouth wrinkling slightly. "Made of a type of parchment, but pretty heavy stuff. That's part of the reason I think it's old, though the fact that you brought it to me tells me that's probably the case. Is it El'aras-made?" He glanced up, then immediately turned his attention back to the book. "No. If it was, the language would be different. I've learned to read the El'aras language fairly well. The hall was helpful."

"I'm sure it was," Gavin said.

"And the more I studied it, the more I came to recognize that there are specific patterns to the El'aras language. I think I can go back even further—I just need to have access to records." He looked up again, settling his hands on the table. "Say, I don't suppose you brought anything else for me."

"Only the book," Gavin said.

"Right." Wrenlow began to flip through the pages again. "I tried reaching out to you a few times. I didn't know if you would be irritated or not, or if you would even hear me."

"No, I didn't hear you," Gavin said. He had wanted to speak to his friend too. He was happy that Wrenlow had stayed behind to find happiness in Yoran, but Gavin still regretted that he had to leave.

"When you didn't answer, I figured that the protection around the city made it difficult. Maybe that was all it was."

"I don't know if it was or not."

"I did try going out to the forest too," Wrenlow went on. He paused on a page, and Gavin leaned forward to examine one of the drawings there. "But Gaspar told me that the range might not be enough. I tried to counter by saying that since the enchantment was El'aras that it wouldn't matter, but you know how Gaspar can be. He gets pretty stubborn, especially when he gets an idea in his head that he thinks is right. He always thinks he's right."

"He usually is," a voice said from behind.

Gavin turned and came face-to-face with his friend.

Gaspar was probably only a few years older than him, but he looked older. Either that, or he acted older. Sometimes with Gaspar, it was difficult to know the difference. Regardless, he had an aura of age about him. He was dressed in a gray cloak, and his hand rested underneath it.

"You got word that I was here," Gavin said.

"It's somewhat hard to sleep when you start chattering in my ear in the middle of the night." Gaspar tapped on his enchantment.

Gavin frowned. "Why do you have that in?"

"Told you that I'd be there if you needed me."

"I..."

"Now, don't get all sappy on me, boy."

Gaspar grabbed a chair and pulled it over to the table, nodding to the two El'aras. "It's been strange around here. Quiet."

"Have you heard anything from Imogen?" Gavin asked.

"Not a word. Rumors out of the east of someone who fits her description, but..." His brow furrowed again, and he frowned even more deeply. "Can't say that I know whether or not those are even true stories. The kinds of things I've been hearing are impossible to believe."

"What kinds of things are those?" Gavin asked.

Gaspar shook his head. "That's not why you're here."

"No. I brought something for Wrenlow. A puzzle for him."

"A dangerous type of puzzle?"

"The type of danger that can suppress El'aras magic," Gavin said.

"That could be dangerous," Gaspar agreed. "Which means it can suppress yours."

"It can, but seeing as how I don't just need magic to fight, I am—"

"You think that your mentor trained you for something like that."

It didn't surprise Gavin that Gaspar would jump to that conclusion so quickly. "I'm not exactly sure if that's the case or not. Tristan wasn't exactly a forthcoming person."

"Not by a long stretch," Gaspar said. "So, what do we have going on here?"

"Just a book. A dangerous man who has my fighting skill, the ability to suppress El'aras magic, and what seems to be a significant quantity of enchantments seems to be after this book—along with some other items, perhaps."

"Why?"

"That's just it," Gavin said. "I'm not exactly sure why."

"Which means you're going after your mentor."

"I am."

"Good."

"Good?" Gavin said, brow arched.

Gaspar nodded. "When was the last time you saw him?"

"Right before I left Yoran."

"And what happened then?"

"He disappeared," Gavin said. "He knew what had happened, and he claimed that whatever prophecy I'd heard was not the prophecy he was concerned about."

"And you believe it?"

"Again, I'm not exactly sure what to believe."

"I see. Well, I was supposed to give you this." Gaspar reached under his cloak and pulled out a small enchantment shaped like a small flat circle with markings along the surface of it. He set it on the table in front of Gavin, then looked up at him and met his eyes. "You have any idea what this is about? After you disappeared, this showed up in my room one day, with a letter attached that had your name on it. Figured you would eventually come back for it. I didn't know it would be quite so soon, but I assumed this enchantment was somehow important. Zella wasn't able to come up with any information about it, which, as you know, is a bit strange for her."

Gavin grabbed the enchantment and held it in his hand. This had to be from Tristan. But why? He turned it over and examined it, and he saw Tristan's mark, confirming his suspicions.

"Zella looked at this?" he asked.

"Looked at it, didn't know anything, but said it's enchanted. Thought that maybe it was sorcery, as her abilities don't always extend to sorcery-made enchantments." Gaspar leaned forward, resting his arms on the table. "Your mentor left it for you, I'm guessing."

Gavin nodded, tapping the symbol on the side. "This is his mark."

"Seems he's planning something else for you."

"Seems he is."

Gavin leaned back and continued looking at the enchantment. He was tempted to activate it, but given that he had no idea what would happen if he did or what kind of power was within it, he didn't want to do so until he had some semblance of an idea.

"Can I see the letter?" he asked.

Gaspar shrugged. He pulled a slip of paper out of his pocket and slid it across the table.

On it were two words: *For Gavin.*

"Like I said, not much else to it," Gaspar explained. "Can't really say what it is or what it is going to do, but I understood that it was supposed to go to you. And so here you are."

Gavin got to his feet.

"Where do you think you're going?" Wrenlow asked, but he didn't look up from the book.

"I need to test this enchantment."

"Well, you can't do that in the city."

"Most people can't. I can."

He started toward the door, and Brandon got to his feet. Gavin shook his head. "Stay here. Enjoy your ale. You as well, Rayena. Why don't you both keep Wrenlow company?"

Wrenlow looked up, holding Gavin's gaze for a moment before nodding. He appreciated that his friend still knew what he wanted. Gavin stepped out into the darkness of night, prepared to activate Tristan's enchantment. What would happen when he did?

CHAPTER THIRTEEN

Darkness seemed to fold and fill the space around Gavin, leaving him surprisingly comforted in it. There was a time when he'd hated the darkness, when he had wanted anything else than to be in it, but now he felt as if the darkness was a place where he could operate easily and openly. He squeezed the enchantment in his hand and focused on his core reserves, but he knew that it was going to take more than that to activate the enchantment. He would have to tap into something greater—he'd have to borrow from the power of the ring.

As expected, Gaspar followed him outside and joined him in the street. "You keeping something from them?"

"Just being cautious."

"The other El'aras have you jumpy?"

"It's not so much the other El'aras individually as it is my experience with them as a people."

Gaspar grunted, shaking his head. "You need to learn to trust, boy. Do you think all of them are like Theren?"

Gavin glanced over, reminded of the conversation he had with Rayena. "It's not all of them, it's just knowing that I have been betrayed before."

"You ever have a lover?"

Gavin laughed slightly. "What kind of question is that?"

"Well, have you?"

"I may have had one or two. Why?"

"You ever been cheated on?"

Gavin frowned. "I don't know. To be honest, I don't usually spend too much time in one place before moving on. Or... I hadn't," he said, peering back to the door.

Gaspar followed the direction of his gaze, then nodded knowingly. "Right. Don't stay in one place too long, don't get attached, don't get hurt. A lot of young men think like that."

"I seem to recall you thinking like that," Gavin said.

"Well, I was a young man once."

"And how long ago was that?" he asked, smiling.

"Careful, boy."

Gavin grinned even bigger. He had been away from his friend for too long, and it *was* good to be back with Gaspar. "Can you get on with what point you were trying to make? I'm assuming you *do* have a point."

"You're damn right I have a point. All I'm saying is that if you've ever been cheated on"—he arched a brow, as if assuming that this had happened to Gavin at some point in his life—"I would bet ten pennies you didn't let that one experience ruin your chance at chasing after another lovely young thing."

"Just ten pennies?"

"That's all I have on me," Gaspar groused.

"I see what you're trying to say."

"I doubt it. You're too stubborn to listen to anything that makes sense. But maybe it don't matter. All I'm trying to say is that you've got figure out who you can work with, who you can trust, and sometimes you just have to make that jump."

"I wouldn't have expected you to be trying to support the El'aras."

"I'm trying to keep you out of trouble, boy."

"Again, something else I wouldn't have expected you to do."

"You really think I want something to happen to you? Gods, I spent all that time trying to keep you safe, keep you alive, and this is what you think of me?"

Gavin chuckled. "Well, you weren't always trying to keep me safe."

"No, you're right. Sometimes you got on my nerves, and I would've been just as happy for the constables to have taken you in, but then you went and made the mistake of working with them."

"I thought it was easier for us to do that."

"Easier for you. Since you've been gone, Chan has been a right pain in my ass."

"Why?"

"Because he thinks that you and I have been in communication."

Gavin's eyes widened, and he started laughing.

Gaspar shot him a glare. "What's so funny about that?"

"Because I suspect you gave him that impression."

"Might be that it was useful to do so," Gaspar said, shrugging. "If he thinks you're coming back at some point, then he's less likely to go chasing after people I want to protect."

"And it probably didn't hurt that I told him that the two of us were going to be in contact while I was gone."

It was Gaspar's turn to frown. "You did?"

Gavin nodded. "I did. I figured that it would be better for you if you didn't have to worry about the constables chasing you down, and better for the enchanters if they felt protected."

"Damn, boy. Never expected you to care so much."

"Yes, you did."

Gaspar nodded. "Yes, I did." He motioned to the enchantment in Gavin's hand. "You going to test that or not?"

"I'm not exactly sure what Tristan left me. It could be dangerous."

"Has he left you anything else that's dangerous?"

"Countless times."

"And this?"

"I don't know. If he left it with you around the same time as he left the other things I've found, then it's entirely possible that he's been trying to coordinate it so that I'll take another job for him."

"I'm starting to think you never stopped working for him."

"I started thinking that a while ago."

Gavin gripped the enchantment, and before dwelling on it too much more, he focused on his core reserves. He pushed power through himself and through the ring, into the enchantment. It reacted slowly, but power began to build, bubbling up through the enchantment and then out.

A strange green-blue ball of energy started to take shape, and it gradually transformed into what looked like a building.

Gavin snorted and shook his head.

"Is that…"

"The Captain's fortress," Gavin finished. He looked over to Gaspar. "Zella didn't know what this did?"

"She couldn't figure it out. None of us wanted to activate it until you came back, especially because we didn't know if doing so would preclude you from using it however he intended you to. And honestly, that just wasn't the time to do it."

Gavin turned to the west, toward the Captain's fortress, where the enchanters were now headquartered. Though he couldn't see it in the darkness, he knew the building was massive and loomed over the western edge of the city.

"Why would he have left you an image like that?"

"Because it's part of a trail that leads back to him," Gavin said.

"How?"

"I don't know. He might have known the book would've been too complicated for me to work through, and he may have anticipated that I would return to Yoran to have Wrenlow help me with it. Or maybe he just thought the two of us had been in contact, and he wanted to send word to me." Gavin shook his head. "I simply have no idea."

"And you think he's there?"

"I think he wants me to go there."

"Well?" Gaspar made a motion along the street.

"Now?"

"You came to the city for answers. You might as well go get them."

Gavin regarded Gaspar for a long moment. "Is that your way of trying to send me away from the city more quickly?"

"You know I have no quarrel with you returning here."

"Just the El'aras."

"All I know is that the last time they were here, the constables got a little wary. We've found a measure of comfort, such as it is. Maybe not easy, but some comfort nonetheless."

"I understand. I'm welcome, but the El'aras aren't?"

"It's not even that," Gaspar said.

Gavin didn't dig any more than that. He didn't want to test Gaspar, and he certainly didn't want to push his friend into giving an answer that he wasn't even sure he wanted to hear.

"Then let's get going." Gavin glanced back to the Dragon and tapped on his enchantment. "Wrenlow?"

"I'm here."

"Gaspar and I are going to run a little errand. I want you to keep those El'aras entertained."

"You don't have to worry about that. They are both happy drinking ale, talking to Jessica, and relaxing. And I think they *both* want to study the book, though they're not saying it."

That wouldn't surprise Gavin, especially with Rayena. She wanted to understand Tristan better. Brandon might have his own reasons, though he'd kept them from Gavin.

"If you see or hear or feel anything that's unusual, send word to me immediately."

There was a pause before Wrenlow spoke again. "You really think that's likely?"

"I don't know what is or isn't likely anymore. I hope it doesn't happen, but I want you to be ready for the possibility."

Gavin could almost see Wrenlow nodding on the other side of the enchantment. "I will."

He motioned for Gaspar to follow him. They hurried through the city, the darkness obscuring the buildings, and they sped along a narrow section of street. In the daytime, there would be quite a bit of foot traffic, with merchants moving through, crowds of locals milling about, and food carts situated all along this area filling the air with mouthwatering aromas. He breathed in, missing much of this. In the distance, a bell sounded.

"I was of two minds about you," Gaspar admitted as they jogged through the streets.

Gavin glanced over to him. "Is that right?"

"I thought that either you would return right away— something that seemed likely, as you'd tried to leave us several times but kept getting pulled back—or you just wouldn't ever return."

"I think that if it were up to Anna, I would not have returned."

"Right. And had you simply disappeared, how would they have reacted?"

"To be honest, I don't know."

"Again, I'm surprised that you came back as quickly as you did. Not disappointed, though."

Gavin glanced over. Gaspar seemed to be moving slower than he had the last time they had been around each other. Maybe it was all the time Gavin had been spending around the El'aras, or perhaps it was that Gaspar had been tied up in the kind of work Gavin had been doing—the kind of work that kept Gaspar on edge.

That edge was gone now. Gavin could see it in his eyes, and he could tell that Gaspar knew it.

"How has it been in the city?" Gavin asked.

"I'm not going to lie to you. It's been quiet. Sometimes quiet is good, and sometimes it can just be... too much. Since Imogen is gone, it has been a bit of the too-quiet kind."

"And you and Desarra?"

Gaspar hesitated for a moment before smiling, which appeared forced. Gavin had been around him long enough to recognize that smile—and the hint of tension behind it.

"Is everything well between the two of you?"

"I don't need to tell you about my love life," Gaspar grumbled.

"I still haven't figured out how to make enchantments, and I'm not sure that I will ever be able to."

"I'm sure we could help you learn, if you really are interested."

There was a time when he would've thought that idea was ridiculous, but now that Gavin had learned about his true connection to power and knew that he was at least partially El'aras, it wasn't nearly as far-fetched as it once would've been.

Gavin shook his head. "My control isn't that good."

"Your strength is, though," Mekel said. "I think you can learn. All of us can. Zella has been making sure that we all have an opportunity to keep mastering these enchantments."

"So, you knew when I returned?"

"I could feel it, but I wasn't the first one who knew."

Gavin reached into his pocket, touching the paper dragon. "Alana."

"Right. She's something else. She has a very different kind of connection to her enchantments than the rest of us, and she knew exactly when you came to the city. I think she could feel the direction you were coming from, even."

Comments like that left Gavin feeling a mixture of guilt and concern about using enchantments made by others, at least when it came to the stone creatures Mekel made or the paper dragons Alana created. If they were still bonded to their crafters in some way, it explained how the enchanters felt it when they were destroyed.

"Did you know that I would come back here?" he asked Mekel.

"I didn't. Zella suspected."

"Is she awake?"

"She is now." He waved Gavin past. "Go on. I think you still know the way."

Gavin nodded, and he headed through the gate. The stone golem followed Mekel as he sealed the gate closed behind him.

"I still remember riding that damn thing away from the city," Gaspar muttered.

"I've ridden one recently."

"You prefer that over the paper dragon?"

"I try to protect the dragon," Gavin said. "Or I did before. Now…"

"You don't think it's safe to use them?"

"I don't know. I don't want to harm their creators if I'm using some part that they put into the enchantments."

"To hear the other enchanters talk of it, it's not so much a matter of leaving a piece of themselves in it as it is connecting to the enchantments. You don't hesitate to use speed or strength or any of the other enchantments you've used before."

"No," Gavin agreed.

"Then don't hesitate to use these more powerful ones. Because they're stronger, it probably means that they have a greater connection to the person who placed the enchantment. That's the reason they can feel what you're doing." Gaspar's logic made sense, but Gavin didn't feel all that much better about it.

"You don't have to come with me."

"Ah, I wasn't going to leave you to do this on your own. And like I said, it has been too quiet ever since you left."

Gavin paused at the front door, turning to him. He could see a slight emptiness in Gaspar's eyes, which suggested that Gaspar had missed the game. Would that be how Gavin felt if he had stayed in Yoran? His whole life had been about testing himself, pushing and trying to learn where he fit, figuring out what he needed to do. If he were to let himself fade...

He wouldn't.

And he didn't know that he could let Gaspar do that either.

"You can come with me," Gavin said. "I could use someone I trust."

"You just have to find others you can trust too."

"You don't want to come with me?"

"I do," Gaspar said, shrugging. "But as you keep reminding me, or at least you did before you left, I don't have your abilities. And seeing as how I'm nothing more than a man who knows how to use enchantments, there isn't much that I'll be able to do."

"Well, you can do more than you let on, but there's still the problem of you being an old man," Gavin said.

"Not so old that I can't—" Gaspar turned, and he bowed slightly. "Zella. It is quite lovely to see you this evening."

The door had opened, and a woman watched them, her dark hair hanging loose to her shoulders. Her sharp jaw was tilted in a tight frown, and her eyes were clear, with a hint of irritation in them. She looked young, but like most enchanters in Yoran, she was older than she appeared.

"Hello, Gaspar," she said. "Gavin, you might as well come in. Either that, or you'll just force your way inside."

"I have no intention of forcing my way in."

"You might not, but we both know that when it comes down to it, your intention is often incompatible with what you end up doing." She stepped aside, and Gavin glanced to Gaspar for a moment before following her inside. Was Zella angry with him for coming?

The enchantment had guided him to the fortress, suggesting that either Tristan was here, or something he wanted Gavin to find was here. Regardless of which one it was, this was the right place to be.

"What is this about?" Zella asked.

She closed the door behind them, and Gavin could practically feel the energy of it sealing them in. There might be an enchantment in it, though it was one he wasn't familiar with. Then again, as the leader of the enchanters in Yoran, Zella would have access to different enchantments than he would.

"It's about this, which Tristan left for me," Gavin said, holding out the enchantment Gaspar had been given. He activated it again, but he found it more difficult to do this time.

"That is what it does?" She frowned, making a small circuit around the enchantment, which depicted the fortress. "It was a message?"

"One of several that were left for me recently," Gavin said. "And I suspect he left something here as well."

"Does the message tell you where?"

Gavin tried to push more power into the enchantment, and the image of the fortress remained, but nothing else happened. He shook his head. "It shows this building and nothing more than that."

"Then how do you intend to find him, or what he left here?" She glanced from him to Gaspar. "That is what you intend, is it not?"

"I suspect so," Gavin said. "Then again, I'm not entirely sure."

Zella motioned for them to follow, and they crossed the entry hall into another space. The room was elegantly appointed, and far more comfortable than it had been when the Captain had occupied the building. A large plush sofa rested in front of a crackling fire. Gavin suspected that Zella had used an enchantment to get the hearth glowing with warmth. Not only had she heated it quickly prior to their arrival, but the fire itself was smokeless and likely enchanted as well.

"Take a seat," she said.

Gavin made his way around to sit on the sofa, and Gaspar stood near the hearth, hands clasped behind his back.

Zella grabbed a chair and took a seat near them. "What do you expect to find?"

"I don't really know," Gavin said. "The enchantment only guided me here. I have a hard time thinking Tristan himself will be here, though." He'd be shocked if Tristan was actually in Yoran. "I suspect he left some way for me to find him."

"And what way do you think that would be?"

Gavin stared at the enchantment that had been left for Gaspar. There weren't answers within it—at least, not easily identifiable answers. He would have to try to work through whatever intention Tristan had in leaving it for him.

"This is Tristan's mark," he said, tapping on the symbol. "Whatever he has hidden here will be marked that way too, so if there's something here in the fortress you've found with that on it, then—"

"This is his mark?" Zella said, brow furrowed. "It's a common enough symbol, at least, without the extra triangle situated atop it. That complicates it and makes it more difficult to activate than enchantments. And less useful, most of the time."

Gavin leaned forward. "You've seen it."

"Of course I have."

"Recently?"

She breathed out, shaking her head. "Why is it that everything is so complicated when it comes to you, Gavin Lorren?" She got to her feet and waved for them to follow.

Zella made her way over to the hearth and pressed something on the stone. The hearth went quiet, the flames extinguished in little more than a heartbeat.

"Follow me," she whispered.

Gavin glanced over to Gaspar, who simply stared where the fire had just been.

"Did you know that was enchanted?" Gaspar asked him.

"I suspected that it was," Gavin said.

What he hadn't expected was what Zella did next.

She tapped on the hearth, though not any part he could see. The floor suddenly lowered, reminding him of what he had seen in the temple, the way the figurine had caused the floor to sink and open the chamber where they had found the second statue. This was similar, only on a much larger scale.

A staircase led down.

"I don't remember this from last time I was here," Gavin said.

"Because it took us quite some time to find it." Zella walked into the hearth and started down the stairs.

Gavin hesitated, but as he moved forward, he didn't feel any heat. Not like he expected. Extinguishing the flames seemed to have immediately put out the heat. That was far more impressive.

He looked behind him to Gaspar. "Well?"

"If you're asking whether I'm going to follow you down there, I don't know if I have much choice."

Gavin descended the stairs into the darkness, toward where he suspected he would find another clue about how to locate Tristan.

A door at the bottom of the steps had a mark on it.

Zella motioned to the symbol. "It's just this."

"What do you mean?"

She shrugged. "There is this door and nothing else.

We've tried to understand what it is and what's behind it, but there has been no way for us to open it."

Gavin was not surprised to see that the symbol on the door was Tristan's mark.

The challenge was going to be finding a way to open it.

CHAPTER FOURTEEN

"You look like you are trying to work through some sort of puzzle," Gaspar said, leaning close to the door and looking over Gavin's shoulder.

"Because I am."

Gavin stared at the symbol etched into the door. It looked larger than the others he'd come across, but there was no doubt in his mind that this was Tristan's. The distinct mark had been carved into the wood, practically branding the door. From where Gavin stood, he could feel power emanating from that symbol, as if Tristan wanted to ensure that anyone who might pass through this place would know that he had placed that mark upon the door.

Gavin handed the enchantment Tristan had left for him to Gaspar, who turned it over in his hand, frowning as he did.

"It's the same symbol," Gaspar said.

"He's left his mark for me to find a few times lately."

"Has he ever done it before?"

"Only one other time," Gavin said. "The same mark is on my foot."

"Really?" Gaspar asked, handing the enchantment back.

Gavin shrugged and took it. "It was an accident that happened when I was younger, while I was training with him. I snuck into his private office and came across something resting on his desk. It was not for me to evaluate, but I tested it anyway."

"And it was hot enough to mark you?"

"I think I activated it," Gavin said, without taking his gaze off the door. "At the time, I didn't know what I was doing. I still don't really understand what happened. Only that I knocked whatever it was off the desk, stepped on it, and—"

Gaspar started laughing. "You stepped on some enchantment that burned you?"

Gavin looked over and glared at his friend. "I didn't think it was that funny."

"Maybe it isn't, but it is to me."

Gavin shook his head. "I need to figure this out. Whatever Tristan left for me is on the other side of this door."

"And what if he didn't leave anything?"

Gavin glanced over to Zella, who stood at the bottom of the stairs, hands clasped in front of her and her face pinched in a tight frown. "You haven't been able to open this?"

"Many have tried," she said. "We have attempted to break through the enchantment, but though we know it's there and that something is behind the door, we haven't been able to succeed. We thought it was something the Captain had been hiding. Many things like that have been left behind from his time here."

Gavin knew that well enough. The Captain had occupied this space as a fortress, keeping enchantments locked away, as well as prisoners. There might be other hidden sections of the building that he had taken for himself.

"Maybe it isn't about Tristan," Gaspar suggested.

"No. It is," Gavin said. "He was here before."

"And he decided to add a special hidden chamber that he might just one day need to use?"

"I'm not saying that. I'm just saying that maybe he realized there was this section here, and he sealed it off thinking he might need to come back. Or perhaps he hid something within it."

Gavin shook his head, still with no more ideas about what Tristan might have done. He started tracing his hands across the door, feeling for the pattern. Its surface was smooth, despite how it appeared. Though it looked as if the symbol had been burned into the wood, it didn't feel like it. He probed with just a hint of his core reserves, pouring energy out of his ring and into the door, but he didn't feel anything from it. Not an enchantment—or at least not one that he could activate.

There had to be some secret here, but what was it? What answer did Tristan want him to find?

Gavin continued to stare at the door, trying unsuccessfully to come up with those answers.

"Maybe it's not for you to open," Gaspar suggested.

"Maybe it isn't," Gavin agreed, "but I can't shake the feeling that he wanted me to find it." He looked over to Gaspar. "Everything else was about me finding it. The temple in Hester. A stone pillar outside Arashil. The book with the sculpture inside."

"There was a book?" Zella asked.

Gavin waved a hand. "You can visit with Wrenlow if you're curious."

"If this man left some archive—"

"I'm not sure how useful it's going to be to the enchanters. To be honest, I'm not sure how useful it's going to be to anyone. It might not be helpful for any of us."

"But it might," Zella said.

Gavin shrugged. With Tristan, it was difficult to know.

He took a deep breath, inhaling the strange smell of the air. Other parts of the fortress were musty, at least on the lower levels where the enchantments had been hidden. The main parts of the fortress were clean, especially where the enchanters had taken hold and exerted their influence. Down here, it wasn't so much musty, damp, or anything that he would've expected in a stone chamber like this. Instead, there was an odd, almost pungent odor to the air, something distinctly familiar.

He shook his head to clear it, then placed both hands to the symbol on the door. He muttered under his breath, trying to think about what Tristan might have done here, and how he would've placed power into the door. There had to be something here that Gavin could uncover that would help him find the key to opening it.

"It's not the ring. It's not me," Gavin said to himself. "And..."

He reached into his pocket, pulled out the small sculpture, and brought it up to the door. Nothing happened. He tried the enchantment that Gaspar had been given, not really expecting much. As he held it up, nothing changed.

He sighed. "That would've been too simple."

"You said you tried your own power through the enchantment he left?" Zella asked.

Gavin nodded. "I can trigger it, but it just shows a map of the building itself."

She moved close, with familiarity born from the times they had worked together over the last year or so. "Not many people can activate enchantments within the city," she said. "And the one that was left with Gaspar was a particularly difficult enchantment. Even for us. I didn't think that there was anything to it."

"Which is why you thought it was made from sorcery."

"Yes, or perhaps another source."

"Another source?" Gaspar asked.

Zella nodded and looked at Gavin, holding her gaze on him.

"El'aras," he said.

She nodded again.

Gavin frowned. "It hasn't been my experience that Tristan knows how to create enchantments like that."

"Would he have to do it himself?"

With something like this, Gavin had a hard time thinking that Tristan would have allowed somebody else to do it. But he might have used enchantments in order to accomplish the same goal. Knowing Tristan, he could have gathered several different enchantments, combining their effects and using them to release the power he intended.

Tristan didn't necessarily have to have control over his own energy to do that, and

Gavin wasn't sure whether Tristan had that level of mastery over his El'aras abilities. His old mentor had made a point of trying to help him learn how to use his core reserves, but did that mean Tristan knew their source? Tristan had always assumed that he had not learned how to control his own power, which was why he needed somebody like Gavin, but perhaps he had known and had simply refrained from doing so.

Gavin held out the enchantment that Gaspar had given him and focused on the symbol on it. He began to push power through it, letting energy flow from him into the mark, activating the enchantment. As he did, he could feel something starting to change. The enchantment took on a pale glow, the same one he had seen when he'd activated it before. Once again, it took on a shape and energy that started to show the image of the fortress.

"Try holding it up to the door," Gaspar suggested.

Gavin angled the enchantment toward the door and pushed even more magic into it. As he did, he started to feel something else—another pattern that was deep within the enchantment. Had he not been pushing so much of himself and so much of the ring into it, he might not have noticed it. He felt it tremble as if buried deep beneath the confines of the enchantment.

He focused on that trembling, and the image of the fortress flickered and started to fade.

"Are you losing it?" Zella asked.

"There's something else inside it," Gavin said, but he kept his focus on the enchantment. The surface of it had grown warm, reminding him of the story he'd just told Gaspar about stepping on a heated enchantment and burning his foot.

What if this was something similar?

The heat built within the enchantment. As he held his hand around it, he squeezed to try to keep control over it, but it was growing too hot.

He dropped it, and it landed on the stone floor. The enchantment began to glow, first with a bright orange light, but then it shifted to a pale blue. Somehow Gavin remained connected to it, even though he was no longer holding it. He had to call through his core reserves and the ring, and he pushed that all out and into the enchantment. It was a strange connection, as if he had linked himself in some way to it.

"What are you doing with that?" Zella asked.

Gavin stared at the enchantment, still able to feel the link. "I think he wanted to keep us from getting to this easily." He guessed that it probably wasn't about him but about keeping others away.

He let more of his core reserves flow through him, through the ring, and into the enchantment. The stone exploded with light, forcing Gavin and the others back several steps. His heel struck the stairs, and he nearly tripped. He used the strength of his core reserves to stabilize himself, and he let out an exasperated laugh as he realized how foolish he was.

Gaspar had fallen and landed on his backside. He grunted as he looked up and gasped, pointing in front of him.

Gavin turned to see where he was pointing and realized that Gaspar was motioning to the door. The entire door had started to glow blue, absorbing some of the light from the enchantment, but it was the mark upon the door —Tristan's symbol—that had taken on a different coloration altogether. Not the blue or even the orange that the enchantment had started with. This was almost a deep golden yellow.

"That's new," Gaspar said, getting to his feet. He flicked a pair of knives around, as if he was ready for the possibility that something sinister might burst free from the door at any moment.

Gavin smiled, as he had his hand on his sword as well.

"What is it doing?" Zella asked. She had taken a step toward the door, and Gavin realized that she had set several golems down on the ground in a ring around the glowing enchantment. Maybe they were Mekel's, or perhaps they were made by one of the other enchanters.

"I think we should stay back from it," Gavin suggested. "I'm not exactly sure what the enchantment is doing, but I can feel something."

He didn't know what he could feel exactly, only that the door was glowing vibrantly as the mark still took on that yellow light.

There was something else here that Gavin had to

uncover, but he had not yet learned what he had come here for. Perhaps he hadn't used the right sequence of enchantments, or maybe he hadn't tried what was needed to open the door.

Tristan had left him this enchantment, but maybe Gavin had another?

He pulled out the statue again and held it up to the door, but nothing changed. He tried pushing power through the enchantment as well, but he didn't feel anything. It left only one other possibility, and he pushed power out from himself, into the glowing mark.

Even that didn't do anything.

"I'm out of ideas," Gavin said.

"This entire place is quite well fortified," Gaspar observed. "I'm curious how he managed to secure it as well as he did."

"It's Tristan," Gavin said.

But because it *was* Tristan, maybe Gaspar was right.

Gavin was the Chain Breaker. That was what Tristan had taught him to be all those years. All those lessons where Gavin had been bound and wrapped in restraints made of rope, leather, and finally metal had taught him how to use power from deep inside him to burst out of any sort of confinement.

Maybe that was a lesson that Tristan wanted to remind him of.

Gavin focused on the door. On the mark. Now he had to be the Door Breaker.

He smiled at the thought as he gathered the power within himself. He focused on channeling his magic through his core reserves and through the ring, then leapt at the door.

He slammed his shoulder into it, and he drove his hand into the mark. The surface of the door was incredibly warm, far more than Gavin had expected it to be, though it wasn't hot. But where he struck the symbol with his hand, it was much warmer than the rest of the door. The door quavered, and cracks began to form along the surface.

"Well, that's one way to do it," Gaspar said.

Gavin fell back, landing next to the enchantment. The glow from within it had started to fade, changing from a pale blue back to a reddish-orange color, and then it went quiet altogether. He reached for it, testing it tentatively, and he found that it was still warm but not hot any longer. He gathered the enchantment, stuffed it into his pocket, and got to his feet.

"Now we have to see what's inside."

"The door is still intact," Zella said.

"For now," Gavin said. "Not for long."

He took a step toward the door and kicked with all the power within himself, bracing with his core reserves and sending strength down his leg so that he didn't shatter it as he made contact. The cracks extended even further, and then the door crumbled, disappearing into a pile of dust.

Darkness greeted them from beyond.

"Any ideas what's on the other side of this?" Gavin asked, not daring to take his attention from the doorway.

"We found the construction records, at least as far as

we have been able to determine," Zella said. "If the Captain had lived, perhaps we would've been able to ask him more questions, but unfortunately—"

"Had the Captain lived, you would not be in the fortress now," Gavin pointed out.

She arched a brow at him. "I think we would have claimed this place as our own eventually. Given what he did to our people and the fact that we had to hide for as long as we did, this was our right."

There was no reason to argue that point, since Gavin agreed with it. This place probably did belong to the enchanters, especially given everything they had gone through and everything that the people of Yoran, including the constables and the Captain, had done to them.

"There's nothing to do but keep going," Gavin said.

He took a step forward, and a strange tingling sensation washed along his skin. He immediately called on his core reserves and braced himself. Anna had taught him this technique, which allowed that energy to flow from some place deep inside him, out through his skin, and all the way through his fingers down into the rest of his body.

In doing so, he created something of an enchantment from within himself.

Everything around them lightened, causing the darkness to fade. The tingling pressure along his skin eased, and Gavin was able to move forward without feeling like he was going to be limited in any way.

He looked back at the others, but Gaspar remained in the doorway.

"I can't go any farther," Gaspar said. "There's some sort of invisible barrier here."

Zella pressed her hand up to it and hissed, pulling back. "And it hurts."

Gavin turned away from them, nodding. "Wait for me. I'll go and investigate."

"Are you sure this is what you want to do, boy?"

"I think I need to. I think Tristan expected me to."

Which was even more reason for Gavin to do it, even if he didn't want to.

He walked down the hall, into the darkness, toward whatever Tristan wanted from him. And he couldn't help but feel as if he was still playing one of Tristan's games.

CHAPTER FIFTEEN

The hall narrowed for only a moment. It took little more than a few steps before it started to widen again, and a sense of pressure washed over Gavin's skin. As he pushed his core reserves out through him, trying to solidify himself, that pressure squeezed around him. There was some other barrier here.

He tapped on his communication enchantment. "Gaspar?" He didn't expect the old thief to be able to hear him, but he wanted to test it. There was no answer. "Wrenlow?"

As before, he didn't expect any sort of answer. But what if he tried using his core reserves to activate the enchantment?

He tapped on it again, and this time he pushed power out through his fingertips into the enchantment. Gavin had rarely tried to do that, but this was an El'aras enchantment that Anna had created for him. Perhaps his own El'aras abilities would add to existing power and allow him to activate it more potently than he would be able to naturally.

The power he channeled surged into the enchantment, and the metal itself grew warmer. It seemed to attach to his core reserves, as if linking to some distant part of himself, like a connection formed between him and the enchantment.

That was new.

Gavin whispered into the enchantment. "Gaspar?"

"I'm here. Damn, boy, I wasn't expecting it to work. I've been yelling your name for the better part of the last few minutes."

"Just be aware," Gavin said. "I added a little bit of myself to this enchantment, at least from my end, which seems to have strengthened it."

"You did what?"

Gavin didn't really understand what he had done, other than try to connect to it. Perhaps it was something that Anna had taught him, and he had finally taken it to heart, but he wasn't entirely sure how to do it consistently. Maybe he could do the same thing with other enchantments, and if he could, then maybe he could strengthen them too. He would feel a link to them—at least if they worked like this.

As he thought about it, he realized that he had done something similar with Tristan's enchantment, the stone wolf, and the paper dragon. He had been able to forge some sort of link between himself and other enchantments, and he believed that this technique he'd learned from Anna was what made a difference.

"I'm in a narrow hallway, but it has widened again," he explained. "There have been two barriers altogether. The second one is probably just like the first, so even if you could've gotten through the first layer, I'm not sure that you would've been able to get through the second, and then..." Gavin shrugged. "I don't know."

"Where do you think it leads?"

"Again, I don't know."

There was silence for a few moments, and then Gaspar spoke up again. "Zella said she was trying to tell us about the records of the construction. There shouldn't be anything here. There was a hidden door in the hearth, but as far as she knew, it led to a doorway and out."

"Out of what?"

"Of the fortress. It was a hidden access point. Only... with the stairs..."

Gavin understood the concern. The stairs shouldn't have been there. Maybe the Captain had added them later, but it was even possible—and surprising—that Tristan might have learned about the hidden access point and modified it himself. Why would he have come back, though?

Gavin looked around. The tunnel had narrowed again, and he felt another sense of pressure on him. This didn't seem the same as when the nihilar oppressed him, where he felt he had to abandon his core reserves. In fact, with this, it almost seemed as if channeling energy through his core reserves could help him push back against it. As he did so, the pressure around him faded.

When the barrier had completely disappeared, he saw

that the room on the other side was much larger than the last one had been. The stone seemed to have changed as well. Before, smooth black stone lined the walls of the hallway, but this was more contoured. The color shifted to gray and then to a faded yellow stone. Was he still in Yoran? The drastic change suggested that he might not be.

He frowned, tapping on his enchantment. "Gaspar? You still there?"

"I can hear you, but you've gotten quieter. It sounds like you're talking into a cup."

Gavin looked behind him. He couldn't see anything other than the darkened walls, but he remembered the pressure he had felt, which had suggested some sort of barrier.

Was it a form of separation that had bound him between one space and another? Tristan had likely placed a barrier in order to prevent anybody else from accessing the space. Or maybe it was something different altogether.

An idea came to him, and he stepped deeper into the chamber. There were rounded walls on either side of him, as well as what looked like a darkened hearth that hadn't been touched in some time. Though it had evidence of old fires, there was nothing active within it now.

A table near the back of the room caught his attention. A single piece of paper rested on top of it. Gavin looked around as he headed over to it. He didn't see any other openings to this chamber other than the way he had entered, but that didn't mean that there wouldn't be someplace hidden. By the time he reached the table, he was convinced he was alone.

He lifted the paper, not surprised to see that Tristan's mark adorned it, and Gavin's name was written below. He flipped open the paper, and a shadow moved at him in a blur of speed.

He spun, immediately unsheathing his sword and catching another blade with his. Gavin danced through the Leier patterns, which were the most effective for him these days. They seemed to connect not only to magic but to some part deep within him, binding his core reserves to the power that the pattern itself was calling on.

The other fighter was incredibly skilled. Gavin twisted, and neither he nor his attacker spoke. It was blade against blade.

He rolled to the side and stabbed upward, thrusting his blade toward his opponent. He missed and spun around, looking for signs of anyone else who may have been waiting too.

It seemed to be just this one.

Gavin pushed power out of his core reserves and through the ring, realizing he wasn't restricted at all. There had been a hint of pressure on him before—not quite the same way as it had felt from the nihilar, but certainly enough that it had created a limitation to using his abilities. Now, there was no more resistance against him, furthering his suspicion that he was not in Yoran.

He ducked a jab, then flowed to his left, quickly reversing course and driving his blade around. Staying low, he swept his sword in a wide arc, using his core reserves as he did and preparing for another attack. He thought about different techniques that might be effective, but he found them less useful.

Imogen had taught him others. She hadn't neces-sarily wanted to teach him, but Gavin had mastered them after having seen the patterns once. At the time, he hadn't understood anything about them other than that they were different sword techniques, but the more he used them, the more he understood that not only were they effective, especially for disrupting sorcery, but there was power within the techniques themselves.

He jumped and drove his sword down. The attacker caught his blade overhead, forcing him toward the ceiling. Gavin pushed off by using his power. The core reserves blasted from within him, and he came to a twisting stop near the barricade at the back of the room.

The attacker did not move toward him. Gavin held his sword at the ready, unsure who this was, though they were incredibly skilled. For a moment, he thought it might be the same attacker he'd faced before, but that didn't seem to be the case. The leader of the nihilar had used his ability to suppress Gavin's core reserves, and that hadn't happened yet.

"Are you with them?" Gavin asked.

They darted toward him. Gavin spun, bringing his blade up and swinging it around, then used a sharp, quick pattern to cut them off. He ducked and rolled under another thrust, and he twisted around.

Gavin flowed from pattern to pattern, and there was something about them that seemed to add to the power of his own core reserves. But it wasn't just the one style. It was the mixture of different types.

He jumped back and held his sword up, the power of the ring blazing through him and through the sword, which lit the room completely. The shadows were pushed back, and the figure of the sword fighter he'd been grappling with became clear.

The person was dressed all in a green, dappled cloak that reminded Gavin of the El'aras, but not quite—almost a mockery of the El'aras. Their height was similar to Gavin's, and their build was muscular. The hood of the cloak covered their face, but Gavin knew who this was.

"Tristan."

He waited, and the figure pulled their hood back. A laugh erupted around the room, and Tristan lowered his blade with a quick flourish before sheathing it.

"It took you long enough."

Gavin hesitated. He had not been one-on-one with Tristan in quite some time. Not only that, but he was trapped in a space he was not in control of, one that he was still trying to understand.

Had all of this been some sort of trap? Tristan's way of getting Gavin out of Yoran, to someplace where he could command him and perhaps use him?

Gavin needed to be careful here, and he didn't sheathe his sword.

Tristan eyed the blade, a smile curling his lips. "Has it come to that?"

"Have you given me a choice?"

Tristan turned his back to Gavin, striding away from

him to the table. He grabbed a chair that Gavin hadn't seen on his first perusal of the room and threw himself down into it. He reached into his pocket and tossed something into the hearth, causing a bright flame to bloom into view. It reminded Gavin of what he had seen in the Captain's fortress, the way that the heat had burned without there really being fire.

Gavin watched him warily. "You wanted me to come here."

"I must say, I hoped you would eventually find me. I've been waiting."

"Waiting?"

"Hiding?" Tristan shrugged. "Perhaps it's both. Regardless, I had hoped you might find me. Now you did." He crossed one leg over the other, and he leaned forward. "You followed the clues?"

Gavin grunted. "You didn't leave me clues so much as you left me a trail."

"It was easier that way. There could be no mistake in this case."

Gavin held onto his blade and increasingly began to realize that it was probably unnecessary. Tristan hadn't made any attempt to attack him since taking a seat, and even if he did, Gavin no longer had to fear Tristan.

Now that Gavin had the power of the ring and the sword, and now that he understood how to use his core reserves better than he suspected Tristan did, he didn't need to fear his former mentor. Which was exactly what Tristan would've wanted from him. He would want to disarm Gavin, to keep him feeling as if he was at a disadvantage.

That would be how Tristan would overpower him.

So even though Gavin figured he wouldn't need his sword, he kept it unsheathed. But he relaxed—just a bit.

He eyed Tristan. "Who is he?"

"Getting down to business right away, are we? You don't want to visit with your old instructor, talk about what I've been doing and why you have—"

Gavin waved his hand and held his gaze on Tristan. "We both know there doesn't need to be a conversation. You wanted me to act. I ended up doing it. And you managed it in such a way that I don't even feel like you were wrong."

That was the part of all of this that surprised him most. When he had been younger, he'd been trained to fight, to kill, and to do so with ruthless efficiency. But since leaving Tristan after his apparent death, Gavin had assumed a different role for himself. He hadn't wanted to kill the same way. Instead, he wanted to have an opportunity to help, which was why he'd carefully selected and taken the jobs he had so that he didn't have to kill all the time. Or perhaps didn't have to kill those who he felt didn't deserve it. And through it all, Gavin had been a pawn in some game Tristan had played.

"Not as much as you think," Tristan said. "There's only so far a heavy hand can go before you start to feel it." He smiled, and darkness glittered in his eyes.

"And the Order of Notharin?"

"I tried to offer a little guidance. I saw that there was going to be a need."

"You trained them to take on the Sul'toral."

He hadn't told Rayena his suspicions that everything Tristan had done with them was to bind them to Gavin ultimately, which he wouldn't put past him. Tristan would've latched on to some existing order, taking it and twisting it to convince people that they were serving a greater good.

"I trained them to do what they needed to do," Tristan said. "And all of them were more than happy to take on that role." He leaned forward, resting his elbows on his knees and his head in his hands. "Much like you."

"Why didn't you just go through the El'aras?" It was a question that Gavin had been asking himself over and over, but he didn't have a good answer for it. He suspected the answer, but he wanted to hear it from Tristan.

"Because they were entrenched in old ideas. And because they believed in a prophecy that was misguided. They had to *see* that it was misguided."

"How did you know?"

"When you escape the people, you begin to see the world." Tristan's voice was soft and low, more introspective than Gavin remembered him being.

"All of this, and you could've just asked me to have a conversation."

"Isn't that what we are doing?"

Gavin stared at him. "It seems that what we're doing is what you want me to do. You wanted me to come here. You wanted me to find the book, the sculpture, and—"

"Did you?" Tristan asked, eyebrows raised.

Gavin frowned, trying to gauge which part Tristan was most interested in. "You didn't think I would?"

"I hoped you would. I hoped you could get them before *they* did."

Gavin nodded. "We have them."

"You need to keep them safe. If they manage to acquire them, they will be able to reach for power they should not have access to."

Gavin backed toward the wall behind him, using that to prepare his defense. He wasn't sure that he was going to need it, but not knowing what Tristan might try, Gavin wasn't about to be caught out in the open.

"I need you to tell me everything," he said.

"About what you dealt with?"

"That's a start. The man I fought knew you. He knew my fighting styles."

Tristan smirked. "Many people know your fighting styles, Gavin."

"He knew *all* of my fighting styles."

Tristan held his gaze but said nothing.

"There aren't any others like me," Gavin said.

"No. There are not."

"Other than him."

"He is not like you, Gavin Lorren."

Tristan leaned back, and he closed his eyes for a moment, as if trying to gather his thoughts. Some of the sternness that Gavin remembered was gone. The lines around the corners of Tristan's eyes were faded, different than they had been, and Gavin was reminded of just how old he might be. Anna had claimed that if Tristan was responsible for taking what he had, then he had to be impossibly old. It seemed hard to believe, and even harder for Gavin to believe that he himself might eventually live that long, assuming that he didn't get killed first. But as he looked at Tristan now, he couldn't help but see the age within him.

"Who is he?" Gavin asked.

"He's a man who wanted to be like you," Tristan finally said. "I trained him nearly a century ago. It was my first attempt."

"At finding the Champion?"

Tristan looked up, then nodded. "I knew the prophecy was a farce by then. At least, I believed it was. I had not yet found the Shard but had been looking, knowing that eventually the Champion and the Shard would have to be brought together in order to prove the prophecy false."

"That was all you wanted?"

"That, along with something else."

"You wanted to destroy the Sul'toral."

Tristan's face darkened, and there was a hint of the anger and rage that Gavin remembered when he was younger. "Yes."

"Why?" Gavin asked.

"Does it matter?"

"It does to me."

Gavin had questioned that for quite some time, pondering whether or not Tristan's motivations mattered, and he still didn't have a clear answer. Tristan had been planning for a long time. Gavin knew that. What he didn't know was what purpose Tristan had in using him. Was there one? Or was he merely a piece of some greater scheme? It surprised him how much that mattered to him.

Tristan tipped his head. "With everything you've experienced, I suppose it does matter, doesn't it? You, the first one where I decided to play a lighter hand—at least, after a while."

Gavin snorted. "That was a lighter hand?"

"You should have seen some of my first attempts."

Gavin shivered, flooded by his own memories of what he'd gone through over the years and how he had been forced to work and fight and act. They'd been painful, brutal, and they had honed him into the fighter he was. What would it have been like for somebody to be pushed even harder? What would they have experienced? How hard would it have been for them?

"And then?" Gavin asked.

"With you, I suspected potential. When I found you, you fit all the criteria."

"What criteria?"

"And you flashed potential immediately," Tristan said, without explaining or answering Gavin's question. "You exceeded my expectations, in fact. You demonstrated skill beyond what I thought you could, so I pushed you. Until I realized I had to stop pushing and to let you do it on your own."

Gavin frowned. "You stopped pushing and started pulling."

"Did I?"

"Maybe pulling the strings."

Tristan shrugged. "I can't deny I tried to influence you. There were times when you didn't take the action I hoped, but also times when you did things far greater than I could ever have thought possible."

"Stop changing the subject. You were telling me about him."

As much as Gavin wanted to know more about himself and what Tristan had been doing with him, he needed to know more about his attacker, the business at hand. He couldn't get caught in the sentimentality of his own desires. That was another of Tristan's lessons.

Tristan smiled, nodding as if he understood. "As I said, he was one of my other attempts. I trained him nearly a century ago."

"Who is he?"

"His name is Chauvan. I don't know if he still goes by that. He disappeared decades ago."

"You mean you lost control of him decades ago."

"Yes."

"Did you ever send me after him before?"

Tristan looked up, holding Gavin's gaze for a long moment, then finally shook his head. "You weren't ready."

"You felt there was somebody I wasn't equipped to handle?"

"I knew he had gone after power."

"Nihilar," Gavin said.

Tristan's gaze narrowed. "You've heard."

"I'm not without my own resources."

"No. I suppose you are not. In that, you have proved even more capable than I expected. It's not only about your resources; it's about your willingness to work with other people."

"I saw your disciple working with others."

"No, you saw him commanding others," Tristan said. "Through fear and intimidation, and a promise of power. That is not how you've worked."

Gavin hesitated. "He has power."

"Not yet."

"It seems like it. I have faced him several times now, and he has a way of suppressing the El'aras magic inside me."

Tristan nodded. "As I said, he's chasing power, but he doesn't have it yet. What he has found are artifacts. Essentially enchantments, remnants of the nihilar. What he's after is something greater. True access to it."

Gavin blinked. If that hadn't been true access to the nihilar, then he couldn't even imagine what that would be like. "What happens if he gains it?"

"There are great powers in the world, Gavin Lorren."

"You don't need to lecture me on powers."

"I suppose I do not. You have encountered Sul'toral and sorcerers—at least most of them—who have chased a dangerous power themselves."

Gavin nodded. "And I've heard of Sarenoth."

"He is but one power. The Sul'toral have gotten close to freeing him over the years, but they've always been thwarted."

"And this nihilar power is—"

"Different," Tristan said. "No less destructive. But it should not be freed either."

"What would happen if it were?"

"You felt what would happen. And if he were to succeed, he would have the ability to suppress all of the El'aras. They would not be able to stand against him."

Gavin had seen how the El'aras had fallen for that power. It wasn't even the complete access to the power that had tempted them but the idea that there would be something greater and a way of using it. But why just the El'aras?

"Is he El'aras," Gavin asked, "or is he something else?"

"He is El'aras, like you. The Champion needs to be."

"Then why would he use a power that could destroy his own?"

"It would not destroy his, it would consume it. And it would allow him to use that power against all who oppose him." Tristan leaned forward, and there was a hard glint in his eyes. "Once he conquers the El'aras, he will take his fight beyond them."

Gavin waited for him to expand on that, but he didn't. "Then why are you here?"

Tristan leaned back, spreading his hands around him. "I'm here because it's safe. At least, as safe as a place can be for me."

"Because he's hunting you."

"He has his people looking."

"And you decided to get me involved."

"I needed your help."

Gavin sensed how difficult it was for Tristan to acknowledge this fact, but he laughed nonetheless. "You want my help. After all these years of forcing me into helping you, now you want me to just agree to it?"

"I thought you would want to offer it."

"Maybe if you had asked me, but you manipulated me into helping. You twisted me into working with you."

"I was only giving you guidance."

Gavin snorted. "You weren't guiding me. You were trying to control me, the way you always controlled me." He stared at him for a moment before turning away.

He had found Tristan. He had gotten the answers to his questions. He had new questions that he wanted answers to, but now he needed to stop Chauvan.

And if he didn't, the El'aras would suffer. Because of Tristan.

"Wait," Tristan said.

"I'm not waiting on you."

"You know what will happen if you let him succeed."

"That's just it. You and I both know I can't let that happen. You saw to it that I could not."

"You know where to begin?"

"I think your book will provide me with guidance," Gavin said. "Especially since he was going after it as well."

He reached for the first of the barriers and started to pass through it, and he felt Tristan come behind him. Gavin spun, immediately calling on his core reserves and pulling power through the ring.

"He was there?" Tristan said.

"You knew he would be."

Tristan shook his head. "I sent you after the book. It wasn't safe for me to keep. I thought that if you could recover it, you could prevent him from finding the key to the nihilar."

"The book is the key?"

"The book shares the key. It's why I left it for you," Tristan said.

"He was already in the temple before I got there," Gavin said.

He waited for Tristan to say something more, but he didn't. Instead, he turned away, muttering to himself.

Gavin remained for a few moments, but frustration got the best of him. "I'm done following your trail."

With that, he passed through the barrier, into the tunnel, and back toward Yoran.

CHAPTER SIXTEEN

When Gavin reached the fortress, he found Zella and Gaspar waiting for him. Both of them appeared on edge, and he realized that Zella had activated the enchantments around the doorway, preparing a series of defenses in case they needed them.

As he stepped through the barrier, he froze. A massive monster made of stone waited right in front of him. "Can I pass?"

"Gavin?" Zella said.

"It's me. I'm here."

She tapped the enchantment, which began to shrink back down into a manageable size, and she plucked it from the ground.

Gavin shook his head, looking to Gaspar. "I need something like that." He took a deep breath, letting it out, and he nodded behind him. "This leads to Tristan."

"As in *the* Tristan?"

"Apparently this tunnel leads to some hidden lair, which is where Tristan is lying low," Gavin said.

"What did he say?"

"I know more about the man I faced, and I know what he's after."

"And?"

"It's worse than I thought."

He started up the stairs, with Zella and Gaspar following him. By the time he stepped through the hearth, the surprise at seeing Tristan had started to fade. Now he needed to make a plan.

He had to figure out what Chauvan and his team were after, how they were planning to go about getting the power of the nihilar, and how he was going to stop it. He had to have the necessary defenses to be able to take on people with incredible power. What Gavin had seen so far was that they were susceptible to enchantments, so perhaps he was in the right place to prepare. He needed to bring whatever help he could to bear.

Gavin paused. "Zella, how many enchantments are you willing to spare?"

"What are you thinking?"

"I'll need hundreds."

He detailed a list of things he could think of; ways of overpowering opponents. Speed. Strength. Impervious skin. Enhanced eyesight. Improved reflexes. Things that only the enchanters were able to make. Then he started brainstorming defensive enchantments.

"I'll need anything Mekel can spare... but I don't want anything to harm him."

She arched a brow. "Harm him?"

"I know that he can feel the enchantments somehow."

"He is aware of them, but they should not hurt," Zella said.

Gavin knew that wasn't true for all enchanters. "Regardless, I need anything he can spare, and anything he's willing to lose."

Zella frowned. "What do you think you're going to face?"

"Fighters more powerful than any I've dealt with before."

"Sorcerers?"

"Not exactly," he said. "More like those who can suppress magic."

He didn't know if they could suppress sorcery or only El'aras magic. If Chauvan had the ability to overwhelm the El'aras, this power might be something that the Sul'-toral would be interested in. After all, it would be another way to fight the El'aras. Maybe Gavin should've stayed and asked more questions of Tristan. He had let his frustration get the best of him and departed prematurely.

But they did have the book. He had to believe that Wrenlow would eventually come up with answers, and they would be able to figure out how to defeat Chauvan.

"I will gather whatever you ask for," Zella said. "How quickly do you think you'll need it?"

"Soon," he replied. "Though I don't know, to be honest. These others are after a kind of power impossible for me to fully understand, and I don't know how close they are to it. I don't think we have much time, though. Hopefully enough that you could replenish our enchantments."

If Chauvan and his people had already been in the temple and had left before...

It might be that they would come after Gavin for the statue and the book. Maybe they wanted both. If so, then the people who had come with him and those who were still here in the city were not safe.

He tapped on the communication enchantment. "Wrenlow?"

"I'm here," Wrenlow answered quickly. "I've heard most of what you're saying, anyway."

"You've heard it?"

"Well, you went quiet for a while, and then you started talking again, and now you're clear. Anyway, I've been trying to work through his book and have been able to come up with a few answers. It's slow going, though. It's an ancient language, and I've pieced it together from various combinations of three different languages that are—"

"Thank you," Gavin said, cutting him off. "We're heading back to you." If he were to let Wrenlow go on, his friend would share everything he knew about those ancient languages, then even more.

He looked over to Zella. "Can you bring the enchantments to the Dragon?"

"You intend to do this quickly."

Gavin nodded. "I fear I need to."

"You need to rest, boy," Gaspar grumbled.

"I might, but I don't know how much time I have. If they succeed—"

"How bad can it be?"

"Well, it might mean the destruction of all El'aras, all sorcerers, perhaps even all enchanters. I don't know if that is what we are dealing with or not, only that I have now seen different attempts at destroying magic. First sorcery and enchantments, and now this."

Gaspar whistled softly. "Fine. You made your point. It can be pretty bad."

Gavin nodded. "That's what it seems." He looked over to Zella. "I'm sorry."

"Why?" she asked.

"Because I brought something else to you."

"Did you?"

"I don't even know." He shook his head. "Tristan is connected somehow, but I don't think that hidden lair is even considered to be in Yoran."

Zella turned and looked toward the hearth. "There are stories about connections like that. I've never seen one."

"Maybe when this is over, I can help you navigate through it." Gavin didn't know if he'd be able to step through the barrier with somebody else, but it would be worth testing. And if Zella offered the help that he was asking for, then he would have to provide her with anything she wanted.

She nodded.

Gavin and Gaspar headed out the front door and through the gate, where Mekel was waiting and watching.

"Already done?" he asked.

"For now," Gavin said. "Zella will have a request for some of your enchantments."

"Of course. You can have as many as you want."

"Anything that won't harm you," Gavin added.

Mekel's face tightened. "They don't necessarily hurt. Well, that's not completely true. They do, or at least some of them do. But it's more like a part of me that gets broken." He frowned, looking over to Gavin. "Does that make sense? It doesn't take anything out of me. I mean, I don't think it does. But it still…"

Gavin clasped him on the shoulder. "I understand. Anything you feel like you can sacrifice. We are going to need as many protections as possible."

"I can go with you," Mekel said.

"What?"

"I can go with you. Wherever you're going. If you need me to help make enchantments, I can do that on the spot."

"I wouldn't ask that of you."

"I want to help," Mekel said, glancing back at the fortress. "Besides, the city is safe. Well, as safe as it can be. And if you feel like it's necessary for you to go and deal with something, then…" He shrugged. "I want to go with you."

Gaspar grabbed Gavin's shirt and pulled him back. "Help like that wouldn't be bad, boy. You've seen what he can make. And I've seen how fast he can make them. You could have an army at your hands in barely more than a few minutes."

Gaspar was right that it might be helpful to have Mekel with him. Gavin wouldn't be able to carry many enchantments with him easily. They might be small, but they were heavy, and there might be ones he could make that Gavin didn't even know he needed.

"Thank you," he said.

Mekel nodded. "I'll talk to her about going."

"Meet us at the Dragon, then."

Gavin and Gaspar strode off, making their way through the streets. Neither of them spoke for a few moments.

"I wasn't the first one Tristan manipulated," Gavin said.

It was strange to learn that, but stranger still was that he didn't know how he felt about it. There was an edge of disappointment within him. It was probably a mistake to feel that way, especially as Tristan had used him for as long as he had, but Gavin couldn't shake that feeling.

"Did you really think you were?"

"To be honest, I hadn't given it much thought. He'd been testing people to create a Champion."

"So you were an experiment?" Gaspar chuckled heartily. "Some experiment."

"I think he believes he perfected it with me."

"I'm not so sure that I agree with his idea of perfection," Gaspar muttered. "But I can see how he would view you as a success."

Gavin glanced over and started to smile. "Are you actually offering me a compliment?"

"Don't let it get to your head, boy," he said, laughing.

They stepped inside the Dragon. Wrenlow was still poring over the book. Rayena and Brandon both sat at the table with a mug of ale in hand, though they were staring intently at each other.

Gavin slowed as he entered, sensing the irritation between them, and he looked from one to the other. "What happened?"

"Nothing," Rayena snapped.

"Oh, they were debating which of them is the better fighter, especially if it came to taking on something called a mugar. Never heard of it." Wrenlow looked up at Gavin. "Have you? I mean, you and I never came across anything like that, but the two of them talk about it as if it's something impressive to be able to take down."

"I don't even need a weapon," Brandon said, and he winked at Gavin. "You know, I probably wrestled a dozen of them when I was younger. Barely more than this high," he said, raising his hand slightly above the floor, then turned his attention to Rayena. "But she likes to think that you need a knife to take them on."

"You have to stick the blade into their spine to control them," she said.

"You can't control them. You just have to force them to do what you need them to do."

Gavin shook his head. "We have a bigger problem." He took a seat and told them about his conversation with Tristan and his concern that they might already be short on time.

Wrenlow returned to studying the book. Gaspar stayed near the back wall of the tavern, and every so often, Gavin glanced over to him. What was his old friend thinking? He didn't say anything, which worried Gavin. He had to have something in mind, but what?

"So, we're running low on time," Brandon said. "We can deal with this, Champion. You taught us how to hold our breath, and—"

"You needed to be taught how to hold your breath?" Wrenlow asked, looking up. That drew more attention from him than anything Gavin had recounted. "Don't most people know how to do that?"

"It's not really holding their breath," Gavin said, and he explained what he meant by that.

Wrenlow nodded slowly. "I see. You taught them how to hold their *magical* breath. That is impressive." He turned his attention back to the book, falling silent once again.

"I have other help coming," Gavin told them.

"What kind of help?" Rayena asked.

"We need something that isn't going to be susceptible to the nihilar. Enchantments aren't, so I have asked for some assistance. As much as we can possibly carry. I figured we needed our own. Speed. Strength. Stone skin."

"I like that one," Wrenlow said, looking up as Brandon glanced over to him. "What? I'm not the fighter Gavin is. When you take a hit, you want to know that you aren't going to get hurt."

"Even with impervious skin, you can still get hurt," Gavin said. "Especially if somebody hits you hard enough."

But it was more than that. If the enchantment started to fade without him knowing, then that was what he really worried about. If he, Brandon, and Rayena were suppressed by the nihilar, there might come a point where he wouldn't be able to push any more of his core reserves into an enchantment to power it. He needed quantity over quality in this case.

"So we have a way of fighting," Rayena said, "but do we even know what they're going to do?" She looked from Brandon to Gavin. "We've followed Tristan's trail, but if that has gone quiet, we won't really know."

"I have no idea," Gavin muttered. He gestured to the book, hoping it might have answers. That was what it was all about.

"It's on me, then?" Wrenlow asked. He smiled tightly. "I've been trying to break down the pieces here. As I said, there is a mixture of terms in three different languages, and things just don't make sense, at least not the way we know them now. I think that with enough time, I should be able to get through it, but you're putting me in a time crunch here and that makes it harder. I'm doing my best."

"We know you are," Gavin said.

"You said something about a temple?"

"That's where we found a statue."

"That's what I thought you said." Wrenlow shook his head, and Gavin knew that he must be onto something. He only got like this when he was chasing a lead, piecing together a puzzle, and trying to figure something out. "The temple is important."

"Because it housed that statue," Gavin said.

"Not just because of that. There has to be something else to it, but I'm not exactly sure what. The temple is referenced here, or at least *a* temple. I'm assuming that's the same one, especially since you had been led there." He flipped open a few pages, coming to stop about a third of the way through the book.

Wrenlow pointed to a drawing of a building. It could be anything, anywhere, but if he had found a reference to the temple, there had to be a reason why. Maybe the book did have some secrets they could use.

"Here," Wrenlow said, and he turned the book around to show Gavin. "This is talking about accessing a key. It's just one step, and apparently there are other keys, but once they are found and used, then some doorway..." He shook his head, frowning. "That's not quite right. Gateway?" His frown deepened. "I don't know. The translation is difficult, and the language is old. So maybe it's a doorway, maybe it's a gateway, or maybe it's—"

"We get the point," Gavin said. "Whatever it is, it opens something."

"Right. It opens something, and it allows a..." Wrenlow paused, turning the book back around to face him, and he began to flip through the pages again. "Well, I'm not exactly sure what it allows. It frees something up. Maybe it's some sort of power? Maybe another enchantment?"

"Nihilar," Gavin said.

Wrenlow tilted his head. "I don't see that anywhere."

"It might not be in there, but that's what they're after. That's the power."

"The power is called 'nihilar'? Do you know what it means?"

"I really don't," Gavin said.

"It's strange." Wrenlow nodded to the book, patting the cover. "It fits with these languages, though. It means—"

"Undoing," a voice said from the doorway.

Gavin spun toward it.

Tristan had entered the Dragon. He was dressed the same as he had been in the hidden chamber, but he had two swords sheathed at his side and a pack slung over his shoulder.

Gaspar straightened, his knives in hand immediately. Rayena jumped to her feet, tipping her head in a bow. The only ones who didn't really react were Brandon, who simply watched Tristan with interest, and Wrenlow, who was still focused on the book.

"'Undoing' seems to make sense," Wrenlow muttered, "but I think there's more to it. It's more layered and nuanced than just that. It is more about unmaking? No. That's not quite right. Maybe it's more about taking. Subserving?" He looked up, and his eyes widened. "Oh. Who are you?"

Gavin snorted. "Wrenlow, this is my old mentor, Tristan."

The door to the kitchen opened, and Jessica paused as she eyed the newcomer. "Great. Another guest."

"You wanted to keep the tavern busy," Gavin said.

She frowned at him. "Not like this, I didn't."

Gavin chuckled. "We can go somewhere else. I know a few other places we can use."

She stepped toward him and jabbed him in the chest with her finger, then set the mug of ale down in front of him. "If you go anywhere else, Gavin Lorren, I will see to it that you never return to the city."

With that, she spun, striding back into the kitchen again.

"Well, at least the two of you worked that out," Wrenlow said.

Gavin ignored him and turned to Tristan. "What are you doing here?"

"You're right. I have been hiding."

"And you decided to come out of hiding and show up at my friend's tavern?"

Tristan glanced around. "Do you think this is the first time I've come?"

Gaspar stiffened. Gavin could imagine the old thief slipping enchantments on and lunging at Tristan, or taking any number of dangerous actions against him.

"What are you doing here now?" Gavin asked.

"When you mentioned the temple, I became concerned."

"Why?"

"I had always thought the book was the only copy. Look at it," Tristan said, motioning to where Wrenlow was studying it. "It had taken me ages to find, to secure, and to protect. Ages where I thought that I had the only copy. No one could read it anyway, so even if they managed to find it, that was only one piece of the puzzle."

Gavin shook his head, trying to make sense of what Tristan was saying. "What are you going on about?"

"You said the people were in the temple."

"Yes."

"You are the only one who would've known how to get to it." He nodded to Gaspar. "You can put away your knives, Gaspar. I don't intend to attack."

Gaspar grunted. "I think I'll hold on to them."

Tristan shrugged and made his way to their table, and he sank down into a chair next to Rayena. She looked at Tristan, and there was an unusual light in her eyes that Gavin couldn't quite read. Was it excitement? Worry? Whatever it was, it was an expression he didn't recognize from her.

"The temple was the only key that I found," Tristan said, glancing over to Wrenlow. "And how long have you had this book?"

"Oh, about an hour or so." Wrenlow turned his attention back to the pages. "Gavin gets irritable if I don't break things down for him quickly enough, so I've been trying to figure it out."

"It has nothing to do with me getting irritable with you," Gavin said.

"You *do* get like that. Well, you did. I haven't seen you in a few months."

Gavin snorted. "Wrenlow is probably the brightest mind that I've ever worked with."

"I can see that," Tristan said. "When I was training you, I had others looking into various aspects of the puzzle. I had hoped—"

Gavin burst out laughing, which caused everybody else to startle and turn toward him. "You wanted others to interpret this book?"

"I wanted to make sure that I understood all of the dangers found within it."

"And that's part of the reason you gathered your coterie of students?"

"One of many," Tristan said.

Gavin had been the primary fighting student, though there had been others. Once he'd defeated all of them, they'd generally disappeared. At the time, he hadn't given much thought to it, but now that he knew what he did about Tristan, he suspected they were other experiments that had failed. Seeing how Gavin had shown promise, Tristan had decided to focus on him. But there had been other students there, like Cyran, who had demonstrated skill with sorcery. And perhaps even others who were prized for different purposes.

"Your friend here would've been an excellent addition," Tristan said.

Wrenlow looked up at that, but his gaze landed on Gavin. He shook his head. "I'm not interested. I'd rather work with Gavin."

Tristan gave a single nod. "I see that."

"Anyway," Gavin said, "you were saying?"

"The temple is one of the keys," Tristan said. "The only one I found. I kept the statue hidden there. I could protect both the temple and the key, and placing those defenses ensured that no one else would even know about it."

"But you brought *me* to the temple."

"Only when you were advanced in your training."

"And you would've brought Chauvan there," Gavin

said, knowing that the man would've gone through a similar sort of training.

Tristan shook his head. "He would not have seen anything."

"Sort of how I didn't see anything?"

"I had not known you did."

Gavin scoffed. "You aren't as all-knowing as you believe yourself to be."

And that might be the problem. Tristan liked to believe that he was in control, that he was manipulating events, but perhaps that was his arrogance speaking and he had done little more than simply delay events.

"So the temple was the first of the keys," Gavin said. "And from what we have found, there are several different ones?"

"Several."

"Three," Wrenlow clarified. "From what I can tell, three keys. Three different languages involved. The keys open the doorway, or gateway, or whatever you call it, and from there—"

"The nihilar is released," Gavin said.

"Maybe. I'm not sure if it's a matter of releasing it or something else."

Maybe it was just about accessing it, Gavin realized. And if that was the case, it was still no better. If they managed to gain power like that, especially given what he'd seen of it so far, the possibilities were far too dangerous. Not only for him, but for anyone who had his kind of power.

The door to the tavern opened, and Mekel strode in

with a massive bag laden with what Gavin could only guess were enchantments.

Gavin couldn't help but wonder how Zella would feel if the El'aras were to succumb to the nihilar. He knew how she felt about the Sorcerers' Society, but this was something else. This was a different threat to the enchanters and the city.

It was important to him, though. Maybe that was enough to make it mean something for Zella.

"She told me you wanted all of these," Mekel said. "There might be nearly a thousand different enchantments. She has them sorted, so it should be pretty easy for you to figure out which ones you need."

Tristan looked over. "That many enchantments?"

"If we're going to take Chauvan and his people on, we might need them," Gavin replied.

"We?"

"I have a feeling that Rayena and Brandon are coming with me."

"I am too," Gaspar said.

Gavin looked over. "Are you sure?"

"I told you things were all quiet here."

"What about Desarra?"

"She will understand."

There was a heaviness to the way he said it. How would Desarra feel when she learned that Gaspar was going to leave? Perhaps it would help both of them. Maybe they could regain the spark they once had.

"Besides," Gaspar continued, "when I heard you chattering in my enchantment, I knew you needed my help.

I'm not letting my friend disappear without helping him."

There was a time when Gavin would've rejected his help. Now, knowing what he had to face, and knowing that it wasn't going to be his El'aras abilities that saved them, he was going to need all the help he could get. And Gaspar was certainly skilled.

"I can come too," Wrenlow said.

Gavin took his friend's hand and shook his head. "I need you to keep working through that book. We need to know everything there is to know about the keys and about how to stop the nihilar and prevent the others from getting through."

"Well, I know the next temple."

"Already?" Tristan said. "I have spent many years attempting to piece all of that together, and you're telling me that you managed to solve it in little more than a few hours?"

Wrenlow shrugged. "What? I figured it out. It's more a matter of knowing the languages, finding the commonalities between them, and then piecing together what we know now with what they might've known then. It starts to work itself out fairly easily. At least, easy enough."

Tristan stared blankly at him.

Gavin bit back a laugh. "Then let's head there, stop Chauvan, and keep the gateway to the nihilar closed."

CHAPTER SEVENTEEN

The sky was still dark as they approached the edge of the city. Gavin suppressed a yawn. He had been going nonstop for a full day, maybe longer, but he didn't think he could slow down. Not yet. Not until they completed this.

As they neared the barricade around the city, Gaspar leaned close to him. "How do you know the order they'll be going in to find these keys?"

"I don't," Gavin said. "But if we find one, we can get there before him and secure it."

"And if we can't?"

"Then… I don't know."

He shook his head and glanced around at their strange group. Tristan had decided to come, and Gavin felt conflicted about it in ways he wasn't sure how to express. There had been so many years where he thought Tristan had died, only to learn that he was alive—and was possibly Gavin's enemy. Now they might be working on the same side, and it was likely that they had *always* been working on the same side.

Or not. That lack of trust made the entire situation incredibly difficult for Gavin. He didn't know whether he could believe Tristan's motives because there always seemed to be some other objective in mind.

What if Tristan wanted the nihilar?

If that was the case, Gavin had to be ready. He had already mourned Tristan once, and if it came down to fighting him and defeating him, then he had already prepared himself for that possibility.

Then there were Brandon and Rayena, two El'aras who had different goals. Rayena was here because of her belief that she had failed the Order, and Brandon had come along because he wanted a chance to fight. Gavin was going to give both of them that opportunity, regardless of whether or not they should do so.

Gaspar and Mekel rounded out the rest of the group. Mekel had joined because he wanted to help Gavin, but Gavin suspected there was more to it than that. He couldn't deny the enchanter's assistance, though. And Gaspar was here because he was Gavin's friend.

He was the one Gavin appreciated the most. He didn't have many friends, or at least he hadn't before coming to Yoran.

"Are you almost there?" Wrenlow's voice popped up in his ear, much clearer and louder than it had before.

"Almost," Gavin said. "And I can hear you just fine."

He could feel his connection to his communication

"Well, I'd be happy to show you, if you were so inclined."

"I am not."

"Is Perisaln part of El'aras lands?" Gavin asked.

"No," Tristan said. He had been mostly quiet during their journey, and this was the first time he'd spoken up. "It's a place that was once forgotten. And these days, none of the El'aras even venture that far."

"Unless they have," Gavin said. He still didn't know how Chauvan had discovered the key to the nihilar, but he must have found something that even Tristan had not uncovered.

"My family once did," Brandon said. "That was the rumor. Or prophecy. I don't know. I remember hearing about it when I was younger. 'The Storen hold the key to a great power.' Though if we did, I never saw it. None of us did. Maybe it was lost in the far north."

He fell silent, and Gavin peered over the dragon's side. The forest continued to loom beneath them, and then it was gone. They passed over a dark section of land, though he couldn't quite tell what it was. It looked like barren rock, and then it changed into what looked to be small, jagged ones. And then finally that shifted.

The scenery was starting to blur with how quickly they were flying. He couldn't imagine what the dragon's speed was, but the creature seemed to be pulling on him. Through their connection, Gavin could feel that not only was the dragon using the power he had pushed into the enchantment, but it seemed to be drawing through his core reserves.

No. Not just his core reserves, but the ring as well. Had he somehow done something to the dragon by channeling power through the ring?

The paper creature started to descend.

"Is it running out of power?" Gaspar asked, leaning close to him.

"I don't think so," Gavin said. "I didn't tell it to do anything. It seems to be doing this on its own."

"The enchantment knows," Tristan said.

Gaspar's eyes widened. "The dragon knows where it's going?"

Gavin rested his hand on the creature's back, and much like he'd felt with Tristan's enchantment, there was an energy that came from the dragon. A distinct sensation of power filled Gavin that he was all too aware of, and it left him questioning whether that power drew strength from him or from what Alana had placed in the enchantment.

"It must," he said.

When they landed, Gavin climbed down and stepped onto what appeared to be broken rock with scrub plants scattered around. A strange, distant rumble came from the north, and the dark clouds became illuminated by a hint of lightning that he hadn't seen when they were flying. The air was humid, almost damp, and unpleasant in a way that wasn't solely due to the moisture. There was something about it that he didn't quite like, though he couldn't put a finger on what or why.

"Perisaln was once a vibrant city," Tristan said, striding away from the dragon. He moved slowly and carefully, and there was something about his posture that had Gavin on edge. "It was a place that had drawn people from all over. This was a trade route." He motioned to a jagged section of rock. "You can almost imagine the road coming through here."

"Did you know it?" Gavin asked.

"Perisaln was a memory, even when I was young."

"What happened?" He looked over at Brandon, wondering if he would know more. If his family had some connection here, it was possible that he might.

Tristan shrugged. "The same that happens to all civilizations. Time shifts. People come and people leave. Things happen. The El'aras withdrew—if they were ever here—and no one else came to replace them."

"Why would there be a temple to the nihilar here?"

Tristan shook his head and frowned at Gavin. "I would not have thought there would be. I have spent centuries looking for information about the nihilar. Centuries trying to ensure the safety of our people."

"Safety?" Gavin asked.

"I'm not after the destruction of the El'aras."

"I'm not sure what you've been after, really."

"Not that," Tristan muttered. "But I won't deny that I have done things in ways the El'aras Council does not prefer."

"I'm sure you have," Gavin said.

"And it has put me at odds with those who think to lead." He nodded to Rayena. "But others see the truth. Others recognize what we need to do. Others have been willing to accompany me in this."

He strode away, and Rayena followed him, with Brandon staying behind her.

Gavin glanced over to Mekel. "Maybe you should activate one or two of your enchantments."

Mekel reached into his pouch, and he pulled out a pair of small figurines, set them on the ground, then activated them. It didn't take long before they evolved into massive stone golems, which marched after him.

Gaspar grabbed Gavin's arm. "Tristan's hiding something."

"I know."

"It has more to do with whatever this is. Maybe it's tied to what he's telling you. He's been looking and has been unable to find it, which must anger him, but I worry it's more than just that."

"I know."

"And you said he was working on trying to train you for centuries?"

"Somebody like me," Gavin said.

"And he's also been looking for this nihilar."

"Apparently."

"Don't you think that it doesn't make a whole lot of sense, though?"

Gavin pursed his lips. "There is quite a bit about all of this that doesn't make sense."

"But this in particular. This doesn't fit."

"Right. We should go, though."

Gaspar shrugged. "What about the dragon?"

"I might leave her like that. She's connected to me, and

I don't think that anybody can use her without my permission."

"Her?"

"You have to stop thinking about these enchantments as if they are something less than what they are," Gavin admonished.

"There you go again, boy. Trying to think that you know something. And here I thought you were making some progress."

Gavin chuckled. They started after the others, and Gaspar pulled a pair of knives from his pocket. He flipped them in his hands from side to side, an intensity in his gaze. It was the first time that Gavin had seen the old Gaspar back. Maybe leaving Yoran had been good for him. Or perhaps it was because they had a common threat.

"I know you have complicated feelings about him, but I don't trust him," Gaspar muttered.

"No," Gavin said. "I don't either, but I think he's trying to help in his own way."

"If he goes after this nihilar himself—"

"Then I will stop him."

Gaspar looked over and held his gaze for a long moment, twirling one knife as he did, an action he made look effortless. It was times like these that Gavin wondered if Gaspar had some aspect of power he hadn't acknowledged. Gavin had already suspected that Gaspar had some magical ability, as many of the constables did, though Gaspar never accessed it openly.

Gaspar slipped his knives back into his sheaths. "He can't be working alone," he said, keeping his gaze on Tristan. "The man you have mentioned. It's been my experience that somebody like that would have to have resources. Someone who is providing them with information. And if he finally started to find these temples, then he would have already uncovered those resources, wouldn't he?"

"Maybe," Gavin said.

"And if that's the case, we have to dig into who is most likely responsible. You've already seen how the sorcerers and the El'aras got along. If a power like that exists that can destroy the El'aras, you can be damn sure the sorcerers will be after it as well."

Gavin breathed out slowly. Gaspar was right.

He started forward, then hesitated as he felt something change. At first, he wasn't sure what it was, but he soon realized exactly what was happening. The ground was trembling, and it was coming from up ahead.

"Tell me you felt that," Gavin said.

"Oh, I felt it, boy."

"Then it means—"

Gavin didn't have a chance to finish. An almost overwhelming pressure began to build around him, suppressing his core reserves.

Chauvan and the others were here.

CHAPTER EIGHTEEN

Gavin hurriedly slipped on enchantments. He'd taken a dozen of each kind that he preferred, prepared for the possibility that he might burn through them rapidly. He slipped ones on for speed, strength, and stone skin, and the power within those enchantments suddenly surged through him.

Behind him, Gaspar grunted. Gavin spun, and Gaspar raced toward him.

"I assume you're enchanted," the old thief said.

"I have to be. I can't use my core reserves."

"You need to stop calling it that."

Gavin and Gaspar jogged and caught up to Brandon, Rayena, and Tristan. All of them had their swords unsheathed. Mekel was crouched down, setting figurines along the ground and activating them quickly. They stretched and grew, filling the space in mere moments. There was an energy here that made Gavin aware of the enchantments forming and taking hold. Could he do something similar? Hopefully there wouldn't be any way for Chauvan and his followers to overwhelm Mekel's creatures.

"The temple is supposed to be here somewhere," Tristan said. "If that's what they're after, they will try to reach the key."

"We don't even know if this is the last key, the second-to-last key, or..." Gavin shook his head. At this point, they didn't have many answers. "Wrenlow? Are you able to hear me still?"

"I can hear you," Wrenlow said. "It's a little faint, though not as bad as I thought it might be. You have to be leagues to the north."

"We're here. We found Perisaln, or at least the dragon did, and now I need you to help us figure out what the book says about getting into the temple."

Wrenlow was quiet for a few moments. "The book doesn't really give me any guidance on how to enter. It just says that it's there, and that you can find the key. Once you do, there is... oh. Wait. There's a picture here, though it's not very detailed."

"Anything you might have," Gavin said.

"I've told you that it's not easy to interpret. Well, not easy for me. I'm trying to help as much as I can, but I can't see anything you could use to get into the temple."

Gavin groaned. "What does it say? Which side does it face?"

"Which side?"

"Do you see an entrance?"

"Why don't you tell me what you're seeing, and I will tell you what I can gather from the picture."

"There's nothing but a pile of rocks."

"That's not quite true," Gaspar said, joining the conversation. "Look over here."

Gavin didn't have his core reserves, so he couldn't use his natural abilities to illuminate the sword, and he still hadn't gained the knack for holding on to his magic continuously anyway. That was part of the reason he was able to adjust to the nihilar suppression of his power as quickly as he did. But he did have an enchantment that might help.

He grabbed one for enhanced eyesight, slipped that on his finger, and everything immediately became brighter. It wasn't quite like daylight but was almost like shades of gray had lightened to show him contours and contrast he couldn't see otherwise.

Gaspar stood about a dozen paces away next to a pile of rock that looked to be tilted to one side. He was tracing his hands over something and frowning to himself.

Gavin joined him. The others were searching elsewhere, but he trusted Gaspar more than anyone here.

"Look at this," Gaspar said. "The language is strange, nothing like I have ever seen before. It looks like a bunch of symbols and shapes, but I don't know what is important and what isn't. I can't read any of this, but it seems like there has to be something significant here."

"What does it look like?" Wrenlow asked. "I could help you interpret it."

"It looks like a series of squiggles, some squares, some intersecting lines."

"Not like that," Wrenlow snapped. "I need actual descriptions. You need to work through each of them."

The ground continued to tremble, and the pressure upon Gavin was building.

"I'm not sure we have time for that," he said.

He looked over to Mekel, who had a dozen of his enchantments now activated. They were starting to form a circle around the group, but none of the creatures had anything to fight. They were basically useless at this point.

"Mekel, do you have any enchantments that might be able to move some stone for us?" He glanced to one of them.

The massive stone creature came over, with Mekel alongside it. "What do you need?"

"Move the rock around that opening there," he said, motioning to where Gaspar stood. He glanced around and realized that Tristan was nowhere to be seen. Rayena must have gone with him, and Brandon...

Brandon was staring off to the south, frowning and looking lost.

Some team this was.

Mekel's golem began to lift the enormous stones, shifting each one and setting it elsewhere. The golem didn't seem to have any difficulty with the stones. Soon, Mekel had more of the golems working together, five of them dragging rock away. The section that Gaspar had found led downward. The golems removed the rock and debris out of the way, but Gavin didn't think they were working quickly enough.

"There has to be some way to blast through it," he muttered.

"Can you do it?" Gaspar asked him.

"I'm not the Stone Breaker."

"I've seen you do it before."

"I have, but this time I don't have access to the same energies I did."

"What about that?" Gaspar asked, gesturing to the ring.

Gavin shrugged. "I can use the ring's power, but it's limited. I will only have one or two shots with it, and I might need to save that."

But he did have impervious skin. Maybe strength and that protective skin combined would help.

He jumped past one of the golems, and he reached for a boulder. Gavin brought his hand up, focused himself, and drove it down, using the power of the enchantment. The stone cracked, splitting with a loud shriek of strange energy. It wasn't just rock, he realized. There was some metal in it. Gavin brought his fist up then down again.

After three blows, he could feel the power in his enchantments already starting to fade. He had about a dozen of each kind. If he was using that much magic with only a few blows, he didn't dare risk wasting all that power—not if they still had to face Chauvan and the nihilar.

Gavin climbed down. "It's not going to work."

"Or is it?" Gaspar said, motioning.

An opening had formed in the stone, which led down into the darkness.

Gavin turned to Mekel. "Keep your golems out here and have them defend this space. Don't let anything but us come out of here."

"I could go with you," Mekel said. "I want to help. After what you did for my people, I feel that I have to do something, whatever it is, to help you."

Gavin started to walk away, but he thought better of it and headed back to Mekel. Gavin had gone to the enchanters in Yoran many times, and they had offered their assistance whenever he asked for it. But he knew that he had to be careful not to take advantage of that. Perhaps he had already.

Now he had to do something else, for Mekel.

"This is how you are going to help," he said. "You and your golems are the best at protecting us. I'm going to need that. You might be the only one able to."

Mekel regarded him for a long moment. Finally, he nodded.

Gavin whistled, and Brandon looked over. "We are going down."

Brandon jogged over to him. "Where did she go?"

Gavin had lost track of where Rayena and Tristan had gone, but he didn't know if they had any time to linger. He had no idea what Chauvan was going to do, but he had a feeling that they were running low on time. As the ground continued to rumble, Gavin couldn't help but feel as if they had to move quickly. The rumbling had to be the result of something Chauvan had done, and though he didn't know what it was, he knew they had to stop it.

He scrambled into the opening. Once inside, a light started to glow softly, revealing smooth walls that reflected some of the light. The unusual glimmer hinted at metal within it, much like what had been found outside.

"Now where?" Brandon asked, shoving his way closer to Gavin.

"Deeper into the tunnel."

They forced their way forward. There was a small gap in the rock, but when it started to thin, Gavin slipped on more enchantments for stone skin and strength, and he punched his way through it. If he had access to his core reserves and El'aras power, he would've been able to break through it more easily. With that much power, he might've been able to blast directly down to it.

The pressure on him, that nihilar energy, continued to squeeze.

"You don't have to come down here," Gavin said to the others.

Brandon frowned. "I have these," he said, holding up a wrist covered with bracelets that were enchanted. "Why do I need anything else?"

Gavin snorted. "I just want to make sure you have enough power. Don't want you to get caught down here."

"I'm not getting caught anywhere. Besides, if I didn't try to take a look at this, my family would never forgive me. We moved from these lands. I don't know if it was Perisaln, but it feels like it could have been. If I can learn anything about my people, I need to bring it back."

He disappeared down the narrowing tunnel, leaving Gavin and Gaspar alone.

"Are you sure you can trust that one?" Gaspar whispered.

"Aren't you the one who is trying to tell me I need to trust?"

"I just wanted to know how much you vetted him. I figured that you must have tried to find out whether or not he's safe for this."

"As much as I could, but there was only so much I was able to do during our travels. Between fighting enchantments, the nihilar, and generally staying alive, I haven't had much time to question my team."

Gaspar arched a brow at him but said nothing.

They followed Brandon, and the opening started to widen. The metal in the walls reflected even more light, and Gavin found himself staring for a moment, trying to understand just what was here.

"I can't help but wonder if all of this was built below the ground," he said, "or if it sank over time. The temple at Hester was like this, with descending stairs."

If he was right, there would be another, similar section of the temple. An opening, then a set of stairs.

The walls started to shake, and the ground beneath Brandon trembled and began to collapse.

"Brandon!" Gavin shouted. He turned back, but boulders were slamming downward. He lunged forward, calling on the power of his El'aras ring and the energy within his enchantments, and he drove himself through the rocks that had nearly toppled onto Brandon.

Gavin tumbled down the stairs the rest of the way, and he came to a skittering stop in a large, open chamber. The trembling persisted, and the pressure upon him continued to build.

He got to his feet and looked around. He was not alone, and he found himself surrounded by five black-robed figures. Gavin sighed and unsheathed his sword.

"You're too late," one of them said. Gavin wasn't sure that this was Chauvan, but he couldn't help but feel as if there was a different power here than he'd experienced before. Could it just be the nihilar pressing down on it?

Gavin brought his sword around toward the figure nearest him as he drew on the power of his enchantments. They blocked him with his black blade. It had to be Chauvan.

"I know all about you," Gavin said.

Chauvan chuckled. "I doubt you know *all* about me."

He twisted and carved his blade at Gavin, who was forced back a step. Gavin had to be careful. He was ringed by the others with Chauvan, and together they used some aspect of the nihilar power to hold them. The ground continued to rumble, making Gavin's footing uneasy.

As they fought, Gavin recognized Chauvan's skill. He moved much like Gavin did, shifting techniques and patterns in a way that forced Gavin to alter his techniques rapidly and cycle through various strategies. Not only did Gavin have to avoid the quick thrusts, but part of him was concerned about whether Chauvan's blade might be poisoned the way Tristan had trained them.

The man twisted. "Did you think that he didn't teach me all of those styles?"

Gavin jumped, drawing on the strength and speed enchantments while coming to land behind his opponent, but Chauvan had already reacted and spun toward him with his sword. Gavin was forced to be on the defensive again.

Chauvan laughed. "Soon this will be over, and so will your pain."

"I don't have any pain."

"Oh, but you do."

Chauvan lunged. The movement was quick, even faster than Gavin could move despite the enchantments he carried. As the blade neared, he slammed his hand down toward it. It would be better to catch it with the top of his hand rather than be disemboweled by it, but instead of the blade striking his hand, it met one of the enchantments he wore. Gavin instinctively found himself forcing power out through it.

For a moment, he thought the weapon had struck his El'aras ring, which he didn't want to lose. As much as he questioned whether he truly deserved the ring, it gave him access to power that he couldn't have otherwise. It strengthened him, allowing him to channel some source of El'aras energy that was far greater than what he had on his own.

But it didn't strike the El'aras ring. It was one of his enchantments for strength.

As it cracked, Gavin's power quickly faded. He tried to turn, but without the enchantment, he was off balance. He stumbled, spinning, and he careened toward one of the nihilar men and almost crashed into him—just as the man sank to the ground.

Brandon locked eyes with Gavin and grinned. "These enchantments are fantastic. I need more of them."

Gavin slipped another bracelet for strength onto his hand, and on a whim, he grabbed one more. He would use as many as he needed in order to destroy Chauvan.

He spun, but Chauvan didn't even react, as if unconcerned. Gavin didn't blame him. Without his core reserves or the El'aras ring, he couldn't counter somebody like this. The man was too fast.

There had to be some way of neutralizing the effect of the nihilar, but he wasn't sure what it was going to take or whether he could even do it.

Gavin darted forward, trying to get to Chauvan and using enchantments to power himself forward. The shadows seemed to fold around his opponent, the way they had when Gavin had first faced him.

He was gone.

Gavin spun around and barely raised his sword in time to block a blow that had come from behind, where Chauvan had reappeared.

The man laughed. "And he thought you could be the Champion? Unfortunately, even a champion can fall. One must find the right power."

"Apparently, you found the power and want to destroy all that you are?"

"I am none of this, but I will be all of it."

Chauvan twisted, and the ground trembled.

Gavin needed more time. Not much, but long enough to disrupt whatever Chauvan thought to use to get to this key.

Thoughts raced through his mind as he tried to think of ways to buy time. Distantly, Gavin was aware that Brandon was fighting several of the nihilar, but facing two at one time meant that he was limited. Gaspar had to be here as well, but how effective would he be?

Chauvan chuckled. "Do you know how long he looked for this?"

"He told me."

"Interesting. He admitted his failings?"

"He told me about you, didn't he?"

If Gavin could make him angry, the emotion might make his foe fight off balance. He doubted that Chauvan was so unskilled as to fall for that trap, though. Tristan would have trained him to be aware of that type of tactic.

Chauvan sneered. "I wonder what he would say about *you*."

"He would say that I was his Champion."

"Perhaps." He jumped back, then brought his blade up.

Gavin prepared to defend against another attack, but it didn't come. Instead, Chauvan slammed his blade down in the center of the room, into the stone. The trembling that Gavin had felt all around him suddenly ceased. Everything went still.

Chauvan looked up, hand still on the sword, and then he twisted it. Some part of the stone itself seemed to turn with the blade.

He locked eyes with Gavin. "And yet you still fail."

Gavin raced toward him as someone shouted his name.

Tristan.

Chauvan struck out with his weapon, pushing Gavin back. Tristan and Rayena entered the chamber, but not from the direction he had come in. They found another entrance?

The two of them strode toward Chauvan. Neither of them unsheathed their blades.

Chauvan pulled his sword from the stone and nodded to Tristan. The shadows around him folded into a point, then stabbed into Rayena's belly. She sank to the ground, and Chauvan and Tristan disappeared within those shadows.

Gavin darted forward, but the shadows surrounded Chauvan and Tristan and blocked him from being able to do anything. When the shadows cleared, they were gone.

He stood in place for a moment, panting. He looked around and saw Gaspar facing two of the nihilar. Gavin jumped toward them, thrusting his blade into one, while Gaspar finished off the other. By the time Gavin spun around, Brandon had taken care of the others.

"What happened?" Gaspar asked.

Gavin reached for Rayena, but she lay motionless. Her eyes were closed, her breathing was slow, but he saw no blood. He scooped her up.

"I'm not sure." He turned back to the center of the room. "Chauvan did something by stabbing his sword into the ground, and then there was a change in the stone. I have no idea what happened, or how he disappeared. And Tristan went with him."

"Why did he do that to her?" Brandon asked. "I thought she trained with him."

Gaspar took Rayena from Gavin. She had sacrificed so much on behalf of the Order that Gavin could scarcely believe that she deserved this. But she wasn't dead. Not yet. Maybe they could help.

Gavin had begun to believe that Tristan wouldn't betray him, that he would actually help them. That had been a mistake, like too many other times he had started to believe that Tristan might actually care.

Why could Gavin trust him, but no one else?

"We need to get out of here," he said.

The ground had started to rumble again, and he had no idea what would happen. It could split open, swallowing them, and then there would be no way of escaping. At least he could call on his core reserves now.

Brandon let out a small laugh, though it faded as he looked over to Rayena. "I've never seen a man blast through stone like that before. Pretty impressive. I guess that's how you got your nickname. You're the breaker of everything."

Gavin looked at the motionless form of Rayena as she rested in Gaspar's arms. "I wasn't enough. Let's go."

They raced along the narrow corridors. His heart hammered as the stone continued to tremble. How much time did they have? Probably not long at all. He needed to keep moving, and when a boulder blocked his way, he hacked at it until it shattered. By the time they exited the temple, he found Mekel standing with one of his stone golems outside the opening. Mekel looked at him, and Gavin shook his head in frustration.

Gavin tapped on the enchantment in his ear. "Wrenlow?"

"What is it? Did you stop him?"

"No. And now we don't have Tristan."

"Oh. Did he—"

"I don't know," Gavin said.

"I suppose you want to know where to go next."

Gavin made his way over to the dragon. He climbed onto the creature's back, running his hand on the paper scales. Frustration filled him. He knew that it shouldn't, that he was only feeding into Tristan's plan for him, but he couldn't help himself. All of this, only to end up betrayed again.

If he failed, and if Chauvan succeeded, what would happen to the rest of the El'aras?

Worse, there was some distant part of him that questioned if it even mattered. The El'aras had retreated from the world for the most part, and all Chauvan intended to do was completely remove them.

Gavin pushed those thoughts away. "That would be helpful," he said to Wrenlow. "We need the third temple. It has to be someplace."

"I'm looking. The last one is difficult. The first two were pretty easy. But then again, he found the first one, and the second one was familiar to me because I've been following some of these old El'aras languages and trying to understand the writing in the hall, thinking that I might—"

"Wrenlow," Gavin said.

"Right. Stay focused. I'm trying. I just wanted to let you know that the first two were easier than this last one. I've been digging into it, and I can't really come up with anything."

"Well, we'll make our way back to you."

"Are you sure you want to?"

"I don't know that there's anything more here for us to do," Gavin said.

"You can wait there until I figure it out."

Thunder rumbled in the distance, and Gavin frowned as he looked up at the sky. "I'm not sure that makes a lot of sense either. I don't know what's out here, but I don't really want to stay exposed while we're waiting. We can head back to you."

The others climbed onto the dragon, none of them saying anything. Gaspar had ahold of Rayena's body, and she was not moving. They took to the air in silence, though Gavin didn't know what there was for them to say. The dragon flew almost solemnly, as if sensing Gavin's mood.

After a moment, Wrenlow piped in again. "I did it. I figured out the third temple. It's in a place not terribly far from Yoran, so if you return, maybe I can come with you."

"It won't be safe for you if we have to take on Chauvan and the others," Gavin said. "I'm not sure I'm going to be enough alone, but I'll have help." The next time he took them on, he was going to have the enchantments working with him. With enough stone golems, he had to believe they could bring down Chauvan. "Where is it?"

"Can't say that I've ever heard of it. It is El'aras as well, at least from what I can piece together."

Gavin's heart started to hammer. "What is it?"

"I think it is pronounced Adashin. Then again, I could be wrong. The language is old and difficult for me to fully interpret."

Gavin stared straight ahead. "No. That's not what it's called. It's called Arashil."

"Oh. You know it. Then you should be able to get there quickly, and then you can stop him."

Gavin shook his head. "It's already too late. If he's gone after Arashil, then he's already accessed that key."

Which meant they were too late. Chauvan would reach the nihilar.

CHAPTER NINETEEN

The dragon circled as Gavin's mind raced to come up with different possibilities. Arashil had to have been some part of it, but if so, why would Tristan have placed the sculpture there? It didn't make any sense. None of it did. But the small figurine and the book had been in Arashil. The larger sculpture had been in Hester. What had been in Perisaln?

Gaspar leaned close to him. "We can still stop this."

Gavin said nothing. He appreciated his friend's confidence, but it was a confidence he didn't feel himself.

"Gavin?"

He looked up from staring out into the distance. He hated the idea of failing, especially at the hands of somebody who had been trained by Tristan too. That competitive drive had always pushed him, and it was pushing him even now. He would not fail.

"What did you find, Wrenlow?"

"I'm not exactly sure. Not yet. There's something here." He fell silent for a few moments, before speaking up again. "I keep digging into these three different temples, and there's something more at each of them."

"I'm starting to think that there is reference to a statue and a book?"

"Not that," Wrenlow said. "I don't see any sign of that, at least not that I've been able to tell so far. I haven't had the opportunity to read through it much, though, so I could be wrong."

That surprised Gavin. If there was no mention of the statues or the book, then why would they have been in those two locations?

They were the two that Tristan was aware of. But he hadn't known about Perisaln. All this time, all the years he'd been looking, Tristan had not been able to find that temple. That had taken Wrenlow's help.

Gavin looked back to where Rayena lay unmoving. They needed to wake her up.

"See if you can't stir her," he said to Gaspar.

He nodded. "I can't tell what happened to her."

"I don't know either." Chauvan had done something to her, but there was no blood, no sign of any attack. She was still alive, but obviously weakened. Had he affected her El'aras magic somehow?

"Anyway," Wrenlow said, his voice difficult to hear over the sound of the wind whipping around them as the dragon circled, "there is something else. Getting to the keys is just part of it. There's one more thing."

Gavin frowned. "What?"

"It's a place for the gateway. Or doorway? Again, I'm not quite sure. The language is difficult for me to read, and it's old enough that I can't tell what this is trying to say."

"Can you tell where it is?"

"That's just it, it looks like it should be in the middle of the different angles formed by the other cities. Or temples. Whatever they are."

Gavin started focusing, thinking about what was there. To his surprise, the dragon started to turn on its own.

"Where are we going?" Gaspar muttered.

"To the gateway, it seems."

"It looks like we're heading back to Yoran."

Gavin nodded. "That's my fear."

Too often, it felt as if everything pulled him back there. That's where his destiny was, somehow, entwined with the fate of the city.

Could this be one more thing that was focused on that place? They had been through enough, hadn't they? Over the time he had been in Yoran, it had been the target of so many different attacks. And he thought it had finally been stabilized.

But what if this was just one more assault?

"It's not the city," Wrenlow said. "At least, it doesn't seem that way. Close enough, but it wouldn't put you in the center of the city. Thankfully. Since it's not in Yoran, you don't have to worry about Davel getting mad at you this time."

Gavin snorted. "I'm sure he'll find a way."

He frowned as the dragon still seemed to be streaking

toward Yoran, and though he tried to figure out just where the dragon was heading, he had a hard time coming up with the answer. If it wasn't Yoran, Gavin didn't know where it was going to be.

"So where what is it, then?" he asked.

"You mentioned some place beyond the city that you traveled to with Anna?"

Gavin froze. "Yes."

"That was an old El'aras place, wasn't it?"

"It very much was."

"And from what I can figure out, it seems like that would be the point of intersect. I can send help. It might take some time to get there, but—"

"No," Gavin said. "Anybody who comes out here and puts themselves against Chauvan and the other followers of the nihilar might not survive."

There was a moment of silence. "You know the people would help you," Wrenlow said.

Gavin swallowed. "I know."

But this was on him. He had followed the trail to Tristan. He had helped with whatever Tristan had intended. And he was the reason that Chauvan would succeed in whatever plan he had.

Now Gavin had to stop him.

He remained tucked down on the dragon as they streaked forward. The others were quiet, and even if they were talking, he wasn't sure he would hear them because of the howling wind.

After a while, Gaspar's voice came through the enchantment. "What will happen if he succeeds?"

Gavin didn't have a good answer. Was it an if or a when?

Gaspar seemed to read his mind. "If, boy. We don't know that he's going to succeed. And if there's anyone who can stop them, it's you."

Gavin sighed. "I was starting to believe that. I was starting to believe I was the culmination of everything Tristan had been trying to accomplish over the years, but I think he was still using me. And maybe Chauvan is what I thought *I* was."

"You have to get Tristan out of your head. He doesn't hold sway over you any longer. I would've never figured you to be someone who would get caught up like that with one person, but I suppose you've known him too long for him to not be important."

Gavin clutched the dragon as they raced forward, his fingers holding the hard paper, the wind threatening to pull him free. "Maybe."

"You got to shake your issues with him, boy. Not exactly sure what it is that has you so knotted up with him, but—"

"You once told me about the woman who taught you your second career."

Gaspar nodded, but he didn't say anything.

"How do you feel about her?"

"Well, she could be tough, but she was my mentor. I think it was different for me with her, though. I didn't go to her when I was young. I went to her when I was looking for something else. A different way, maybe."

Perhaps that was all it was. Gavin's issues with Tristan

stemmed from the fact that he was the father figure Gavin never had. Giving up on Tristan was like giving up on his father.

"I just don't—"

"What is that?" Brandon's voice rang out above the wind, and Gavin craned his neck to see.

In the distance, there was a bloom of shadows along the ground, seeming to absorb the little light that was there. Gavin could make out the city of Yoran from afar, lights glowing in several windows, but the old El'aras ruins were what caught his attention. That was where they were going now.

He leaned toward the dragon. "I need you to set us down outside of it."

The creature circled and began to descend. As they slowly neared the ground, Gavin jumped free and unsheathed his sword. The others climbed off and only Rayena remained. They spread out, swords at the ready, enchantments in place.

Gavin frowned for a moment and tapped on the dragon. "Circle above us. If it looks like we need help, dive down to me."

"Do you really think the dragon is going to understand what you're asking of it?" Gaspar asked.

Gavin ignored him and continued speaking to the dragon. "Maybe you leave that one behind. Or you can eat him."

Gaspar scoffed. "It's an enchantment. It doesn't need to eat."

"Don't listen to him."

The dragon turned its head, and for a moment, it locked eyes with Gavin. There was a surge of the connected energy between them, and then it took to the air again, massive paper wings carrying it into the sky until it circled overhead.

"You know that's not alive, don't you?" Gaspar insisted.

Gavin brushed off the comment, turning to Mekel. "I need your enchantments to surround this entire area."

"Where are we?" he asked.

"We are just outside the borders of Yoran. There's an old El'aras ruin out here, which connects to the city through the tunnels."

Mekel's eyes widened. "Why here?"

"I've been asking that question for a while."

It all had to be linked to this place, but maybe it was because of the connection to the nihilar. Or maybe it was simply that the El'aras had made this place important. Or perhaps it was even older than that. Gavin had no idea what ancient powers had existed here and whether anything about that mattered. None of that was his concern right now.

"We can have the enchantments encircle the space, but it's not going to help us unless we know what's there," Gaspar said.

Gavin had already thought of that. He pulled the three paper ravens from his pocket, set them on the ground, and tapped each of them. As they unfolded, growing large enough to be nearly the same size as real ravens, he connected to them. The images that came from them suddenly surged in his mind.

"We will use the ravens to help guide us," he explained.

"Inside of that?"

Images of dark clouds formed in front of him—the nihilar, he assumed—and he didn't think that the paper ravens would suffer inside the ruins. He didn't know, though.

"So far, we've seen that enchantments aren't diminished," he said. "At least, not those created by the enchanters. I don't know if sorcery enchantments or El'aras-made ones are affected."

He hadn't spoken to Wrenlow or Gaspar about using the communication enchantment Anna had made while they fought Chauvan, so there was a real possibility that the El'aras enchantments wouldn't work. The magic was different, and it came from a different place and had a different use. The nihilar might only selectively suppress El'aras magic.

"And then what?" Gaspar said.

"We find Chauvan and Tristan, and then we stop them."

"Are you sure you're up for this, boy?"

Gavin turned to him. "I am."

Mekel finished stacking enchantments on the ground. He had placed nearly three dozen, and he quickly went to work, touching each of them to active them. They all started stretching, elongating, and growing. They were different shapes, but almost all of them were made out of stone. He sent the first of them marching away.

"I triggered them to focus on anyone who isn't us," Mekel said.

Brandon started laughing. "And what happens if you have friends who decide to join?"

"No one else is coming," Gavin said.

Brandon looked over and cocked his head to the side, his frown deepening. "This is it? Just the us, taking on whatever this is?" He motioned to the dark cloud nearby.

It seemed impossible. And Gavin agreed.

They were attempting to go after the nihilar, thinking that they could take down all of what lay ahead. But was it just the three of them? They would have Mekel's enchantments. They would have the power Gavin could summon. They would have…

Something crackled in his ear.

"Just wait a little longer," Wrenlow said. His voice sounded clear, and louder than it had been.

"What are you doing?" Gavin asked.

"I'm not letting you risk yourself like this. You've helped so many people. They're coming to help you this time."

"This isn't about protecting Yoran."

"No. It's about protecting your people."

Gavin turned to see the stout and heavily muscled form of Davel Chan riding on what looked to be a small wooden wagon, one that was self-propelled. His dozens of enchantments encircling his wrists and fingers seemed to glitter with their own light. He jumped down, nodding to the others who were on several dozen similar wooden wagons. They carried constables and enchanters, all armed with heavy enchantments and weapons.

"What are you doing?" Gavin said to Davel, pulling

him to the side. "This isn't your fight. Gods, I don't even know if this is my fight. It's about protecting my people."

The darkness near him continued to build, and though he couldn't feel anything from within it, he suspected that whatever Chauvan intended would happen fairly soon.

"You helped protect mine," Davel said.

"I protected your city."

"Those were my people. You didn't have to stay in Yoran, but even when the fight wasn't your own, you protected them. I figure I might as well repay the favor."

"This isn't going to be anything like what we've dealt with before."

"Oh, I'm sure that's true. Every time you and I get tangled up in something, it ends up worse than the last one. But seeing as how we are just outside of Yoran, we might end up dealing with this anyway."

"So, it's not all about helping me."

"I wouldn't be outside the city if it weren't."

Gavin regarded Davel for a long moment, trying to decide what to say, but maybe he should just be thankful. This was how Tristan, and others who had faced him before, had always underestimated him. It wasn't about the magic, the power, or being the Chain Breaker that had mattered at all. It was about the people and the teams he had managed to create.

And he wouldn't be facing Chauvan on his own.

Gavin nodded to Davel, then turned to Mekel. "You're going to need to make sure they don't attack any of the constables or enchanters as well."

"Already done."

Gavin looked around. "Davel, we should have each of your people pair up with one of the golems. The combination should offer a bit of protection. And if the enchantments work the way I think they do, we should be able to power through the attackers."

And it was more than just that. He believed that by using the combination, they would be able to overwhelm their opponents.

Davel's constables separated, moving out and taking up positions around the stone pillars scattered about the ancient El'aras ruins. Davel stayed near Gavin and Gaspar, with Brandon just a step behind.

"Well," Gaspar said, "are you going to deploy your ravens?"

"I will. I'm just waiting a moment."

"And then?"

"We have to be prepared."

Gaspar snorted. "We will be. But will you?"

Gavin glanced over, and he nodded slowly, knowing what Gaspar wanted him to be ready for. It was more than just preparing for what he was going to have to face. It was about readying to confront Tristan, and all of Gavin's conflicted emotions when it came to him.

He looked down at the ravens, then tipped his head. Some connection between them triggered, and the ravens took flight, circling for a moment before diving toward the cloud around them. Gavin didn't know what was going to happen as soon as the ravens struck the dark shadows that swirled around the ruins, but he thought they would be able to make it through.

He closed his eyes and focused on the images he saw from them. When they reached the darkness, Gavin didn't see much of anything. The ravens looked at the world in a different way. One of them saw gradations in heat, another saw things in different shadows, and the third saw slightly desaturated colorations. Gavin could use the three images and piece them together in his mind, and he'd done that in the past to help him fight. But he'd also seen the ravens fail.

The birds penetrated the fog, and the shadows that remained pushed against them, as if the ravens were struggling against some great power. Gavin tried to reach for his core reserves, and he breathed a sigh of relief that the nihilar hadn't tried to suppress his magic yet. He was not expecting that to last for much longer. Eventually, they would turn their attention to him—unless he didn't matter.

His vision with the ravens started to clear, and an image of the ruins took shape. This was one of the first places he had ever used the ravens, and they circled above as though they knew where they needed to go.

They showed him an image of the nihilar. Dozens upon dozens of them. More than Gavin had expected.

"What are you seeing, boy?" Gaspar asked.

"We might be overmatched," he said, not opening his eyes out of fear of becoming distracted from the images. "There are quite a few more of these attackers than I had expected..."

But where were Chauvan and Tristan? The rest of the nihilar were around the ruins, but he didn't see those two.

"They have to be underground somewhere," Gavin said, mostly to himself.

"What?" Gaspar said.

Gavin opened his eyes. "The same as we've seen at the other temples. They go underground. That's where we have to head." He looked to Mekel. "Whenever you're ready, signal to your enchantments." He turned to Davel. "And you?"

Davel offered a hint of a smile. "What about me? My people already know what they need to do."

Gavin glanced over to Gaspar. "Then it's time."

"Let's get it over with."

With a coordinated surge, they all started forward. It surprised Gavin how quickly everybody managed to move in sync, knowing what they needed to do almost as if they were of one mind. The stone enchantments and the constables walked into the dark cloud.

Gavin looked over to Brandon. "This is going to be painful."

"You loaded me up," he said, holding up both arms. They were covered in enchantments from wrist to elbow. "I think I'll be fine."

Gavin hoped that would be the case.

The pressure of the nihilar hit him immediately as he stepped forward. He recognized how that squeezed him and knew exactly what was happening, but he didn't know if he was going to be able to withstand it for too long. He could feel the energy, the effort, and he could feel some part of it pressing down on him, the power all around him oppressive.

him. When he used his core reserves, he had no difficulty, but this was something different.

He stumbled, and the stone enchantment moved toward him. Gavin instinctively brought his hands up, and the golem stopped, frozen in place. Part of him could feel a connection. He hadn't been fully aware of it before, but now he could, distinct and buried within him.

"What happened?" Gaspar asked.

"It seems to have responded to me."

"Well, that *is* unexpected."

"Now we need to go and—"

Other enchantments appeared on either side of them.

"Attack them," Gavin commanded. He tried to put some of his power into the words, having no idea if it would even work, but the golem stormed toward the nearest one.

A strange battle began among the creatures, all made out of rock and earth, and he stood back and watched. The massive stone golems drove enormous fists at each other, the sound a terrible thunder that rumbled. Chunks of stone and debris rained down as the monsters fought, like mountains beating one another.

"This isn't over," Gaspar said.

Gavin shook himself out of watching the bizarre spectacle. "You're right. I need to get moving."

He stumbled forward before righting himself, and he was able to gain control over the movements he had been struggling with as he continued forward. He looked up at the dark beam of power shooting into the sky. It still seemed as though it were pushing power out, squeezing down on him.

"I need to get rid of that pressure," Gavin said. "The nihilar is just too much for me."

Gaspar grunted. "You don't need to worry about that. Focus on stopping the other two."

"If it's only two." Gavin took a deep breath, reached into his cloak pockets, and grabbed several more enchantments. He slapped them onto his wrists and slid a few rings onto his fingers. "Let's go."

"You sound like you're marching into death."

"I feel like we are."

As they walked forward, the sounds of the battle rang out behind them. Stone smacked against stone; the crashing power of the monstrous enchantments battling one another. He was tempted to turn and watch, but he ignored it and raced ahead. He could feel something as he did, some energy within him, and started to worry that perhaps the nihilar was shifting.

Then he saw Tristan, who stood alone.

Where was Chauvan?

Gavin approached slowly, gripping his sword. Anger started to fill him. Gaspar joined him, and Gavin was thankful for his friend. He felt grateful that he didn't have to do this by himself, but he was not even sure if he was ready to take on Tristan if it came down to it.

"Tristan!" Gavin shouted. "You used me again."

Tristan turned, glancing past him toward the beam of energy shooting up from the center of the boulders—from deep within the El'aras hall. The light poured into the darkness of the night. Gavin advanced carefully.

"I thought I could do this," Tristan said. He didn't look over or try to attack. He seemed tense in a way that Gavin had rarely seen before. "I thought that I could be the Champion, but when it became clear, I started searching for others."

"Why?"

"You learned about the prophecy here."

Gavin kept distance between him and Tristan, worried about what he might try. This all felt like some ploy, which left him uneasy. "The prophecy the Sul'toral created."

"I told you there was another. A greater one that involves all of the El'aras, and it included the nihilar."

"The great shadow," Gavin said.

Tristan looked over to him. "Partly. That is only one aspect of it."

"I don't understand."

"I couldn't find Perisaln. I used you, Gavin. I'm sorry, but it was necessary."

"Because you wanted to be here for this."

"Because *you* needed to be here for this."

Faster than Gavin could react, Tristan sped forward and lashed out, grabbing his wrist. Though Gavin tried to pull back, he could not break free of Tristan's grip. Gaspar tried to get to them, but Tristan had some enchantment in hand that pushed out with a surge of power that prevented him from doing so. With a jerk, Tristan pulled on Gavin, tossing him into the darkness.

Gavin cried out, but there was no pain. There was only the sensation of falling, a strange burning that worked through him, and then he landed.

He glanced around at a place he had been before. He knew what was here, and he had even been inside the main chamber. The power he felt around him was also familiar. It tried to blaze through him, to eradicate the El'aras part of him. He resisted the temptation to call on his core reserves. If he did, he knew what would happen.

Gavin squeezed his sword. He had shifted it so that he now held it with the hand that bore the El'aras ring. Some part of that ring constricted him painfully, like a warning to him.

He tapped on his enchantment, calling out to Gaspar and to Wrenlow, but he didn't really expect them to answer. Even though he had used his El'aras abilities to connect to and enhance the enchantment in some way, he didn't think it would work when suppressed by the nihilar.

Gavin looked around and saw no signs of Chauvan, but he knew the man had to be here. Though he had been unsuccessful when they had faced each other, he wasn't afraid, but he recognized a superior opponent. If Gavin had access to his full potential—his El'aras abilities, his core reserves, the ring—it would be a different matter.

But Chauvan was in his element here.

And Gavin was alone.

Could that have been what Tristan wanted all along? Pit his two potential Champions against each other?

Gavin had gotten further than Chauvan. At least, he

believed he had, but what if he had not? He had managed to find the sword and the ring, and he had become known as the El'aras Champion, but Chauvan had gained access to the nihilar. Maybe they were both Tristan's Champions.

He made his way along the hall, which was narrow with a low ceiling. He remembered his walk through here last time, how he had been readying himself and his team to face a Sul'toral. He'd come with people he felt unsure of, rather than the team he would have preferred, but it had been a team nonetheless.

And now he was here on his own.

He wanted his people, but perhaps it was better that this was just him.

Gavin knew exactly how to find the large chamber where he had faced the Sul'toral previously. Perhaps that Sul'toral had known about the nihilar. Or maybe this was all just chance. The sorcerer had been after Anna, after the Shard, at the time. All because he believed there was something significant about Yoran.

"I wasn't sure if you would come."

To Gavin's enchanted eyes, the darkness seemed to fill everything, though there were contours of light within it. He reached into his pocket, grabbed a couple of enchantments, and dropped them behind him. He had no idea if he could activate them, but he wanted to be prepared for the possibility that he might be able to. So far, the enchantments he carried on him were not deactivated by the nihilar. Perhaps they would not be.

"I didn't have much of a choice. Tristan wanted me to be here."

"One Champion versus another." The hood on Chauvan's black cloak was pulled up, obscuring his face. He started to laugh, his voice dark and filled with anger. "I was close before you found it."

"Before I found the statue?"

"Before you found the ring. I would've been the true Champion."

"I'm sorry to disappoint you."

"Oh, you did not. You might've made it easier for me to fulfill my destiny."

Chauvan lunged at him, and Gavin was ready. He had been drawing on his enchantments, and he had placed so many on himself that he would have speed and strength and stone skin. He would need all of it. It wasn't the same as having the power of the El'aras ring, nor was it the same as having access to his core reserves, but it was a start.

Gavin met him blade for blade. Flurries of movement came fast, furious, the kind of fighting that only two masters could manage. The sound of their swords clanging against each other filled the entirety of this space.

They bounced back and paused their fighting.

Chauvan chuckled. "He taught you well."

"And you."

"You must have some appreciation for how difficult it is to find an adequate sparring partner."

Gavin shrugged. "Some."

Chauvan launched himself forward, and Gavin reacted by twisting, slashing, and bringing his blade around, forced into a series of quick movements. The only thing that had been effective for him before had been the Leier fighting style, but as he danced backward in those techniques, Chauvan matched him.

His opponent let out a small laugh. "It took me a while to piece this one together. An interesting style. Who did you learn it from?"

"A friend."

Gavin darted toward him, pulling on his enchantments that granted him speed and strength. When he reached Chauvan, he tried to drive his blade into the man's stomach but missed. Chauvan grabbed for Gavin's wrist, and Gavin jerked back, then went tumbling off to the side.

"I have never had much use for friends."

"I hadn't either," Gavin said. "I learned otherwise."

"You learn to depend on those who will disappoint you."

"I learned to depend on those who can help me."

Chauvan laughed again. His voice was hard and angry, and Gavin clenched his fists. He had to push down his hatred, though. Chauvan was trying to get to him.

When he leapt at Gavin again, Gavin was controlled and ready. He spun, sweeping his blade down, and at the last moment, he twisted it around. He used a mixture of Leier with Hiv, two styles that were seemingly incompatible, but he created something new. He brought his sword up and was rewarded with a grunt.

He thought Chauvan would drop his blade, but Gavin was wrong. The man had been trained by Tristan, just as Gavin had. He would have learned to suppress pain or any reaction, and he would have learned that there was no stopping until the fight was won or you were dead.

A blow to Gavin's side forced the sword out of his hand. As it went skittering away, he immediately switched into a grappling style, trying to sweep toward Chauvan, but he was blocked. He brought his fist up to connect with Chauvan's chin, but his opponent twisted, impossibly fast.

Perhaps the man was enchanted, or maybe he still had access to his magic—his core reserves, El'aras abilities, or whatever it was that granted his power. Regardless, Gavin couldn't get to him.

Chauvan pushed him away. "And you were supposed to be a Champion."

He lunged for Gavin, who kicked and swept his leg around, but Chauvan grabbed it. He forced Gavin down.

"You remember what it was like when you were first learning from him?" He grabbed Gavin's wrist and bent his arm behind his back.

Gavin was prepared to break his own arm if necessary to get free. He could fight one-handed and with his legs.

Chauvan seemed to know what Gavin intended, and he slammed him down onto the ground. Gavin's head bounced off the stone, and for a moment, everything went black. It happened for the briefest moment, but long enough that Gavin lost track of everything.

He felt hands on him, but then they were gone. So was the pressure. Gavin rolled over, rubbing his head. Chauvan had not only disarmed him but beaten him far faster than he'd been beaten in years.

Maybe if he had his core reserves, or access to the El'aras ring—

The ring was gone. Impossible. Gavin had never been able to take the ring off, despite trying many times.

He forced everything out of his mind and leapt to his feet. Chauvan stood before him, holding a slender silver pole, and he started to place the ring onto it.

"What are you doing?" Gavin said.

"I am going to become the true Champion."

Chauvan dropped the ring onto the pole, and darkness began to fill the object and move into the ring. Gavin jumped up, unmindful of anything else. His body hurt, his head still throbbed from where he'd struck the ground, but he couldn't focus on any of that.

He wanted his core reserves, but they didn't react to him. All he had were enchantments.

The enchantments.

He had the stone golems.

Gavin thought about the connection he hoped had formed when he had touched some and set them on the ground. He concentrated deep within himself. All he needed was a faint stir of his core reserves. The nihilar was designed to suppress that, but Gavin was the Chain Breaker. He was the Champion.

He continued to let that energy fill him, and he pushed against the resistance within himself. The nihilar energy was trying to tamp down some part of him, but he didn't need to let it flow all throughout his body. He needed to connect to those enchantments he had already joined with.

He slammed that power out, and there was a bulging sensation that allowed him to feel how the nihilar was trying to hold him down.

But he was the Chain Breaker, and with one more push, Gavin exploded past the resistance.

It was gone.

The enchantments rumbled, trembling to life. He could feel them doing so.

He brought his fist forward, slamming into Chauvan. The man blocked, but Gavin was not done. He swung his knee around with a sense of control.

Gavin had fought Tristan and defeated him. Chauvan had never done so.

He grabbed for the other man, reaching for the hand holding on to the pole. Chauvan punched Gavin, who ignored it and absorbed the blow. A kick landed in Gavin's side, and he strained against it.

Everything within him hurt. He didn't know how much of that was the nihilar suppression and how much of it was the pummeling, but none of that mattered now.

Chauvan gripped Gavin's hand and started to bend it back, but Gavin knew his opponent couldn't let go of the pole. Chauvan brought one hand up, then drove it down on Gavin's forearm. His arm snapped, and Gavin cried out.

He immediately pushed past the pain and reminded himself that he still had one good arm. He wrapped it around Chauvan, who managed to shove Gavin and drive a fist into his chest, far harder than he should have been able to do.

Chauvan gripped the pole, something in his hand. Gavin tried crawling toward him but stopped when he realized that darkness was flowing into the silver pole, into the ring, and then back out.

Somehow, he'd stolen the statue from Gavin. Had Tristan helped with that?

He couldn't keep what was happening straight in his head. Everything felt like a painful jumble.

"You were no Champion," Gavin said.

He tried to get up, but he had injured his leg in the fall. He managed to stagger onto his one good leg, with one arm broken. But he would keep fighting.

Chauvan snorted. "At least he taught you not to give up. That was a lesson we all had to learn."

"He taught me more than that."

The ground trembled. It was similar to what had happened in Perisaln and in Arashil. He didn't remember it happening in Hester, but perhaps it had. It had to be the effect of whatever Chauvan intended to do.

The trembling persisted, deep, moving.

His enchantments were coming toward him.

Chauvan scoffed. "Really? You think you can use sorcery against me? I can suppress anything you use against me."

"Not sorcery. And it's not El'aras."

With Chauvan distracted, Gavin had only a moment to react. He had to get to that pole. Whatever else he did, taking that was going to be how he could stop Chauvan and all of this. He had no idea what would happen with it or what might happen if the power of the nihilar poured into the ring, but he suspected that if it succeeded, something terrible would happen to the El'aras ring—and then the El'aras.

He had felt the way the nihilar had tried to overwhelm him, the way it had attempted to burn off his own core reserves. And even now, he could feel how that energy was there, buried, trying to overpower him. Gavin wanted nothing more than to get past it, but he didn't know if he could.

He let the enchantments march toward Chauvan, knowing he would have to time this right. There was one thing he could try. If he could push off on his good leg, he might be able to flip, grab the ring, and then—

He had to hope that it would be enough.

The stone enchantments converged on Chauvan. When the nearest one reached him, Chauvan kicked once, and the enchantment shattered.

Gavin hated acknowledging how impressive that was.

He needed more time, so he waited and watched as two more enchantments neared. Chauvan turned toward one of them and kicked again, shattering it. Surprisingly, Gavin could feel it as the enchantment broke apart. It was as if when he had connected to it, he had linked to the pain that would come, like Mekel had described.

Two more enchantments were coming, which he could feel marching in his mind. He silently instructed them to pick up the pace, to move more quickly.

Chauvan turned, preparing to attack the enchantments, and Gavin used that moment. He jumped with his good leg. Chauvan spun around, likely assuming that

Gavin was lunging toward him, but Gavin didn't. He grabbed for the pole with his good arm, focused on everything within him, and jerked.

But Chauvan was stronger. Or had better enchantments.

Gavin's hand slipped up the length of the pole, until he reached the ring. He managed to pull it free, but darkness came with it and wrapped around the ring. Gavin tumbled to the ground, squeezing the ring in his hand, and it slipped onto his finger. With a panic, he tried to remove it, but despite prying and pulling at it, it wouldn't come free.

He began to feel something different.

The nihilar. He was certain of it.

It began to flow through the ring, through him, but strangely, it also unlocked something. It was almost as if the nihilar energy within the ring allowed Gavin to access the magic inside of it and his own core reserves. Some aspect of the nihilar seeped outward, a cold, burning sensation that felt familiar. It drifted down into his core reserves like it was trying to flow into it and blaze through it.

And there might be something else he could do.

He thought about that power, the way he had linked to the enchantments, and he pushed his core reserves out. Rather than fighting, he intentionally bridged that.

The cold burning flared within part of his mind. Part of him.

Chauvan could control the nihilar. Which meant Gavin could now as well.

He got to his feet, and Chauvan turned to him. He had made quick work of the stone enchantments.

"That's *my* prize," Chauvan said dangerously.

"Not any longer."

Gavin focused on the power within it, knowing that he had to draw upon the nihilar, regardless of whether he wanted to or not. He could feel that power coming from deep within him.

As Chauvan dove toward him, Gavin reacted without knowing what he was doing. He pulled on the power that filled him, a strange sort of energy he felt warring with his El'aras abilities. The two parts of his magic were battling, but he knew he had to unite them. He could only explode power outward, which created a barrier around him.

Chauvan stopped in his tracks, then tried to break through and pound at him. Gavin wasn't sure what would happen if Chauvan succeeded. He didn't like his chances in being able to withstand another attack. His leg hurt, and his arm was a useless wreck. He needed time to recover.

Chauvan glowered at him. "Do you think you have control over it? You aren't the real Champion. You can't know what it's like. You can't know what it takes."

"I have the ring. I have the sword. I think that makes me the real Champion."

The ring and the blade. They both had to be part of it.

The sword lay on the ground out of reach, and he focused. One good jump. That's all it would take.

He feigned moving in the opposite direction, and Chauvan reacted to it. Gavin jumped toward the sword, and when he grabbed it, he jerked around while already pouring power out of him. The blade seemed to take on a different quality than it had before, filled with a gray light —not the blazing blue he'd seen before, not the darkness of the shadows, but some mix of the two.

Chauvan watched him. "I will claim them. And then I will destroy you."

The ground trembled, and he cocked his head.

Gavin smirked at him. "I imagine you're wondering what that is. That's the enchantment you thought to use against me. I've called him to me, along with the others my friends have. If you think you can break through my meager control over the nihilar before they get down here, then I invite you to give it a shot." Gavin shifted his weight on his good foot and dared him.

Chauvan stormed toward him. There was power in the way he charged, the kind that Gavin would probably struggle to withstand even when healthy, not injured the way he was now. But he had something new within him now.

Gavin brought the blade up, calling on the nihilar power through him and through the ring, and he exploded outward.

A strange tremble rippled in the air, but when it was gone… and so was Chauvan.

Gavin crumpled to the ground.

CHAPTER TWENTY-ONE

Gavin lay still for a moment. He couldn't get to his feet, and his arm hurt even more. He seemed to have injured it again when he fell to the ground, but he didn't care. Chauvan was gone. The dark beam of energy that had been shooting out of the chamber had eased, but now it seemed to be swirling around the ring, as if all of that power was getting drawn into it.

As it did, he realized something. He thought this had been about the book and the statue, but maybe they were only part of it. The statue had been useful, and the book had provided instructions, but it had been more about the sword and the ring.

He looked up and laughed, unable to understand what was happening. The sword was an El'aras blade. The statue... Gavin suspected that it was the nihilar. And the ring seemed to bind them together.

Could one of them be the item of power Brandon had

mentioned? The statue had been in Hester. The ring and the sword had been in Yoran, but not always.

They were all connected. He was sure of it.

The ground continued to rumble, and he barely managed to look up as Brandon, Mekel, and Gaspar barreled into the room. Tristan was with them, though Gaspar shot him a hard look with every step that he took.

"What happened?" Gaspar asked.

Gavin winced as Gaspar reached for him, not wanting to get up. He wasn't sure he should be moving yet.

"I defeated him," he said, then looked at Tristan. "If there was any question about who the real Champion is, I wanted to put that to rest."

Tristan regarded him for a long moment. "Did you think that was what it was about?"

"You wanted me to fight him. You wanted to know."

Tristan shook his head. "No. I needed you to be the true Champion."

"Right." Gavin glanced back over to Gaspar. "He's not gone. Well, he's gone for now, but I suspect he's coming back."

"Then what will you do?"

"I need to understand all of this."

"The ring?" Gaspar asked.

Brandon frowned as he looked at the ring but remained silent.

"My El'aras ability," Gavin answered. "And the ring. And the nihilar. All of it. Somehow, it is all bound to me, and bound to the power I was able to use. I'm not exactly sure what it is, only that I have it."

"The true Champion," Tristan said.

Gavin shot him another look.

"Let's get you out of here, back to the city," Gaspar said. "You can rest. The others are taken care of. Davel and his people are finishing them off, and I think he intends to drag them back to the city."

"Not Yoran," Gavin said. "I don't think the power there will be enough to suppress them."

"That's just it. The strange power they had seemed to have disappeared."

"I don't understand."

Gaspar shrugged. "Neither do we."

"Because the true Champion has come," Tristan said. He was smiling at him, and it left Gavin unsettled. It was almost as if he had actually wanted this. Gavin had a hard time believing that. Instead, he thought that perhaps Tristan wanted to play all angles. "You needed it. Why do you think I sent you after the statue?"

Gavin's brow furrowed. "I thought you wanted *him* to have it."

"He thought he could have power he should not have. I told you that I have been trying to find the Champion for centuries."

"You were looking for something else."

"I was looking for the real one. Because, as I told you, what is coming is worse."

"Worse than the nihilar?"

"The nihilar is another myth that the El'aras have long believed. What is it but power?" He nodded to Gavin. "You must feel that. I am sure that you can."

Strangely, Gavin could. When he had been transported into this space, he had felt the way the nihilar had attempted to burn through him, to rip free his El'aras abilities. But now that he had the ring with the nihilar power and could feel that energy within himself, he couldn't help but wonder if it was merely another power—or if it was something worse.

He could feel how that power linked to him, though he had no idea what it might do, only that by using something similar to how he had linked to the enchantments, he had found a way to control something different. Something dangerous and possibly deadly.

He had to understand it. He didn't know what it meant for him to be this true Champion. He was El'aras, though.

"I suppose you think you are going to help me understand it?" he asked.

Tristan smiled tightly. "I have studied this more than anyone else."

"I'm sure there are El'aras priests who have looked into this."

"No priests have dared."

Gavin took a deep breath and tried to put weight on his foot, and nearly collapsed. Gaspar quickly helped him up.

"What do you think?" Gavin asked him.

"I don't think he has shared everything with you, and he never has. I think he is still trying to manipulate you."

"I agree."

Gaspar sighed. "And I think you're going to need help."

Gavin looked over to Tristan. Could he trust Tristan to

help him? His old mentor had betrayed him over and over again, but he may not have a choice.

"You might have to help Rayena. I don't know what happened to her."

Tristan frowned and shook his head. "I won't be able to. You are going to have to. Now that you have control over it, you are the only one who can save her."

Gavin didn't know if he could trust Tristan, but he did know that Rayena deserved more than this. She wanted to help her people. He might not agree with her on everything the Order did, and he knew that she might not even know how she was supposed to serve, but this wasn't to be her fate.

"I'll do that, and then I think I need to return to the El'aras," he said. Rayena could go back with him. Maybe there was more that could be done for her. He wasn't sure, though.

"I think you need to," Gaspar said.

It had been hard coming back to Yoran. Harder than Gavin would've expected. He had prepared himself for being away from them, and seeing his friends again had brought back memories he had enjoyed, ones that left him thinking about what life might have been like were he to have something resembling normalcy.

But that wasn't where he belonged. He wasn't from Yoran. They weren't his people.

Were they?

Davel had said that Gavin had not needed to protect Yoran because they weren't his people, but maybe his people were the ones he chose. He would still protect the city. For now, though, he needed to understand his people. The others. And he needed to be ready for whatever Chauvan might do again.

"He's not done chasing power, is he?" Gavin asked, looking over to Tristan.

"He will still want what you have."

"And there will be something worse."

Tristan nodded.

As much as that pained Gavin to realize, he didn't think Tristan was lying about that. He had seen it. Events beginning to coalesce. Things happening too frequently to be chance. The Sul'toral making their presence known. Power coming forth all throughout this part of the world.

He didn't know what it meant, but he felt increasingly certain that he was going to have to play a role in it. And given what he had just experienced, Gavin thought that he had to. Not only to help with the El'aras, but to help with the people of Yoran. As far as he knew, he wasn't done here either.

"Once I heal enough, I'm going to head back to Anna and the other El'aras. Tristan is coming with me," Gavin said. He regarded Tristan, expecting him to argue, but he didn't. Tristan simply met his gaze.

Could this be some other machination Tristan had in mind? Some other part of a plan where he would be brought back to the El'aras? Even if it was, Gavin wasn't sure that it mattered.

"I figured as much," Gaspar said. "I think you need someone you can trust when you do."

"I can't trust him."

"I know. Which is why I'm coming with you."

Gavin looked over, shaking his head. "Not here. You won't know anyone. And Desarra—"

"Will get along quite well without me. For a little while." Gaspar chuckled, but he turned to Tristan, and all of that emotion drained away as darkness burned in his eyes. "You have a blind spot when it comes to him," he said to Gavin. "And you need somebody to bounce ideas off of, especially in a place you don't know. Since I don't know what's going on either, the two of us can decide how much of it is right and how much of it is bullshit. Besides, since you modified that enchantment, I wonder if we might even be able to get the kid to help."

"I heard that," Wrenlow's voice piped up. "I could come."

"No," Gavin said. "I'm going to need somebody in Yoran who can keep an eye on things for me. Besides, Olivia would definitely kill me if you did."

Wrenlow chuckled.

"Even if I go back to Yoran," Gaspar said, "it's not like I'm stranded there. You'll have the paper dragon. And…" He reached into his pocket and pulled out several pieces of folded paper, showing them to Gavin. "I might have a few myself."

Gavin snorted.

Maybe this plan would work.

He had not liked leaving Yoran before, but partly that was because he hadn't wanted to leave his friends. Now that he felt increasingly certain that there was a danger coming that he needed to be ready for, he was also sure that he needed to have somebody he could trust with him.

After everything he and Gaspar had been through, he trusted the man. And he could use Wrenlow's help too.

Gavin turned to Tristan. "You are going to tell me everything you know about the nihilar, the prophecy you've heard, and what you have been doing."

Tristan held his gaze. "If you think you're ready."

"You have made me ready."

Tristan tipped his head slightly. "You're right. I did."

Coming next in The Chain Breaker: A Champion Falls

Read more about Imogen's adventures in an exciting new series: Unbonded - First of the Blade book 1.

SERIES BY D.K. HOLMBERG

The Chain Breaker Series

The Chain Breaker

The Dark Sorcerer

First of the Blade

The Executioner's Song Series

The Executioner's Song

The Dragonwalkers Series

The Dragonwalker

The Dragon Misfits

Elemental Warrior Series:

Elemental Academy

The Elemental Warrior

The Cloud Warrior Saga

The Endless War

The Dark Ability Series

The Shadow Accords

The Collector Chronicles

The Dark Ability

The Sighted Assassin

The Elder Stones Saga

The Lost Prophecy Series
The Teralin Sword
The Lost Prophecy

The Volatar Saga Series
The Volatar Saga

The Book of Maladies Series
The Book of Maladies

The Lost Garden Series
The Lost Garden

Printed in Great Britain
by Amazon